NIGHTBLADE

A BOOK OF UNDERREALM

GARRETT
ROBINSON

NIGHTBLADE

Garrett Robinson

The author greatly appreciates you taking the time to read his work. Please leave a review wherever you bought the book or on Goodreads.com.

Interior Design: Legacy Books, Inc.
Publisher: Legacy Books, Inc.
Editors: Karen Conlin, Cassie Dean
Cover Artist: Sutthiwat Dechakamphu

1. Fantasy - Epic 2. Fantasy - Dark 3. Fantasy - New Adult

Second Edition

Published by Legacy Books

To my wife
Who gave me this idea

To my children
Who just make life better

To Johnny, Sean and Dave
Who told me to write

And to my Rebels
Don't forget why you left the woods

GET THE NEXT BOOK

You're about to read *Nightblade*, the first book in the Nightblade Epic.

You can get an ebook copy of *Mystic*, the next book in the series, absolutely free. Just sign up for email updates from Legacy Books. You'll also get exclusive deals and sales on our titles.

Want to keep reading? Visit the link below now:

Underrealm.net/free-mystic

NIGHTBLADE

A BOOK OF UNDERREALM

GARRETT ROBINSON

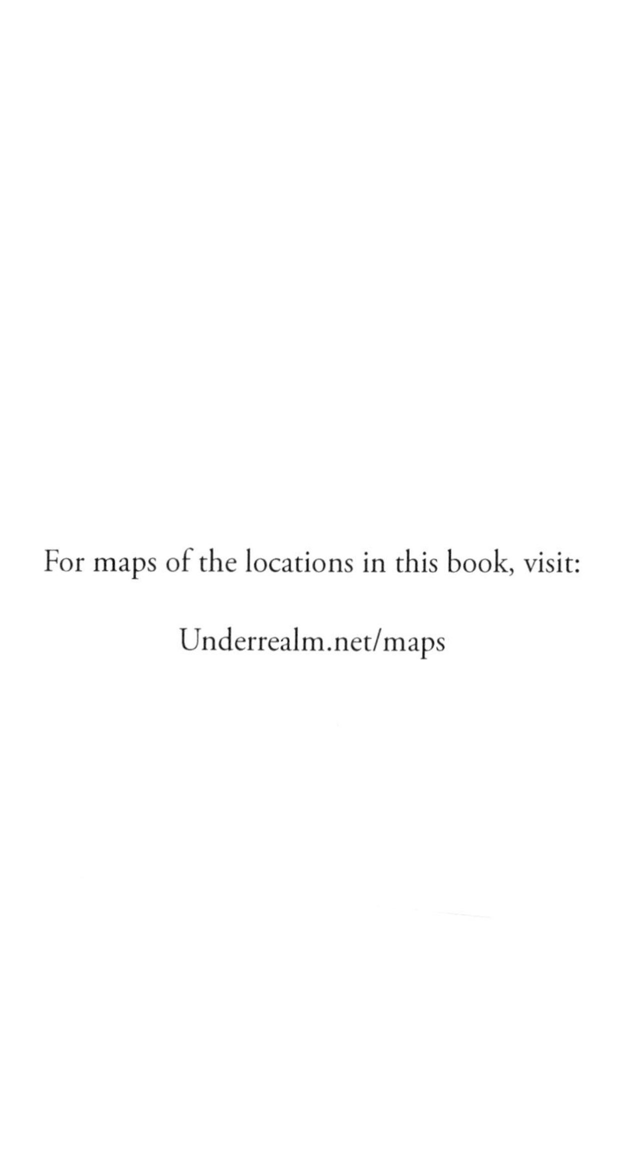

For maps of the locations in this book, visit:

Underrealm.net/maps

ONE

LOREN LET HER AXE FALL, AND THE LOG SPLIT WITH the sound of a skull cracking open.

She heaved a sigh and hoisted the axe to her shoulder. One hand rose to wipe sweat from her filthy brow, streaking it with dirt. She surveyed the pile of logs that awaited the kiss of her axe. There were many. Far too many, if she had any hope of going to the village dance that night. Loren did not care overmuch for dances, but certainly she preferred them to chopping logs.

Only a dance could unite the village where Loren had been raised, a thin scattering of homes too small to warrant a name, nestled in the Birchwood Forest of Selvan. The dwellings were so sparse, so thinly spread, that often she went days without speaking to any other villager. Other than Chet, of course.

She let her gaze wander, looking upon her tiny house, where a thin plume of grey drifted from the smokestack. Loren had worked all day without seeing her mother, the one person who could rescue her from several more hours of backbreaking labor. But Mother had sweet cakes and buns to prepare, hoping to lure with taste what Loren had not attracted with looks.

Far past the house, Chet emerged from the smithy and hailed Loren with a shout. She gave a wan smile and a wave. Dear, foolish Chet. He would happily have taken her to wife, though she stood three fingers taller and could beat him in arm wrestling. But Chet could not bring the dowry her parents demanded, and Loren feared the young man would waste away with his relentless affection.

She wondered often what would happen if her parents did find a worthy suitor. What would Chet think? No, Loren could imagine what he would think. But what would he do?

"Why do you stand there gawking, girl?"

Her father's voice dripped with malice. Before answering, Loren stooped and batted the halved log aside with the blunt end of her axe. She fetched another and stood it upright before she dared raise her eyes to his.

"I am sorry, Father," she mumbled. "But I only rested a moment."

"Why, work is still to be done?" he growled.

He stepped in close, the way he liked to—close enough to strike at a moment's notice, close enough for Loren to faint from the stench of his sweat. Now he blocked her from chopping the log.

She took a half-step back. Her father followed. Loren gulped, her whole body tensing in anticipation of a strike. Her arms burned with the bruises he had left the day before.

Over her father's shoulder she could see Chet. The boy had stopped walking, his eyes fixed upon her, a dark look on his face. Loren prayed he would be wise enough to stay away.

Mayhap distraction would work. "Father, Mother said I am to ready for the dance. If I do not, she will be angry."

"And you think I will not be, if you persist in disobedience?" said her father. His voice had grown very like a snarl. "You think to prance about in a gown while I break my back doing your work?"

She knew better than to deny it. "I do not want to go. Only Mother—"

"You chop," he said. "And if you rest again before your fingers bleed, I will slice them open myself."

He did not move. Loren had to step around him to bring her axe down on the log. Her father waited for her to split two more before finally stumping off to vanish behind Miss Aisley's house.

Chet still stood, staring at Loren. She gave him a weak smile and a quick wave before lowering her head. When she raised her eyes, Chet had gone.

The fear in Loren's gut churned to rage. As always, she loathed herself for it, hated that she could only summon such anger when her father's hands no longer threatened. If once she could bring it to bear when he stood close and the axe lay in her hands. . .

She stamped the thought down. *You have a murderer's heart*, she hissed in her mind. If ever she gave in to such dark thoughts, constables would kill her slow and accurse her name across the kingdom.

Thoughts of constables turned her mind to the wide lands beyond the Birchwood, lands that seemed as far out of reach as the tops of the trees. Loren could scarce remember a time before her unceasing dreams of wandering the world. Always her reveries had contained great cities, strange mountains whose names she did not know, and swift rivers chasing endless leagues.

Now her waking dream ran further. Loren saw herself in a cloak of black with a dagger at her waist, perched atop a spirited palfrey. Its harness bore gold, as well as emeralds the color of her eyes. She slipped into a city and robbed its nobles blind before vanishing with the morning mist. And as she slid out through the city's gates, guards quaked in fear and whispered the word *Nightblade*.

Her mind shied away. Years had taught Loren to ignore childish wishes. She was fifteen now, and a woman grown. She had no time for flights of fancy that could bring only pain, the knotted ache of desire without hope. If ever she had dreamed of escaping her parents, that dream had withered long ago.

The axe fell, the log split, and she knocked the pieces aside. She moved to the pile and stooped to pick up another.

As she grasped the log and stood, Loren saw a thin figure in a bright blue coat. It darted through the woods at the edge of the clearing. The man—for she could see it was a man now—scurried from tree to tree like a hunted animal, looking over his shoulder before vanishing into the forest.

Loren glanced again towards the village. She saw her father nowhere, and no villager looked her way.

That blue coat was no woodsman's garment. The man came from beyond the forest, from the lands Loren had seen only in her dreams. What was he doing? Where was he going?

She knew only one way to find out.

Anxiety roiled in her gut. Her mind raced with the possibilities of what would happen if her parents caught her. But a voice within cried *Go!*

Loren flung her axe to the ground and ran into the woods where the flash of a blue coat had vanished.

TWO

By the time Loren reached the trees, the man had disappeared. She knelt and inspected the ground where she had last seen him. Crushed blades of grass told the tale of his flight. She threw a final, hesitant look over her shoulder but saw no one.

She would leave for only a moment, and return before anyone could tell she had gone. A little while, that was all.

Her feet fell swift but silent as a tomb. Loren prided herself on her woodcraft, and knew how to move swiftly while avoiding detection.

Only a little while passed before she saw the man again. His telltale blue coat stood out like a beacon fire between the brown trunks. Loren slowed her pace to match his and peeked out only when he moved.

She needed only a few glances to take his measure. Neither short nor tall, his height matched her own, though he looked more than twice her age. He wore his dark curled hair longer than most men in the village. Dirt covered his every fingerbreadth. His boots looked fit for the road, but his clothes bore rips and tears from travel.

A town man, then, or even one from a city. Loren wondered at his purpose. Running from something, certainly. The filth of his clothes spoke of hiding in ditches and under the roots of trees. He bore a panicked look that Loren knew well from the eyes of prey she hunted. His furtive feet, his jerking hands, every movement showed fear. Loren looked behind as they ran, but could see no sign of pursuit.

Eventually she grew careless. The man turned when she stood exposed, and his eyes fell upon her. He gave a strangled sort of yelp, redoubled his pace, and vanished.

"Wait!" she cried, too late. He was gone, and her voice would not carry far in the forest.

But if he hoped to evade her, he would find that a folly. Loren had seen his unease beneath the trees, his steps more used to streets and floors than the ground of a forest.

She struck wide, making for a thick copse of birches she knew stood nearby. The man would avoid them, but Loren could pick her way through the trunks as if she were walking an open road.

Her feet devoured ground faster and faster, her breath rising in excitement. She could hear her heartbeat in her ears. She was a wolf on the hunt, and her blue-coated rabbit could not escape her.

She burst out the other side of the copse, exulting at the look of shock upon his face. She gave a cry of joy—but it turned to a yelp as the man raised his hands, eyes glowing, and fire bolted towards her.

Loren skidded on her heels and crashed to the ground. But at the last moment, the man twisted his hands. The firebolt turned aside and crashed harmlessly into the dirt. Loren flinched at the impact, and though a wave of heat washed across her face, she shivered.

"What do you think you are doing?" A pale white glow faded from the man's eyes. "I nearly killed you!"

For a moment, Loren shook too hard to reply. The man's shoulders heaved with deep breaths, his eyes locked on hers. They were a curious color: a light brown verging on grey, a sharp contrast against the dark curls of his hair. She could see now that he wore a short blade on his belt, from which also hung a few pouches of leather. But one of them was cloth, and it hung small and curiously heavy; it bore coin, Loren suspected. She composed herself and stood, brushing soil from the seat of her pants.

"Why are you running?" was the first thing she could think to ask.

The man blinked as though reminded of something. He looked behind him, but the forest lay empty.

"No one is there," said Loren. Her own breath still came steady. It took more than such a light run to rob her of her wind. "I kept a careful watch as I followed. No one pursues you."

The man snorted. "Oh, they do. You may sleep assured of it and bet your last coin, if a gambler you might be."

"Not I. But foresters have little opportunity to wager with wizards."

One of his eyebrows arched. "Though ample opportunity to raise daughters with quick tongues and quicker eyes, it would seem."

"You *are* a wizard, then."

"You saw my flame. It renders your guess less impressive."

"A firemage as well. Your flight is curious, then, for who could you fear?"

He glanced behind him once more, and his feet twitched as though itching to run. "A man need not fear his pursuers to wish them no harm. Though it may look ignoble to flee, who would praise my honor if I caught constables in a blaze?"

Loren's eyes grew wide. She cleared her throat and tried to look calm. "Constables? Are you . . . dangerous, then?"

His mouth twisted in a smile before he barked a sharp laugh. "Dangerous? A slain patch of dirt lies at hand to prove it. Were I a touch slower, the dirt's fate would have befallen your remarkable green eyes."

Loren blinked. "What about my eyes?"

"I mean no insult. I said they are remarkable, not ugly. I have never seen their color."

Loren felt a growing frustration. Her hands rose of their own accord to tug at her hair. The man was trying to distract her.

"I have not forgotten my question, firemage. Why do the constables pursue you?"

His face grew dark, and for a moment Loren felt afraid. But the shadow passed, and he tossed back his hair. "You will withstand their questions better if you do not know."

"Whence do you come, then?" Loren pressed. "Where are you bound?"

He only looked over his shoulder again.

She had to get him talking. "I am Loren, a daughter of the family Nelda. If your purpose must remain a secret, surely you can tell me your name. I am sure the constables are free enough with it."

"That they are," he muttered. "It is Xain. Well met."

He gave no family. Loren knew a thousand reasons for that, but her first thought was *bastard*. The word sent a thrill through her. No husbandless mother bore a child within the Birchwood—fathers and hefty axes saw to that.

"Well met, Xain. How closely are you pursued, and for how long?"

Xain looked at her curiously. "For a child, you bear remarkably little fear."

Loren stood straighter for the moment. "A child? No one my age can beat me at arm wrestling, nor can any two years older in the village. Nor can they climb as high, nor run as fast. What would I fear from you and your pretty blue coat?"

Xain balked, and then laughed as he looked down at his coat. "When one must flee in haste, one must seize upon the garment closest to hand."

He had distracted her again. Mayhap she could turn the tables upon him. Loren thought hard about what she knew. He had come from the east, and made for a southwesterly course. The east road ran straight through two cities to the bay of the High King's Seat. And the closest town to the southwest was . . .

"Cabrus," she said, gratified to see him give a little start. "You make for Cabrus. There is nothing else the way you are going."

Xain glowered, and she knew that she was right. "The road is long," he grumbled. "Cabrus is scarcely a dot on the great maps of Underrealm."

"A place may be a way-stop, yet men make for it when occasion rises," said Loren. "And you do not deny it. But you will never reach it."

His nostrils flared, and his hands clenched at his sides. A little shiver ran down the small of her back. "Do you mean to lead the constables to me, then?" he said in a grim voice.

Loren shook her head. "I bear you no ill will, and you saved me from the flame."

"I sent it after you also."

She shrugged. "A weight on both scales clears the account. But only your boots can bear the long road to Cabrus. Your stomach will not, even if those pouches at your belt hold nothing but salted meat, which I doubt. After the Melnar, you will find no other fresh water on the road. Thirst and hunger will claim you before you can glimpse the walls of Cabrus."

Xain frowned. He held forth a finger and whispered a word. His eyes glowed with pale white light, and blue fire sprang to life above his fingertip. "I can hunt. A bolt of fire or thunder will serve as well as an arrow; the squirrels know no difference."

Loren's cheeks flushed. "Water, then. I do not think you can draw the rain from the sky, unless you are Dorren in disguise."

He smiled at that. "You have me there. Mayhap you are correct, and the constables will catch me. I can always beg them for a drink. They are most accommodating once you are within their grasp."

Loren felt her pulse quicken. A half-forgotten dream tugged at the back of her mind, a destiny she had long abandoned.

"Mayhap you will not need their courtesy. If you stay here, I shall run and fetch you water and provisions, enough to make the journey."

"Why?" said Xain. He looked over his shoulder again.

"Because I want you to bring me with you."

He took a quick step backwards. "That is what I feared. No. I will not."

"Then you will never reach Cabrus."

Xain's mouth soured. "I will find a way. I have made it this far."

"Following the King's road and the river that runs beside it, I do not doubt," Loren said.

Xain growled and ran a hand through his hair. "You are a foolish girl if you think to follow me on an adventure. I am wanted, and not for a feast of honor. If they find you with me, it will go ill for you."

Loren avoided his eyes, uneasy. Then she unlaced the cuff of her sleeve and pulled it to her elbow. Black welts and bruises shone like beacon fires against her pale skin.

She saw a flash in his eyes—not only anger, but recognition.

"I will await you an hour," he grumbled. "Then I move south without you, and if I die of thirst, so be it."

"I shall take less than half that," said Loren. She turned and vanished between the trunks of the birches, hoping it looked as magical to him as his fire did to her.

THREE

Loren approached her village quick and quiet, wary of meeting her parents. Many villagers had gathered in the open space to the west. There the sun as it set cast everything in a ruddy glow long into the evening, perfect for merry gatherings. Such a party would soon be afoot. Some folk readied stout tables for food, and young children tramped a wide space in the grass for dancing. But Loren did not see her mother or father.

Her heart sank. Their absence meant they would be in the house, the place she needed to go.

She flitted from tree to tree like a bird, keenly aware of the passing time. It took longer than she wanted to reach the village's east end where her house sat far from any other.

There Loren saw something she did not expect: two strangers in brown and red garb. Chet stood by them, along with Bo, another young man from the village. Chet's eyes were hooded and his brows close, but Bo spoke animatedly and gestured all around. The strangers listened patiently, only occasionally offering comment or a prompting question.

The constables, thought Loren. They had to be. It would be too great a coincidence for any other strangers to arrive today. She had to fetch her supplies and be off quickly. She did not think anyone else in the village had seen Xain, but the constables might yet find his trail leading southwest.

Although . . .

She thought hard for a moment, reached a decision, and emerged from the trees. Chet's face brightened as he saw her.

"Loren!" said Bo. "These men are constables. I have never seen a constable in the village before, have you?"

"Not once." Loren dusted her hands as though she had just come from the axe. She stuck a hand out to the men. "Well met, strangers. What brings you so far from any building made of stone?"

One of the constables stood tall and thin, but muscular as any village man. The other was at least two hands shorter, but his chest was barrel-wide and muscle bulged beneath his clothes. Both had boiled leather pauldrons and breastplates dyed a dull red and worn over long, simple tunics of brown. The taller one stared at Loren's outstretched hand, but his companion reached across and took her wrist in a firm grip.

"Well met," he said. "I am Corin, and my dour companion is Bern. We seek a man traveling through these lands. When last we saw him he headed this way, and we wondered if he had come to your village."

Loren's eyes widened. "A man in a blue coat?"

They all started. "You have seen him?" growled Bern, the taller constable.

"In the woods, yes," said Loren, nodding with vigor. "As I foraged for herbs, I saw him amid the trees. He fled when he saw me, and I could not keep his pace. I soon lost sight of him."

From the corner of her eye, Loren saw Chet's face grow stony. He knew no foreign man could escape her in these woods. But he was not such a fool as to counter her before the constables.

"When was this?" said Corin. "My lady, this man must be brought to his justice. Tell me, when and where did he run?"

Loren laughed, putting just the right amount of giggle into it. "Oh, you are too kind, constable. You know well I am no lady." She made a great show of thinking hard upon his question. "It could not have been more than a quarter hour since I saw him. As for where, he fled that way, though his path swung wildly about."

She thrust a finger to the north and east, directly away from the birch copse where Xain awaited her.

Corin and Bern traded glances. Corin gave her an earnest half-bow. "You have provided our lord a great service. If indeed we should find the wizard, we will return with a purse of his gratitude."

"A wizard?" said Loren, her eyes shooting wide. "Truly?"

"A purse?" said Bo.

Bern scowled at his shorter companion. "My friend speaks with a looser tongue than he might. Our lord would prefer that the lot of you forget his words."

"Of course," said Loren. "I will say nothing. Nor will the boys, lest they catch my ready hand." She stepped forwards to hold a stern fist beneath Bo's nose, and he grimaced. Chet needed no such encouragement, she knew.

The constables ran off with a final hasty thank you. Bo wandered towards the dance preparations, leaving Chet to fix Loren with a knowing look.

"The man outran you?" His tone betrayed nothing.

Loren shrugged. "Well, I did not give him full chase. How was I to know he was worth a purse? I tired of my run and gave in, for why should I continue?"

Chet's arms folded, and his eyes eased. To further his mind down the proper path, she smiled and set a warm hand on his arm before making for the village. He did not follow, for which she was grateful. She had no desire to lie more than she must, and time grew ever shorter.

"Loren!"

Her heart dropped to her boots. The bruises on her arm flared with pain. Her father stood there, his face twisted and mean with fury.

"Your logs lie idle, and your axe with them."

She tried to talk, but her throat cracked like desert sand. She tried again. "Constables, Father," she said, gesturing vaguely. "Two constables came in search of a man."

His eyes did not waver. "What worth are two constables and their man? If they find him, will they chop your logs for you?"

"They offered a purse."

He stepped towards her. It was all Loren could do to remain rooted. She wanted to flee, to vanish into the woods and beg Xain to take her even without the supplies. But she stayed. She would not run. Her father got close, the way he liked, and she craned her neck to see him.

"I will return to the logs, Father." Loren could not keep the quaver from her words. If she could only make him let her go, she could take what she needed and slip away, never more to fear his meaty arms or rank breath.

"You will go to the house," he said in a growling whisper. "That is twice you have tried to leave me your job, and twice too many. You will go to the house, and I will give you a lesson. Next time, your feet will stay planted, and your arms will swing."

"I do not need a lesson, Father — "

His fist met her gut. Loren's nose crashed into his shoulder as her body tried to double over in reflex. It was not his hardest blow. He would save that for the house.

"You are far too free with your tongue when speaking to your elders," her father hissed. "To the house. Now."

She heard Chet's footsteps and looked up to see the boy striding towards them, his face a mask of fury. She met his eyes, pleading without words for him to turn around. He ignored her.

And then Loren heard a voice she was seldom relieved to hear: her mother, shrilling in the forest air. "Loren, where is your dress, you witless child?"

Loren fell a step back. Her father turned. "She's still chopping for me." He thrust a meaty finger in her face. "She will need to go all night at the rate her lazy hands move."

"And how do you think we will get her wed? Not when you never let her try her luck with a man."

"The men can come to her," said her father stubbornly. "Let them watch her chop. A man needs a strong woman who can work."

With her father distracted, Loren risked another look at Chet. He had stopped his advance, but he stood with folded arms and anger clear in his features. He would not leave so long as her father stood by.

"A man does, and a man knows it, but a man does a different sort of knowing when he chooses a wife." Loren's mother strode up to her father and shoved her face into his, full of all the anger Loren could never summon. At the same time, her sharp-nailed fingers seized Loren's bicep, pinching into the skin. "We will never get the dowry without some boy who can afford it seeing her whirl about in a skirt. Loren, you get in the house and get that dress on. Tear it, and I will lock you in the house for an hour with your father, and blow a treehorn to cover the noise."

Loren gulped and glanced fearfully at her father.

"What are you looking at him for?" her mother screeched. "Go!"

Loren remembered Xain and went. As she retreated, her parents' conversation dissolved to bitter, hate-filled argument behind her. She did not know if Chet still stood guard, but she dared not look back to see.

The moment she passed through her front door, anger swelled in her gut. She should have struck back. Her father's wrath would have burned like flame, but Chet would have stepped in. Together they could have beaten her father to within a breath of his life, and mayhap beyond. And Chet would not be a kinslayer if he did.

But such thoughts would not help, not when Xain waited and nearly half the hour he promised her had passed.

Loren threw from her bed the ridiculous green gown her mother had bought. Its arms, like those of her tunic, hung long to hide bruises. She threw it to the floor, ground dirt into it with her boot heel, and spat on the pretty cloth for good measure. Then she went to gather the things she needed.

First she took her father's smelly, thick cloak of dark green. She donned her own cloak, throwing the cowl back to let her black hair spill down her back. In her parents' room sat a cupboard, and from its top cabinet Loren took her father's travel sack. His cloak went into the sack, forming a soft lining around the interior. Two skins of water sat near the front door. She threw them into the sack. Food she took next: salted meats and several loaves of good hard bread, still fragrant from Miss Aisley's oven.

Loren thought of Miss Aisley with a pang of regret, and her thoughts turned to those in the village that she would miss. Dear, foolish Chet, of course, and old Kris, who was decent to her when she did not wish to go home. But the names she would miss far underweighed the others—those who heard and saw what her parents did to her and never raised a finger, or even frowned.

She would be well quit of the Birchwood Forest. It would not miss her.

Loren hesitated before her final acquisition. It sat tucked in an old chest atop a shelf in the kitchen. The chest held useless knickknacks in the main, but one item she might use. A long and curved dagger, its sheath made of leather cracked with age. As a young girl she had drawn it, and then she hid it away before her mother could know. The blade bore strange, twisting marks engraved in black. It was a weapon, no hunting or cooking knife, as any fool could see.

The night she drew the dagger was the first night she lay on her straw pallet and imagined herself in a black cloak. It was the night she first whispered the word *Nightblade*.

Now, though, she feared to lift it. Could she really take it? Loren knew little of such things, and yet she would have wagered the dagger cost more than her parents' whole house. Then again, they might never notice it had gone. Not in all her life had Loren seen them bring it forth from the chest.

Her hand closed around the dagger's hilt. She almost threw it in the sack, but at the last moment she paused. Untying her simple rope belt, she ran it through the sheath's loop.

With the dagger at her waist, Loren felt like a different person. Now, truly and forever, she was Nightblade.

But she had wasted too much time. She needed only one thing more before returning to Xain. The wizard could hunt with his fire, yes. But Loren would not let herself fall under his care. What if the wizard left her upon reaching Cabrus? Or died on the road? No. She must be able to forage for herself.

She needed a bow, and she knew where to get one.

Loren dropped her brown cloak over the dagger and slipped out the door, making for the trees once again.

FOUR

Loren hoped to find Chet away from home, but that hope fell when she found him out back fletching an arrow with a knife and gutstring. She could not hope to avoid him. But she still had her tongue, and it had served her once already. She stepped from the trees.

Chet's stern face softened at the sight of her. His close-cropped hair glowed golden in the sun, and his bare arms glistened with his work.

Upon past years, she had thought to take Chet for a husband, dowry or no. They would find a way to pay it, or they would run away together. But that dream had grown dimmer and dimmer as the years passed, and had guttered out when his mother fell ill. Now, two years later, the sickness kept her as close to and as far from death as ever. Chet could never muster Loren's dowry as a huntsman, and he would never leave his home to run away—not then, and not now with Loren and Xain.

All these thoughts flitted in and out of her head in an instant, and then she put on the expression she knew she must wear: unconcerned and gently happy to see him. "Should you not be dressing for the dance?"

"The same could be said for you. That cloak is not the dress your mother chose, I think."

Loren shrugged. "I must wash before donning it. I make for the river to bathe before making myself a fair young flower."

Chet put down his arrow a little too hastily and stood. "I will come. This is dull work, and does little to calm my anger."

She knew Chet's temper burned bright and long, though it took ages to stoke. Loren had often wondered what would happen if her father sparked it true, but now she would never know.

Loren cocked her head and narrowed her eyes. "I think you presume much. A woman's bathing is no time nor place for a young, fair-haired man who holds her in no bond of marriage."

That had the required effect: Chet's face turned red as a berry. "I meant . . . I would wait behind the bank, of course."

Loren laughed lightly. "Do not fret so. Will you dance with me tonight?"

"Of course. And will you, with me?" He stepped closer.

"I would not have asked if I meant to cruelly refuse. But my parents might object. They require such a great dowry, and may refuse to let me dance with one who cannot offer it."

Chet glowered. "Not even they could not deny me so simple a thing as a dance."

Loren both loved and bemoaned how easily she could sway his mood—a symptom of young love, she supposed. She had long known she could, but she rarely had the need. And just now, it would not do to have him *too* angry.

"Fetch me your own dowry," Loren said. "Weave it of dandelions and lilacs, and place it upon my head. Then I will give you your dance, and you can give me mine."

He flushed again, but gentler this time. "A crown of pretty flowers for a pretty flower of a girl? This I can do, and gladly. But no dandelions and lilacs lie near the river."

"I am astute in my planning, then."

He chuckled. "Very well. I will see you at the dance. Denying myself the sight of your dress will sweeten the pleasure of its revelation. Ready your hair for my dowry."

"I will." She touched his arm as she had before—for the last time, she realized. Her fingers lingered for just a moment.

He wandered off to the southeast. Loren watched him go, catching a spring in his step that had not been there before. She kept a gentle smile in case he turned around, but inside she quailed. Chet, her only true friend in all the world. Chet, foolishly and incurably in love with her. She would miss him more than all the rest, more than the Birchwood itself.

As soon as he had gone, Loren slipped in the back door of his house. His mother's room lay quiet and still. Loren chanced a look through the door and found her asleep. That was fortunate. A sudden scream might undo everything.

Loren went to the rack on the wall and pulled down one of Chet's hunting bows. She took the one of poorest make—it would serve for rabbits and squirrels, and she needed nothing grander. Loren strung it quickly and slung it on her back, and then stooped to a low shelf where two full quivers rested. She took one, but she left the other. She would not make Chet a pauper, unable to hunt. She would take only what she must.

Nightblade must always have such honor, she thought.

It was time to go. Loren had what she needed, and would not have to rely on the wizard to hunt for her. Her throat grew dry. This was goodbye forever; she was leaving home to fend for herself out among the nine lands. How could this be, when only that morning her greatest aspiration had been to find a way out of chopping logs?

She made for the back door, and disaster struck.

The door swung open, and Chet's father, Liam, stepped into the frame. Old and stooped, he was a genial man but never seemed to notice Loren's existence. That was not the case now. He froze on the spot and gawked at her, his watery eyes growing wider. He opened his mouth to cry out.

Loren had the bow in her hands. Before she could think, she leapt forwards and slammed the wood into his temple. His eyes fluttered and closed as he fell to the dirt floor, an angry red welt blooming to life on his forehead.

She stifled her cry with the back of her hand and dropped to one knee. Frantically she placed her palm on his chest—and felt a strong heartbeat. Her own pulse skipped in relief.

Her eyes went to the bruise on his head. *Chet.* He could have forgiven Loren for fleeing the village without telling him. But he could never forgive this. Could he?

It does not matter, she thought. Soon she would be in the forest, never to return. Loren shot to her feet and ran out the door.

She made it to the trees and almost kept going. But at the last moment, she could not leave without a final look. So she stopped beneath the low branches of an oak and turned to her home one last time. Her eyes roved across the simple houses, the smoke from the smithy, the pile of wood outside her house, her father.

Her father.

He stood by the chopping block, Loren's axe in his hand. And just as her eyes found him, he saw her.

He stood dumbstruck for a moment. He took in her cloak, the sack hanging from her shoulders, the bow slung across her back. His face contorted in fury.

Loren turned and ran into the woods. As soon as the village fell out of sight, the terror in her veins turned to rage, far too late to do her any good.

FIVE

She pounded through the woods, wasting no time to cover her trail or silence her footfalls. She could hide her trail from most, but her father, too, called the forest home. He had spent many more years beneath its boughs than Loren had, and she knew he could track her easily. She would have to rely on speed and hope that his age would give her the advantage.

Every odd noise sent a gout of terror through her. But then she would reflect upon the sound and realize it was only a bird taking flight, or a doe fleeing from her footsteps. Even in her terror and her haste, Loren's instincts could sense what her mind could not.

It seemed an eternity before she saw the white bark of the birches far ahead. The summer sun beat down through the leaves, and sweat soaked every part of her. She weaved between them, jerking away whenever her travel sack caught on branches. Finally she slung it off her back to carry at her side. In a short breathless while she emerged from the copse to find the forest empty.

Panic seized her. Her hour had not yet passed. Where had Xain gone? She scanned the ground for his trail, but then she heard the snap of a twig, and he rose from behind a fallen log.

"I am pursued," she said quickly.

His eyes flashed. "The constables?"

"No, I sent them the other direction. But my father spied me as I left the village."

He muttered a curse. Loren thrust a hand into her travel sack, wrapped it around her father's cloak, and tugged.

"Here. Leave your coat—it will get in the way, and shine like the sun besides. Put this on."

He obeyed without question, dropping the garment into the dirt and donning her father's green cloak. She saw his nose wrinkle at the smell, but he made no comment.

"Come, and quickly," she said. "Try to follow my path exactly. The track I take us on will be difficult to follow. Mayhap we can lose him."

"I have no quarrel with your father," growled Xain. "We should split up, or you should stay."

Loren's stomach spun circles. "I had no quarrel with your constables, and yet I saved you from them. You cannot leave me!"

His eyes darted back and forth. "Very well. But if he should catch us, I will not raise a hand against him first."

He will raise his, I assure you, she thought. But she said nothing. Xain would go with her, as long as she did not scare him off.

As they went south, the land fell away before them. The slope of the ground lent them speed, and Loren used it to their advantage. Once the land began to level again, she swerved suddenly right and up a low rise. At the top, broken rocks formed a sort of circle. The Giant's Crown, some called it, and the ground grew hard and stony beyond. She followed the rocky terrain as long as she dared, but when it turned north she abandoned it and plunged again into the trees.

Before long, a small stream sprang up at their feet. They ran down its speedy flow, splashing through the shallows at the edge. It slowed them somewhat, but water bore no marks of passage. When the stream turned north, Loren led Xain out of the water again.

Here the trees were sparser, and they had to run long distances over open ground. Loren imagined she could feel her father's eyes on her back as she ran. Her steps came faster and faster still, but soon Xain began to flag behind her. She had to slow her pace to match him, and every step seemed an irredeemable loss.

"You must hurry," she said. "He will find us."

Xain did not bother with an answer. He could move no faster, and they both knew it. After a time, his ankle caught upon a protruding root. He stumbled, and in that moment her father struck.

He leapt from the shadows between two thick oaks. A meaty hand lashed out, cracking against Loren's cheek. She fell to the ground with a cry and struggled up before he could pin her down. But he did not come for her. When she rose, Loren saw him atop Xain instead, wrapping an arm around the thinner man's throat. Xain's face turned red and then edged towards purple. He fought to bring a hand around, scrabbling for her father's face, but her father caught the hand and twisted it, prompting a screech of agony.

Loren's mind turned to ice at the cry. Never had her father hurt another in her presence—except when he fought her mother, and then Loren only wanted each to hurt the other as much as possible. But now he threatened to crush the life from her chance at escape, the first man Loren had ever hoped might save her from the life of pain and obscurity she feared.

Icy rage turned white-hot, and Loren drew the dagger. She leapt at her father with the blade held high. But he saw her coming and released Xain, scrabbling to his knees and away from her wild swing.

He rose and roared like a bear brought to bay. The sound dampened Loren's sudden burst of fury, and she hesitated. That moment was enough, and like a snake her father lunged. One hand gripped her wrist to hold the dagger helpless, and his other curled into a fist that he drove into her face.

Stars erupted at the edge of her vision, and Loren stumbled back. Her father squeezed her wrist until the dagger dropped to the grass, and then let her follow it. She gasped at the pain in her eye, blinking as she fought to clear her vision.

"Spawn of soiled seed," said her father between heavy pants. "You have been a plague and a pox upon me since the day you first clawed air into your lungs."

He kicked her. The hard leather of his boots felt like a falling tree trunk. Loren screamed and tried to roll away, but he only kicked her in the back.

She could not see. She could not think. Where was she? Who was this man, and why did he want to hurt her so? Why did some part of her mind cry that he should love her, pick her up and cradle her in his arms and promise to take the pain away? Instead he only gave her more.

Loren's eyes fell on Xain, who crouched a few paces away. The wizard's lips moved, and his eyes began to glow. A hand curled at his side, and Loren saw the flash of fire within it.

"No!" she cried through the red haze that clouded her vision. "Do not kill him!"

Xain froze. His lips stopped moving, and the fire wisped out in his palm.

The shout drew her father's gaze. His ugly, beady eyes fell on the wizard, and his lips split in a grimace, revealing spots of blood.

He leapt catlike upon Xain and bore the wizard to the ground. This time he wrapped his hands around the wizard's throat, digging his fingers in deep. Xain's eyes bugged forth as though they would burst from their sockets. He gasped a phrase, and blue lightning sprang into being, but it vanished before he could unleash it.

Loren's heart broke. Xain would not have been here if not for her. He might have died on the way to Cabrus, and he might not. But she had brought him to this place, and then brought her father's wrath to follow them. And now Xain would die for it.

She could not allow it. Loren saw the dagger lying near her fingers, and she thought of her childish dreams.

Nightblade could not allow it.

Loren fought to her knees. Her bow still hung on her back, and by some grace of the gods its string was whole. Her fingers felt like wood, but she forced them around the bowshaft and pulled it free. Shakily she brought an arrow to string and half-drew before taking two stumbling steps forwards. This time, her father had eyes for nothing but Xain.

Loren kicked as hard as she could, and something in her father's face broke under her boot heel.

He fell away, rolling over and over to put distance between them as he screamed in rage. In a blink he regained his feet, but there he paused. Loren's arrow rested at full draw, aiming straight for his heart.

Slowly, her father's hamfist hands came up on either side of his head. The higher they climbed, the greater grew the fury in his eyes.

"No more." The words left Loren in a whisper. "No more will you torment me. I am leaving, Father, and I mean never to return."

"You mean to defy me? You will do your duty as a daughter or—"

She pulled just a little harder on the bow, another bit of draw. Her father's voice fell to silence.

"You have never done your duty as a father," she said. "I feel I owe you nothing."

"You owe me everything. I could have killed you in the cradle. I could have killed you when

I woke up today, and moved my bowels on your corpse. I made you, and now I see I made you worthless."

His words should have stung, but she was beyond them. They were only a stronger flavor of the same things he had said all her life. And in this moment, now that another fate beckoned, she stood under his sway no longer.

"Then when I leave, you shall suffer no great loss." Her icy eyes met her father's boiling rage.

Xain had finally regained his breath, and he came to stand at Loren's side. He muttered, and as his eyes glowed white, a ball of lightning hovered in his grasp.

"You think you can escape me?" her father said, changing tack. "I learned these lands years before I spilled you between your mother's legs. Nowhere in Selvan can you hide from me. Ready yourself for sleepless nights by a bright fire. For if you close your eyes in sleep, if for even a moment you let yourself sit in darkness—"

Loren loosed the shaft. It sank into her father's thigh. He collapsed to the ground without a scream, but with a gut-deep grunt of pain.

"Chase us now," said Loren.

She turned and walked away from him, stopping for only a moment to retrieve the dagger and replace it in its sheath. She did not turn to see if Xain followed her, but after a moment she heard footfalls behind her.

Her father did scream then, in rage more than pain. The hateful sound followed them for a long while, long past the time when she could no longer understand the words. Finally it died away just as they reached the flat plain between the forest's southern edge and the King's road beyond it.

The sun hung low in the sky by the time they reached it. Loren had only seen the road twice in her life. Its hard-packed dirt felt odd beneath her feet. Not far beyond, they heard the whispering sigh of the Melnar as it babbled its way towards the High King's Seat.

"The King's road at last," said Xain. They were the first words he had spoken since the fight, and they came hesitant and raspy from his throat. His bruises would long remain, Loren knew. She feared to see the marks on her own ribs, and whispered a quick prayer of thanks that nothing had been broken.

But the road would not let her think of the hurt for long. "Does the road reach as far as they say?"

"I do not know what you have been told," said Xain, "but I would imagine it is longer. Follow it west from here, and you will come to every capital city in the nine lands. Follow it east, and soon enough you will find yourself at the High King's Seat."

"But we do not go that way."

He frowned. "No. We do not travel upon the road at all. Fast though our path might be upon it, watchful eyes would spy us far too easily. We must cut across and follow its course, but far from its edge."

Loren nodded. "How far will we go tonight?"

"Your arrow was well placed. We need not fear your father's pursuit. And if I know constables, we will not see them until the morrow, if then. We will make for the river and camp upon its bank."

Loren would have traveled all night, eager to prove her willingness and her worth as a traveling companion. But her heart nearly melted in relief at Xain's words. A bone-weariness had set upon her. For the first time she had stood up to her father, and she had emerged alive, though not unscathed. Her mind had not yet decided what to think of the encounter, and had settled instead for a comfortable numbness that drained her of energy.

She led the way across the road. Xain did an odd thing as he followed her: he skittered across the packed dirt, stepping lightly as though placing a foot upon it would invite the watchful eyes of every constable in Selvan. Once they had crossed, he resumed his stiff gait.

The sun neared the horizon as they reached the bank of the Melnar. Loren walked downstream until she found a large rock beside which to camp, and then returned and led Xain to the place. She threw her travel sack upon the dirt and fell beside it, resting her head on the soft, silty dirt of the riverbank.

Xain slumped against the rock, and for a long time they sat there, neither speaking nor looking at each other. Eventually Loren felt her stomach rumble, and so she dug into the pack and fetched some salted meat. She cut it with the hunting knife she always kept in her boot—the dagger at her belt was meant for a different kind of flesh—and split it with Xain.

She pulled out more salted meat and one waterskin for him. He drank thirstily, and then refilled it from the flowing river. He chewed sparingly at the meat, and then wrapped the remainder to place it in the bags hanging at his belt. Loren felt great relief to see the wizard ration himself. She would not have to mother him, at least.

The sun had vanished beneath the horizon, but dull orange still glowed in the sky when Xain finally spoke. "Will you never return home?"

Loren thought hard upon it. "He will die. Not from today—that arrow wound will heal long before his temper does. But one day he will, as will my mother. We never grow younger. I could return once they have passed. But why would I?"

"Do you have no other . . . no. I am in the wrong to ask. Some wounds must wait before we can clean them."

She wondered what that meant. "What of you? You do not seem on a course that bears return. What will you do? Run forever?"

He did not answer, only turned away and lay upon the ground with a little pillow made from torn grass. He fell asleep faster than she could believe.

Loren built her own grass pillow and lay upon it, but sleep would not come. She could only stare at the numberless stars as they sprang to life in the inky night sky. Her mind raced and stood still all at once.

She could not think of home. She could not remember her mother's face. She could recall Chet, but not his voice. And she could not envision Cabrus or any place else that lay ahead, either. There was only the here and now, and the quiet bubbling of the Melnar close at hand.

She did not remember drifting off, but before she knew it she had fallen asleep upon her pillow of grass. And when she woke, Xain had taken his meat and his water skin and gone, leaving her alone by the riverbank.

SIX

LOREN WAITED FOR NEARLY AN HOUR BEFORE SHE came to accept that Xain would not return.

She spent the time eating more of her rations. She drank from the waterskin, careful not to overfill herself, and replenished it from the river. And she poked gingerly at the bruises on her ribs and around her eye, probing their extent.

When Xain still had not appeared, she cupped river water in her hands to see her reflection. The skin around her left eye had grown black. She let the water seep through her fingers.

All the while, her eyes avoided the empty spot where Xain had slept.

At last she forced herself to rise. He was gone, and he was not coming back. She expected the revelation to come with doubt or fear. Instead, her insides turned to ice, and doubt became resolution. She stowed her waterskin in the travel sack and slung it over her shoulder. Then, her hand gliding along her dagger's hilt, she set off west along the river.

The Melnar stretched wide beside her, babbling and whispering as it ran the opposite direction of her course. She focused on it to keep her thoughts from Xain, but then it felt as if the river dragged her backwards. So she tried to think of nothing at all. Fortunately, she traveled through a foreign land that lay beautiful in the early morning. She let her eyes roam the rolling terrain and the glow of pink in the eastern sky, focusing her mind upon the land around her.

It had few trees compared to the Birchwood, affording her excellent visibility in every direction. She walked atop the line of hills between the Melnar and the King's road, where she could see the dark line of the Birchwood on the northern horizon. But soon she realized that while she remained upon that raised land, others could see her as well. The thought sobered her, and she descended the south side of the hills to walk the riverbank instead.

She could not still her mind forever, and at last she thought of her father. He had no doubt returned to the village by now. If the constables too had returned, Father would tell them about his fight with Xain and Loren. The constables would come, and until Loren was far away she must remain cautious.

Long before midday, Loren reached the road's great turn south. It swung left and crossed the river by means of a great stone bridge that robbed her of breath. The stones stood at least five paces high from the surface of the water, and they were shaped like river willows given form by human hands, grown from the earth's roots. Just beneath the bridge itself, they joined in great arches that supported the King's road, curving across the top of the river's swells like the path of a thrown rock. The pillars were wet and dark, while the stones of the railing were caked with a white crust.

"How could such a thing ever come from human hands?" said Loren. "How could they build such towers of stone in the deep, deep water?"

She realized no one was around to hear, and her cheeks flushed as her hand went to the dagger's hilt.

"Well, for lack of anyone better, I shall talk to you, then. Though I think the wonder of this bridge is lost upon you."

The dagger said nothing.

"I must give you a name," she muttered, glancing over her shoulder. "But mayhap it can wait until I have more time to think, and I no longer fear the pounding of boots behind me."

Loren expected the bridge to shake like the rickety wood-and-rope bridges common to the Birchwood. But it stayed solid as the road. It unnerved her to walk across the stone and see the water swirl five paces below.

Immediately she cut off and away from the road. Trees grew plentiful again, and she dipped into the space between their trunks. She kept walking until the ground rose and she could scarcely see the road to the west. Then she struck south, following the road's straight course and keeping it just on the edge of eyesight.

In the Birchwood, Loren had often walked beneath trees that stood twenty paces or taller. Here, she barely saw a one that reached more than eight.

"Though I am grateful for their company, these trees are bare saplings next to the ones from home," she murmured, her finger brushing the dagger.

Midday came and went, and the sun began its slow journey back to the earth. Loren felt a gnawing in her stomach and reached for the travel sack where her meat and bread waited. But just then, she spotted a telltale patch of brown fur beneath a nearby shrub. Quiet as a ghost, she pulled her bow from her back and nocked an arrow.

Silent she drew, and silent let fly. The rabbit gave a thin death scream.

She dressed it quickly and struck a small fire. The rabbit tasted delicious, so she ate as much as she could—long past the point of enjoyment. Salted meat would last her long if she rationed it carefully, but on an uncertain road a wise traveler ate sparingly from reserves. She drank carefully, too, taking only a small sip of water.

Still limbs brought thoughts of Xain, urgent and unwelcome. Loren pushed down a sour feeling as the rabbit lost its savor. Soon she stamped out the dying embers of her fire and resumed her trek south.

The rest of the day passed without event, but Loren felt a curious sense of urgency growing. It spurred her legs until she no longer walked but half-ran through the woods. She thought she might feel better if she *did* see the constables, if only to end her aching uncertainty. What if they trailed her in hiding, waiting to see if she would reunite with Xain? She felt eyes boring into her back and hoped she imagined them.

As the sun neared the horizon, she decided that she must rest. If the constables indeed trailed her, she would gain nothing by pushing on through the night. She would only waste precious hours of sleep and dull her senses the next day. With no one to trade night watches, she spent her last hour's walk in search of a hidden place to sleep.

She found it at last in a thick oak. The sun's last sliver had vanished only a moment ago. Four paces from the forest floor, a large black hollow gaped. She hooked arms and legs around the trunk and shimmied up, to poke a cautious eye above the last branch. The hollow lay empty.

Climbing atop the branch, she inspected the hollow more closely. Indeed, it was empty of anything save ants. Loren could stand ants, especially small ones such as these, which did not bite.

By running her legs along the thick branch, she could lean into the heart of the tree and rest. She wished for a rope to tie herself in, but she could not conjure one up now. Her arms she wedged against the hollow to better hold herself in place.

As soon as she stilled, Loren's mind leapt to Xain despite herself. She feared her thoughts might keep her from a restful sleep. But moonslight pierced the leafy canopy to fall upon her outstretched legs, and her sight grew hazy upon the cool silver glow. Weariness soon claimed her.

She woke in the morning to a stiff back, though less so than she had feared. Sliding gently from the hollow, she climbed hand over foot down the oak's branches. She felt no hunger, but her urine smelled. That made her drink more water than she would have liked. She could not drink so much every day, but neither could she afford to grow too dry upon the road. Water loss could creep upon the unwary traveler, leaving them weak.

Her thirst sated, she decided to visit the road before traveling on—a quick glance only, to see what could be seen.

She reached the road at the crest of a hill and hunched low as she walked out onto it, scanning the land in all directions. But her eyes found no travelers on either foot or horseback.

With a small sigh of relief Loren palmed the dagger's hilt. "Luck is with us still," she muttered.

As if in answer to her words, a small smudge appeared to the north. It grew larger as she watched, unable to move. Soon she dropped to her stomach in the dirt, for she could see what raised the cloud of dust: two men on horseback, riding south hard and fast along the road.

SEVEN

Loren scuttled for the trees, keeping as low as she could. The forest enveloped her like an old friend, and she felt safer the moment she came beneath its shadow. She plunged farther into the brush that covered the forest floor.

But as soon as she lost sight of the road, Loren paused. She could not be sure the men were constables, though something in her heart said they were. If so, she should keep an eye on them. But how could she ensure they would not spot her?

Just south of where she stood, the land rose steeply to form a low ridge that ran alongside the road for what looked like many leagues. Loren made her choice and ran for the rise. The trees grew thinner as soon as the ground climbed, forcing her to dart from cover to cover. Finally she stood atop the ridge, a large cave at her back descending into the earth. She stepped behind the trunk of a tree and then poked an eye around it to look north.

The men had drawn near. They drove their horses hard, and the beasts' flanks were streaked with white. They would pass her in a little while. She need only hide and wait. Once they left her behind, her journey to Cabrus would be made in safety.

Loren slid a hand along the dagger's hilt. "A good scare, certainly, but nothing to worry about. We are safe."

She moved back behind the tree and slid down against its trunk—and her heart nearly stopped.

The ground quivered under the impact of heavy feet. Not three paces away, a bear emerged from the mouth of the cave. Its nose twitched as it snuffled the air, tiny eyes fixed on Loren. Black fur stuck out in great bristles as its hackles rose. Two cubs cowered behind their mother's hind legs, looking at Loren with equal parts curiosity and fear.

Her throat went dry as she slowly stood. Her hand slid to the dagger, but she dismissed it. *A fool's hope,* she thought. The dagger would serve no better against the bear than would her fingernails.

But the Birchwood held many bears, and Loren knew what to do. It would mean exposing herself to the road again, but that seemed preferable to serving as the bear's supper.

She sidestepped away from the tree and took several steps backwards. At her movement, the bear hunched down slightly and growled. But it did not advance.

Slowly Loren backed down the slope, never taking her eyes from the beast. Another step. Another. If she could only get far enough, she could run without the bear giving chase.

On the next step, her foot caught on a rock. The slope worked against her, and she nearly crashed to the ground. The sudden movement startled the bear, and it took two great steps forwards with a roar. Even at a distance, Loren could smell the reek of its breath.

She risked a glance over her shoulder. The constables had stopped their mounts on the road adjacent to where she stood. As she watched, they spurred their horses into the woods towards her.

Mayhap they thought her some chance girl in trouble and did not recognize her from the forest. But they would know as soon as they saw her close. She must leave, and quickly.

An idea sprang into her mind. She stomped the ground as hard as she could, throwing her hands into the air and bellowing an angry roar.

Most bears would have backed away, but this one had cubs. The bear took two half-steps and then broke into a run. The ground shook, and Loren's legs tensed in readiness.

Just before the bear reached her, Loren leapt to the side. It could not stop quickly enough, and the loose soil gave way beneath its feet. The bear tumbled and rolled head over paws down the slope. A great plume of dust followed it down.

Loren could take no time to exult in her quick thinking. She ran up the ridge as fast as she could. The cubs fled into the cave in terror, but Loren paid them no mind.

She reached the top of the ridge and plunged down its far side, her feet lent sudden speed by the slope. Just as she passed over the top, she heard loud shouting behind her, joined by a roar. The constables had encountered the bear. Mayhap it would occupy them long enough for Loren to make good on her escape.

She forced herself to slow, though every part of her screamed to go faster. Her quick wits would mean nothing if she fell and broke a leg—or her neck. She picked her way on solid ground and rocks, avoiding any patch of ground that looked like it might slide out from beneath her.

But despite her caution, bad luck caught Loren at last. A rock she had thought was sturdy shifted and tumbled beneath her foot. Loren went down with a cry. She twisted to land on her front and planted her hands in the turf. It hurt, but she knew the bow on her back would not withstand a tumble.

The bow. She could find a high spot in a tree, wait for the constables to approach, and then plant shafts within them before they knew what had happened.

As quickly as she thought it, Loren cast the idea aside. Even if she could shoot with such skill, Nightblade did not—*could* not—murder. Especially not constables who were only doing their duty.

Her only hope lay in escape. So she pushed off the ground, wincing at the sting in her palms, and kept running.

Before long she heard the thunder of hoofbeats coming down the slope behind her. They had either evaded the bear or killed it. She risked a glance over her shoulder but could not see them through the trees. That was good; neither could they see her. But she could not outrun them forever.

Loren scanned the forest and saw something that might help: a fallen trunk with a hole beneath it. She dove in, careful not to snap the bow against the entrance.

Not a moment too soon. The thundering hooves grew louder, and then they were upon her. But she had hidden in time. She saw a flash of red boiled leather between the trees a few paces away, and the hoofbeats receded.

Loren waited until she could no longer hear the horses, and then she waited longer still. In the sudden silence of the woods, her pulse sounded like rolling thunder. When she felt sure they must be gone, she slid out from beneath the log.

A cluster of firethorn stood nearby, unruly but straight as a hedge. It ran south, crosswise to the slope. Loren ducked behind it and slid along on hands and knees. In silence and shadow she crept, poking her head above the tops of the bushes every few moments to look for the constables.

Now that she had a moment to observe, she could see that this side of the ridge ran down to a different, smaller road. This one, too, ran south as far as she could see, though she imagined it had to cut west and join with the main road eventually.

She must gamble now; either the constables would make for this smaller road and follow it, hoping to catch her, or they would climb the ridge and make for the King's road once again. That seemed the likelier course. They had only seen her, not Xain. They might surmise she had separated from the wizard, and if so they would return to the main road in hope of catching him.

Then Loren realized that the forest around her had grown too quiet.

An arrow sped from between the trees to *thunk* into a tree beside her. Loren's body jerked in surprise. She dropped flat and slid beneath the firethorn. The arrow had come from above. Somehow the constables had circled around to her rear. She had underestimated their woodcraft, mayhap for the last time.

Why would they try to kill her? They wanted Xain, not her.

As if in reply to the thought, she heard Corin's voice. "Stay your hand! Leave her whole!"

Bern, the one with a harsher look, shouted a reply that Loren could not make out. Crashing footsteps sounded from up the ridge, much higher than she had feared. Mayhap she could yet evade them.

Once she passed beneath the firethorn, she rose to flee in a crouching run. Now that she had their measure as woodsmen, she would withhold nothing.

She used every trick she had learned from a lifetime in the Birchwood. Her thoughts faded to a dull murmur, and instinct took over. Her feet found only the hardest ground, and she twisted and weaved to avoid snapping any branch. She wrapped her cloak tight, letting its brown fade her into the forest. The sounds behind faded away as she pressed on.

There was the road—and now she could see a caravan, its wagons sitting in a rough line. People in bright clothing sat clustered in a group at the front. Men in shirts of mail and shining helms stood guard around them.

But the back of the caravan lay nearly unattended.

Loren made for the tree line. Many paces of open space stretched between the forest and the wagons, but that could not be helped. If she could make it to one of the wagons unseen . . .

The closest guard turned and walked away, and she seized her chance. She broke from the trees and raced across the rocky ground, as fast as she dared while staying deadly silent. Her cowl flew back, and her raven hair streamed in her wake.

She expected at any moment to hear a cry of alarm or the sound of drawn steel. None came. Loren reached the back of the rearmost wagon and slipped down the line to the third from the last. Still no one, guards or constables, was in sight. Without a sound, she leapt up and over the wagon's edge into the waiting shadows.

EIGHT

LOREN INSPECTED HER SURROUNDINGS WITH HASTE. Bolts of cloth lay on wooden shelves that lined either side of the wagon, and a thin aisle ran up the center.

A merchant's caravan. She hoped that would help. From what Loren knew of the rich, they did not appreciate the eyes of the law and had skill at turning them away. But even a cursory look would find her, here. The merchants had packed their racks too tightly for Loren to slip in among them.

She almost turned and left, but then she heard footsteps outside, near the wagon. Her heart skipped a beat, and she slipped deeper into the wagon. Then she saw that she had been wrong before: one shelf near the front of the wagon was empty. Loren slid onto it, squeezing back as far from the aisle as she could manage.

A great shout sounded outside, followed by the hiss of drawn steel. For a moment, Loren feared she had been discovered. But the sounds retreated, and she realized the caravan had spotted the constables. She heard hooves approach and pull to a stop not far from her wagon.

"We are men of the king of Selvan, about his business," came Corin's burbling voice.

"And what business has the king with us?" came a sharp reply—a woman's voice.

"We pursue a man and a girl." This time it was Bern who spoke. "They fled us south on the King's road. We spotted the girl on that ridge. She may have come among you."

"No girl came," said the woman. "We have seen no one since yesterday. Who is this man you seek?"

"He is between our heights," said Bern. "He may have worn a blue coat, or a dark green cloak. His hair hangs long and curled."

"We saw him, or one like him," said the woman.

Loren put a hand over her mouth to stifle a gasp.

"When?" said Corin.

"Yesterday. Just after the sun had set. He came upon our camp at night and offered us fair payment for a horse. He refused to rest the night, though we offered him hospitality. Instead he rode on, south along this road."

The constables remained silent a long moment, or if they spoke Loren could not hear their words.

"He did not have a girl with him?" Corin said at last. "She would have been young, in forester's garb."

"Of course he did not," said Bern. "We just saw her."

"No one came with him," said the woman. "Alone he arrived, and alone left. Nor have we seen any other since. If you pursued him, I am sorry to have sold him the horse, but we could not have known he deserved justice."

"Of course, my lady," said Corin. "Last night, you say?"

"I do."

"Then we must away. We thank you—"

"Hold," said Bern. "The girl is near."

Again they fell quiet, though this time Loren felt sure the constables must be speaking softly. That proved true, as their voices gradually swelled in anger. Finally Bern spoke again, loud and clear.

"If you have not seen her, it will not matter if we search your wagons."

"They carry only goods for trade," said the woman, indignant.

When Corin spoke, he sounded as though he held anger in check. "My stalwart friend is mayhap overeager. But the girl could have arrived without your knowledge and stowed herself away."

Loren searched around her in panic. They might not see her from the wagon's rear, but then again they might, and if they came inside the wagon they would find her for certain.

"Come now," said the woman. "Our guards stand vigilant. She is not here."

"Let us see, then," said Bern. His voice had taken on a mean edge that Loren did not like.

Her eyes roved again over the inside of the wagon. No better hiding place presented itself. But as she glanced at the floor, her gaze caught on something. A shaft of sunlight fell upon a board that protruded from the wagon's floor. She leaned out and prodded it with her fingers. It was loose. She lifted, and a large panel rose silently.

Beneath lay a compartment, cunningly hidden. Within sat several packages wrapped in brown cloth. But more important, plenty of space remained for Loren to hide herself. Like a snake she slid into the compartment. Then she held the wood panel steady on all her fingers, lowering it into place without a sound. She could not be sure it lay flush, but she could do no better.

Loren heard the constables move down the caravan towards her wagon, drawing closer. She heard a gruff snort, and then the wagon shook. Heavy boots thudded onto its floor, and Loren barely kept from yelping in fright.

Through the cracks in the panel above her, Loren spied Bern's grim features. The constable walked up the length of the wagon, peering into every corner. He stuck his nose right into the shelf where she had hidden a moment before. At last he turned and stalked towards the wagon's rear. The whole thing shook again as he clambered out.

The constables moved slowly away. Loren waited breathless; each passing moment felt like an eon. At long last she heard conversation again, though it was too far off to make out, and then came the thunder of galloping hooves. Still she waited, listening for some clue or sign of safety.

Instead she heard voices. One a man's, deep and booming, and the other belonged to the woman she had heard earlier.

"They found none of the compartments?" said the woman.

"None, my lady," replied the guard. "We followed them every moment. They never so much as glanced at their feet."

"That is good. Though it was too close a thing regardless. I do not like surprises."

"Nor I, my lady," said the man.

Their conversation ceased. Loren thought they must have moved away. After a short while of silence, she reached up to lift the panel off. A quick glance told her no one stood behind the wagon to see, so she slid out of the compartment and replaced the panel before creeping to the back of the wagon.

Now guards stood in thin-stretched rows down both sides of the caravan, all of them facing outward. Her escape would prove more difficult than her arrival, it would seem.

But as Loren surveyed their positions, trying to work out the best angle by which to leave, a child appeared from nowhere. She sprang up from below the edge of the wagon's back panel, a tiny thing with skin as black as night. Yellow brocade glinted on a muted purple gown, matching the shine of her innocent eyes wide as dinner plates. They grew wider still as she gaped at Loren.

"Who are you?" cried the girl. "Are you the one the constables sought?"

Loren fled for the front of the wagon. It had a smaller opening than the rear, but still large enough to slip through. But as she dropped to the ground, she found herself facing a pace of bared steel.

She froze. Her eyes traveled up the length of the sword to the man who held it. He dwarfed any person she had ever seen. His skin, like the girl's, nearly glowed in its darkness. But Loren could scarcely look away from his eyes, for they were solemn and uncompromising as stone. He wore a shirt of chain and a silver helmet like the other guards, but also steel pauldrons wrought with gold inlay.

Loren took him in for a moment, and then her knees buckled and she collapsed to the ground. She cowered at the steel point of his sword, ready to leap forwards and plunge into her chest.

"Who are you?" said the man. She recognized the booming voice from earlier.

"I . . . I . . ." The word *Nightblade* leapt into her mind and vanished like a puff of smoke.

"Gregor! Lower your blade."

A woman arrived, and Loren could hear it was the one who had spoken before. Her voice was even more distinct in the open air. From her eyes and the shape of her face, Loren knew at once that this must be the mother of the little girl she had seen. But where the girl was all bounce and innocence, in the woman's face Loren saw a grim determination more steely than her captain's sword. And at her command, that sword dropped, its point sinking into the grass.

The woman strode forwards, swirling her dress around her with a flourish. Like a wizard's trick, the little girl appeared just behind her mother's legs. Loren thought at once of the bear cubs.

"You are the girl the constables sought, I imagine," said the woman. No trace of a question lined her words.

"I . . . I am," said Loren, finding her voice at last. More of her wits gathered to her, and she hastily added, "My lady."

"Help her up."

Gregor seized Loren's shoulders and hauled her to her feet. To Loren it felt as though he could fling her into the sky, but he set her down almost gently on her heels. The woman gestured with two fingers. Gregor took three steps back, quick and yet unhurried. The woman stepped forwards to take his place. Her hand leapt out to cup Loren's chin and tilt it up. She studied Loren's face for a moment.

"How came you by that eye? Not from the constables, I hope."

"No," said Loren, unsure how to take this. She winced as the woman probed her bruises with a finger. "That gift I received before their pursuit began."

"Hmm." The woman removed her hand and stepped back. "Do you choose to withhold your name?"

Loren blinked before bowing. "I am Loren, my lady, of the family Nelda."

"Damaris," said the woman, inclining her head. "Of the family Yerrin. Well met."

"And you," said Loren, keeping her head and most of her body bent. She could not shake a keen awareness of Gregor and his sword.

"Oh, stand, girl," said Damaris. "I am a merchant, not the queen."

Loren straightened. "Thank you."

"You are pursued, and rather hotly, it seems," Damaris went on. "Tell me why."

"They spoke the truth. I traveled with the wiz—" Loren clamped her mouth shut, her cheeks flaming red. "With the man they sought."

Damaris' nostrils flared. "I thought I heard a secret hidden in their words, but a wizard? That is remarkable. I suppose I should count myself lucky the man did not cast us all in fire and steal the horse he needed." Her eyes flicked past Loren to the wagon. "But tell me. The constables were thorough. How did they miss you?"

Loren heard something in Damaris' tone, and thought she knew what it might be. "I found a loose board in the wagon's floor, my lady. I hid myself beneath it."

"In that wagon?" said Damaris, pointing.

"Yes, my lady."

Damaris' voice took on an undercurrent of steel. "And did you see anything else concealed within the floor?"

Once again, Loren heard the meaning beneath the words. And so she said, "Not a thing, my lady. The compartment lay empty, with plenty of room to stretch my legs."

Damaris relaxed, lips twitching in a smile. "It is such a pleasure to find wit and charm in a chance stranger."

Loren bowed again. "My lady is too kind. I give only the truth."

The tension on the air melted away, and Damaris' daughter emerged again to study Loren. Her wide eyes roved up and down. Loren had the uncomfortable feeling of being a sow under inspection.

"Will we give her to the constables, Mother?" said the girl.

Loren's heart slid into her throat, but Damaris shook her head. "We will not. They sought the wizard more keenly, I think, and he abandoned her. Sending this girl into the hands of the law would gain us no profit."

Loren seized upon Damaris' hidden meaning.

I know of the hidden compartments and what lies within them, she thought. *If they give me to the constables, I might speak of them.*

It gave her a sense of security. When two strangers walked together outside of the King's law, neither could gain much from betrayal of the other.

Then she had a second thought and realized that might not be so. If such knowledge indeed proved dangerous, Loren's corpse would serve Damaris better than her presence. Loren's eyes flitted to Gregor and the bare steel in his huge gloved fist.

As though she read Loren's mind, Damaris shook her head. "You have nothing to fear, girl. Not needlessly do we spill blood. Such policy serves one who lives by the sword, but rarely is it profitable to those who live by the coin." Again she motioned with two fingers. Gregor slid his sword into its scabbard—though too slowly for Loren's comfort.

"Thank you, my lady. It would seem I am in your debt."

"I have given you nothing," Damaris replied. "I have merely neglected to take anything away. Now, where are you bound?"

Loren thought of a lie she might tell, but the thought went too long, and so she abandoned it for the truth. "Cabrus."

"And your wizard friend?"

"Cabrus as well."

"Do you seek for him, then?"

That gave Loren pause. Did she? Loren did not know. She only knew that she had begun her journey with Cabrus in mind, and nothing had given her cause to change course. But Xain? Mayhap she would find him, but she would not be surprised if he had quit her forever.

"I do not, my lady. He seemed eager to part ways with me, and I have no reason to think that may have changed in the day that has passed since."

"And did *he* give you that kiss upon your face?"

Loren shook her head quickly. "No. In fact, he rescued me from . . ." She nearly said *my father,* but something held her tongue. Damaris did not need to know, and doubtless did not want to.

Instead she said, "I was trapped. Xain provided the means of my escape. Though I know not why he left, I bear him no ill will."

Damaris nodded. "Very well. If Cabrus be your destination, then our paths lie upon the same road. You will travel with us, at least for now."

Loren swayed on her feet. "I would not impose myself as a burden upon you, my lady."

"No. You would not." Damaris turned with a whirl of her dress and left, Gregor close on her heels.

The daughter remained. Her eyes gazed wide and white, striking Loren again with their intensity. Dark brown irises made the whites all the more prominent.

After her mother had passed out of earshot, the girl stepped forwards. "I am Annis," she said.

Loren bowed. "I am Loren, of the family Nelda. Well met."

"I know who you are," said the girl, giggling. "You told Mother."

"Still, manners are never out of place."

Annis' smile dampened as they roamed Loren's face. "I do not think the one who gave you that eye had very good manners."

Loren's hand rose to her left eye, brushing gingerly against the dark bruise. "No, he did not."

"Are you a great fighter? Have you killed many men?"

"With this?" Loren laughed and pointed at the bow. "This is no bow for fighting, nothing worthy of a great name. Squirrelbane, you might call it." But she felt keenly aware of the dagger on her belt, and she drew her cloak a little closer. She did not think anyone had seen the blade, and it might be best to keep it that way.

Annis giggled again, oblivious. "You are funny. Come. You may ride with me in my carriage."

Loren followed her towards the front of the caravan. But as she neared the lead wagon, she felt a keen gaze upon her. Glancing up, Loren saw Gregor's dark and solemn eyes fixed upon her. Though she met his look, he did not turn away.

NINE

The caravan rang with the shouts of Yerrin guards preparing to leave. Annis had a carriage near the front. Loren balked at the sight of it, well crafted all in stained mahogany.

"I do not wish to impose on your mother's hospitality," said Loren. "Surely she would rather ride with you alone."

But Annis only laughed and showed Loren inside, where she found the carriage empty.

"I have my own carriage," said Annis. "I do not ride in Mother's unless I have some reason to, for it is terribly boring there. Mother and Gregor speak only of the road south, while Mother and Gretchen talk of nothing but the accounting books and how much profit they have made upon the road."

"Have you traveled far upon it?"

Annis shrugged. "This is my first journey. I do not know how far is far, you might say. Only this summer has Mother consented to my presence on the caravan. I have lived upon the High King's Seat all my life."

Loren gawked. "The High King's Seat? I have heard it is a place of wonder. Are the streets truly laid with marble?"

"Goodness no," said Annis with a titter. "Only cobblestones, like any city." Then her mouth twisted in doubt. "Well, like I imagine any city would be. We have only passed two upon the road, and one reeked with plague. Mother did not let me open my window, much less leave the carriage."

Loren shuddered. She had never known plague, but some of the village elders had told tales. A great sickness had swept across Selvan in a time before her parents were born, and the Birchwood had not gone unscathed.

"But I speak too much of myself," said Annis. "Mother and my tutors say that is always my way. Tell me of yourself. What do you seek in Cabrus?"

Loren felt her guard rise. "I come from the Birchwood. It is a great forest, the greatest in Selvan."

"Odd," said Annis, turning to look out the window. "I have not heard of it."

"You have seen it," said Loren, "if you rode along the Melnar or the King's road. It runs beside the road from the High King's Seat until the road crosses the river."

"Oh, I think I remember," said Annis. Her gaze wandered out the window.

"You could not have helped but see it," said Loren, feeling her hackles rise.

"And how did you come by that?" said Annis, pointing once again to Loren's black eye.

Loren felt taken aback. The girl's manner was frank to the point of rudeness, her questions brief and to the bone. Rather than answer, Loren said, "How old are you?"

"I have seen twelve years."

Loren smirked. "Ah. Still a child, then."

That produced the desired effect. Annis straightened on her bench, her brows drawing together and her lips pinching in an angry scowl. "I am not a child! I am nearly full-grown, for most in my family do not grow tall. And I am half again as clever as any of my tutor's other pupils. He has told me."

Loren leaned against her cushions and raised her hands, smiling easily. "I meant no offense."

Annis' face relaxed somewhat. But her eyes no longer wandered as though Loren had ceased to entertain her.

Feeling more at ease, Loren decided she might as well answer the child's question. What could it matter? Her father lay in their house far away now, no doubt nursing the wound in his thigh.

"As for my eye, my father gave it to me," said Loren. Annis' mouth opened into a small *o*. "He did not take kindly to my desire to leave home. He pursued me, and when he found me he gave me this. And more."

Loren twisted in her seat and lifted the edge of her tunic to reveal her ribs. Bruises stood bold against the pale white of her skin. Other, older bruises shone yellow, former gifts from her father's meaty fists. Loren pulled the shirt up higher, until

Annis could see the bruises that ran across her chest and all along her back.

Annis squeaked and leapt across the carriage to yank Loren's tunic down. She released the garment like a snake and withdrew, sinking into the purple cushions of the carriage seat.

"What is wrong?" said Loren. "I did not mean to frighten you."

"Frighten me?" squeaked Annis. "I . . . why not just strip naked?"

Loren blinked.

"What, do all the peasants of your village walk nude beneath the sun? Are you savages?"

A scowl twisted Loren's features. "I can say at least that we are not partial to insults. What is the matter? We are women both, and you are too young for courting."

Annis stuck her nose in the air. "In civilized circles, we do not go around parading our bodies. It is unseemly."

Loren snorted. "Very well. I shall not trouble you with my savage customs and peasant's body."

She pushed away from the bench and threw open the carriage door, striding out onto the grass. After a moment the carriage door slammed shut again.

Loren walked for the rest of the day. The caravan moved in no great hurry, and so she easily kept the pace of the horses. Soon she forgot her annoyance with Annis and was able to enjoy again the sights of the strange land around her. The ridge she had crossed soon turned into a low mountain range that ran south, following the course of the road—or rather, she supposed, the road followed the mountains.

Every so often she looked back towards the caravan to see Gregor studying her from under his gleaming helm. Soon she had to make up her mind to ignore him. How could Loren blame him for being suspicious of a mysterious girl pursued by constables?

Eventually the sun neared the tops of the mountains, and the wagons pulled to a stop. Unlike at the midday meal, this time they pulled into a tight circle by the side of the road. Guards dismounted and began to erect a large purple tent amid the wagons. Loren did not need to guess who would sleep there.

She decided to head for the trees while some light remained. Damaris had offered food, but Loren did not want to endanger her hospitality by burdening the caravan's supplies. And if Annis had spoken to her mother, they might already be inclined to see Loren leave. But before she could set off for the woods, she heard footsteps and turned to find Annis.

The girl stood there, hands clasped behind her back and gaze fixed on the ground. She looked for all the world like a village child about to be chastised. Loren almost smirked.

"I am sorry I insulted you. I did not mean it. Only . . . we are not so free with ourselves as you are."

"No apology is necessary," said Loren, feeling gracious as she bowed. "I should not have presumed to be so forward."

Annis looked up at last. "You are not angry with me, then?"

Loren sighed inwardly. She could not help the thought that Annis would anger her again before the road ended. But she smiled. "Of course not. I make for the woods to catch myself dinner. When I return, would you sup with me?"

Annis' eyes widened, as they had when Loren first saw her. "Of course! I would be delighted!"

Loren left her with a smile and made for the woods. She soon saw a squirrel and a rabbit, but both her shots went wide, and she lost one of the arrows. Then she spotted a quail just as the last light died in the sky. Her arrow flew true, and she picked up the bird to bring it back to camp.

She built a small fire and began plucking. But before she had the quail ready for the fire, she felt a presence in the darkness. She looked up and squinted. Damaris' dark face appeared, her eyes glinting in the flickering flames.

"Did you find our provisions unsatisfactory?" said the merchant. "I could have had one of my men fetch a bird, if you wished."

Loren laid the quail down and stood quickly to bow. "No, of course not, my lady. I did not want to impose upon your generosity any more than I already have. Free passage south is a great gift, and I would not ask you to feed me as well."

"Yet you do not even take our passage in truth, for you spent much of the day on your feet."

Loren blushed, feeling somehow off-balance. Had she delivered some insult? These people had strange customs, and she seemed to break them at every turn. "I have never been in a carriage before, and I found the motion disorienting." She did not think it would help to say that Annis had called her a savage.

"I shall tell the driver to be more gentle, then." Damaris' voice betrayed no emotion, yet Loren some felt that she had angered the merchant.

"I will happily ride tomorrow, my lady." Loren bowed low. "And I apologize if I offered any insult."

"Oh, do not trouble yourself. Now, Annis has taken it into her head to sup with you. I told her that you likely wished to be left alone."

Annis appeared behind her mother's legs, like a goblin leaping from the dark. "She does not, Mother! She *asked* me!"

"She would be most welcome," said Loren quickly. "I did offer. But I would never think to pull her from your company."

"Oh, I think it is good for her to spend time with others. Indeed, I often have trouble prying her from my side." The merchant's stern look seemed to melt away, and a warm smile spread across her features. Rather than feel reassured, Loren felt even more unsettled.

Annis squealed and leapt forwards, sitting on the ground beside the fire without a second thought for her fine purple dress. Damaris inclined her head, and then turned to vanish into the darkness.

"What did you catch?" said Annis, leaning forwards.

"It is a quail. It will be ready soon." She picked the bird back up and resumed her plucking.

"Are you a good hunter?"

"I can feed myself. But I learned from a boy in my village whose skill dwarfed my own. He can bring a stag down at full sprint. He . . ."

With memories of Chet came a lance of pain. Loren stopped talking and bowed her head over the quail, pretending to work. Annis did not seem to notice.

"Tell me about your forest. Did you like it there? I have only ever seen the Seat. This is my first time in the wilderness."

Loren would hardly have called this tame land a "wilderness," but she thought better than to say so. "The forest was a good home to me," she said. "But the people within it were less kind. My parents notably so."

Annis' face fell. "Were they very cruel? They seem like the wicked stepparents you hear of in stories."

Loren snorted. "In stories, the parents lock the daughter in a high tower to keep her from true love. They do not beat the daughter for failing to chop enough logs. They do not whip the daughter for mussing her dress."

Loren's fingers had grown tight around her hunting knife. She forced them to loosen.

"How could you stand it?" said Annis. "I think I would have gone mad."

Loren smiled. She looked into the darkness to either side of her as though searching for an eavesdropper. "I might have done. Did you ever think of that, my little lady?" She flipped her knife over the back of her palm, and drops of blood spattered the dirt.

Annis gave a little squeal. "How did you learn to do that? I wish I could flip a knife!"

Loren chuckled and turned back to the quail. She carved off long strips of its flesh and impaled them on sticks she had gathered from the ground, and then propped the sticks up to cook over the fire. "That little trick, and a fair few stories, I learned from an old man named Bracken."

"Bracken?" Annis cocked her head and narrowed her eyes.

Loren raised her hands. "I doubt he gave his true name. He used to say that true names held power, and that only fools gave theirs away. He was old when my parents were children, and he came to our village in autumn every year. He carried a great sack filled with metal pans and hunting knives and old boots. He would trade them in the village, but never for coin. Always he traded for food or trinkets or a nice strong bow."

"A peddler!"

Loren cocked her head. "I do not know that word."

"He was a peddler," said Annis, drawing up straight and puffing out her chest in pride. "They move from town to town, selling and trading. They often tell stories as well. 'Tall as a peddler's tale,' we say on the Seat."

Loren shrugged. "Well, Bracken told tales, true enough. Simple tales of things happening in the nine lands today, and grand tales of knights and dragons from faraway yesteryears. When I went out to fell trees, often he would follow, sitting in a crook or hollow to spin his stories."

"I love stories of dragons," said Annis. "Is it true they are still to be found out in the world?"

Loren gave a little smile. "Truly? Dragons? I did not take you for one who sought to be a mighty warrior."

Annis smiled. "My tutors said the same thing. Soon I turned it into a joke, and said that I only liked the dragons because they had so much gold, just like my family."

Loren chuckled. "I like a quick wit."

"But come, tell me. Did you have favorite stories? Did you like to hear of the princesses who overcame their wicked stepparents? You must have hoped to escape, as they did."

Loren sat silent for a moment. She feared it unwise to speak of her purpose with just anyone. But Annis was only a child. Who would believe her? And if they did, what then? Loren had done nothing wrong. Yet.

She leaned forwards and pulled the sticks of quail from the fire. "Have you heard the tale of Mennet the Mist?"

Annis took a stick, her eyes alight, and leaned back to wrap her arms around her knees. She took a large bite and chewed noisily. "No. Who was he?"

"There never lived a greater thief than Mennet the Mist," said Loren, trying to mimic Bracken's voice when he began a tale. "They say he struck a deal with the shadows themselves. He wove them into a cloak to melt into any darkness and appear in another shadow wherever he wanted. Even in the vaults of cruel kings and tyrants."

"Ooh," said Annis. "He was a good man, then?"

"Not always," said Loren, shaking her head. "He grew up poor and barefoot in the streets of some city—I forget which. He fell in with cutthroats and brigands, and when he grew older he lived as a highwayman, waylaying caravans. Like this one."

Annis looked over her shoulder into the night. Bracken would have been proud.

"But one day, as he and his men rode through the land in search of more plentiful bounty, they came upon a village. The king in that land treated his subjects poorly and met any insolence with fire and sword. Some man in the village had delivered insult, and so the king sent his army to burn the place to ashes.

"Some of Mennet's men wanted to ignore the fire. Others wanted to steal what they could. But Mennet spurred his horse into the town, for he had heard a babe's cry. He found her in a house in the middle of the village, her parents having fled or lying cold in the dirt. Mennet leapt through a window and scooped her up, but fire blocked his escape. That is when he pleaded with the shadows he had befriended all his life, and they enveloped him. The house collapsed, and Mennet's men thought he had died. But then he stepped from the shadows of the trees, the babe in his arms. Terrified, all the men fled.

"Mennet had finished his days as a highwayman, and he turned his talents to doing good. First he stole the King's gold and brought it to the villagers who had lost their homes, repaying them ten times for the damage.

"Then he traveled across the land seeking other wrongs and turning them right. If a nobleman plotted the death of his lord, he might find his private letters taken and constables soon knocking at his door. If one of the nine kings plotted rebellion against the High King, Mennet would know, and the traitor would find the other lands united against him."

"I would wager that he slipped his sharp blades into more than a few backs as well," said Annis.

Loren shook her head quickly. "No. Mennet never took a life. He preferred cleverness to strength, speed to skill with a blade. No one could bring him to a fight—they found themselves outmaneuvered first, their weapons vanished, their men unwilling to battle. Mennet held that only kings could judge, and then only if justice lay on their side. And so when they abandoned justice, Mennet turned it upon them, and even then he refused to swing its righteous sword. He never saw it as his place."

Annis sat in silence for a moment, chewing her quail. Then, in a small voice, she said, "Do you mean to find Mennet, then?"

Loren stared at the flames. "He lived many and more a yesteryear ago. No. The world has not seen his like in an eon. But when Bracken told me those tales, they stayed in my mind. And whenever Father grew angry and struck me, when my mother shrilled and pinched and locked me in a cupboard, I remembered Mennet. I remembered that he did more good with his mind and his words than any king with a mighty sword and an army at his back. My father seemed weak then, my mother foolish. And I hoped that one day I could escape and become the kind of person they should have been."

Annis considered that. "Where is Bracken now?"

"Three years ago, he stopped coming. He must have died. He was very old."

The air dropped to silence again. Loren realized that she had not yet touched the quail, and Annis had eaten nearly half of it. "Are you going to eat all my hard-won bird?"

Annis smirked and took another bite. "Only if you refuse to."

Loren picked up a stick, eating without seeing the food in her fingers. She could see only the fire, the red shape of it leaping up and down, swaying with every gust of wind.

TEN

AFTER THEY ATE, LOREN TRIED TO FIND A PLACE TO sleep. But it felt strange to lie in firelight, surrounded by strange guards with long blades. After a time she rose and took herself beyond the line of wagons. Then her head rested easily upon the ground, and she soon fell asleep.

The next morning dawned bright and early, and Loren woke before most in the camp. She felt no surprise to see Gregor had risen earlier still, and as soon as she stood his gaze snapped to her. She gave him a little wave. He did not so much as blink.

The caravan seemed to take an eternity to get moving, and Loren nearly screamed from impatience. But eventually the drivers mounted their seats and spurred the horses south.

Loren had grown somewhat bored with the countryside, so she spent her time inspecting the caravan instead. The two carriages led the way, followed by a dozen wagons of varying sizes. The two biggest wagons had eight wheels each and were nearly as wide as the road.

Loren let her course run back and forth across the column, peering into the backs of the wagons. She wondered how many of them hid packages swaddled in brown cloth.

What could be so valuable that Damaris would hide it from the constables? Something outside the King's law, no doubt, but Loren had no faintest idea of what that could be.

Annis tried walking with her, but she soon tired. "I do not know how you do this for hours and hours," she said, cheeks puffing in and out with each breath. "I can scarcely keep pace with the wagons."

"The drivers hardly touch their reins."

"The horses seem not to need it," said Annis. Soon she abandoned Loren and retired to her carriage.

After some hours had passed, Damaris emerged and mounted a horse that Gregor brought to her. She rode beside the caravan, sometimes spurring to a gallop and ranging ahead at the edge of eyesight, sometimes content to walk her mount beside the wagons. Wherever she went, Gregor came close behind on his own steed. Loren watched with interest.

After some time, Damaris turned her horse towards Loren. She reined in a pace away, while Gregor sat just behind her, his eyes never leaving Loren's face.

"You seem quite interested in our horses," said Damaris.

Loren flushed. "Where I come from, no one owns a steed for riding, but only plow horses and the like. I have seen riders only rarely, though I always dreamed of owning a horse of my own."

"Would you like to ride?" said Damaris.

For a moment, Loren could not speak. "I . . . I am afraid I would only embarrass myself. I have never sat a saddle."

"It is not so hard. And you wear the right clothing for it. You need not ride sidesaddle, as I do." Damaris slid from the horse's back and drew its reins into one hand as she approached.

"I . . . you do not look . . ." Loren's heart raced as the horse neared. It stared at her with wide and gentle eyes, like great pools of black water.

"Come," said Damaris. "He is gentle, I promise. Give me your bow."

Loren unslung the bow from her back and handed it over, never taking her eyes from the horse.

"Raise your foot."

Loren obeyed without thinking. Damaris seized her boot and placed it in the stirrup before moving Loren's hand to the saddle horn.

"Now step up. Imagine you are climbing a rock. The horse will remain as steady as that."

Loren took a deep breath and pushed. She swung her leg up and over, and before she knew it she had gained the saddle. She sat there for a moment, both hands wrapped around the pommel, too terrified to budge.

"Your other foot," said Damaris.

Loren looked down. Her right boot hung loose. Flushing, she placed it in the stirrup. "Thank you," she said in a small voice.

"Come now. I will walk with you."

Damaris tugged on the reins and walked forwards. Loren did not anticipate the sudden motion and nearly pitched backwards, but somehow she kept her balance. The saddle bounced uncomfortably against her rear. She feared that if the horse increased its pace even a little, it would send her flying. And yet, she rode. She was sitting a horse, for the first time in her life.

"You sit too high and try too hard for balance," said Damaris. "Bend your back somewhat to lower your weight, and cling tighter with your thighs. Do not fear to hold the horse's neck. It will not mind unless you tug too hard on the mane."

Damaris pushed Loren's leg to demonstrate, and then hunched her own body lower to show her how to sit. Loren tried it and felt the saddle's impacts lessen. Unbidden, a grin spread across her face.

"It is so gentle! I thought it would be harder."

"Well, you are only walking, after all." A smile had crept into Damaris' words. "Travel at this speed grants little benefit, other than freedom from your burdens."

They walked that way for a while, Gregor close to Loren's right, Damaris walking to her left. With every passing moment she felt more comfortable with the rolling motion of the horse's back. But after a time, she felt a soreness creeping up her legs, the muscles growing tense and knotted. Her bottom felt bruised.

"I thank you greatly, my lady," said Loren earnestly. "But mayhap I shall walk again. If I stay here too long, I fear I will lose the use of my legs."

Damaris chuckled. "You take to horseback easily, but you might be right. It is not wise to overexert oneself on the first day. But before you dismount, you must try trotting. Gregor."

The man rode up, and Damaris passed him the reins over the horse's neck. He seized them in one hand. Loren's stomach did a somersault.

"Remember, balance yourself with the horse's neck." Damaris stepped away and gave the horse's haunch a gentle slap.

The horse broke into a trot, but to Loren it seemed the earth buckled beneath her. She wrapped her legs around the horse's belly and bent over its back, gripping its coat as hard as she could with both hands. Somehow she stayed on, but the saddle horn slammed into her stomach until she cried out with the pain.

Gregor tugged the reins, and both horses came to a swift stop. Loren shook for a moment, unable to move. Finally she pulled her right foot from the stirrup and swung it over. At the last moment her left boot caught in its stirrup, and she fell over backwards to the ground. She felt her face grow beet red.

Damaris approached, holding out Loren's bow. "A fair effort, for your first time. Do not be discouraged. No one learns to ride well in an hour, or even a day."

"Th-thank you again, my lady," said Loren. "You are too kind. But I think I will walk by the wagons now."

Damaris smiled and remounted. "Very well. If you are still with us tomorrow, we will try again."

She and Gregor rode off. Terrified as she might have been, riding a horse had been a lifelong dream come true. Even as she winced at her aching legs, she envied Damaris as the merchant cantered away.

Midday came, and the caravan halted for lunch. They moved so slowly that Loren would have preferred to eat on the road, but of course such was not her place to suggest. Annis disembarked from her carriage and came to eat with her again. Loren did not enjoy the thought of hunting with her body so sore, and so she gratefully accepted Annis' offer of food.

"You looked so funny on the horse!" said Annis. "I fared much worse than you on my first day. But then, I was much younger."

"I hope to do it again," said Loren. "I have always wanted a horse of my own."

"To roam the land as a wealthy thief," said Annis, a light growing in her eyes. "Riding from town to town with a bag of gold on your back. It sounds glorious."

Loren looked at Annis askance. "I recall speaking no such words. Some might call that a foolish wish, and few would see glory in it."

"Oh, come now," said Annis, leaning in close and dropping her voice to a murmur. "You cannot fool me. After all that talk of Mennet last night? That is your wish, is it not? To become a great righter of wrongs? I could see the light in your eyes when you spoke of it."

Loren swallowed hard and focused on her food. *Fool!* she thought. She had been too free with her words, and Annis seemed less starry-eyed than Loren had thought.

"I desire no such thing. I think Mennet used his skills honorably. But only an idiot would seek to win her fortune through thievery."

"Or speak so openly about it if she did," said Annis with a wink. The girl was not half so silly as she seemed, for all her prudishness. "You thought little before you spoke, and you should guard your tongue more closely. But I am not fooled by your naysaying now. And I may be able to help with your first conquest."

Annis reached into a fold in her cloak and withdrew a small leather purse. She tossed it gently in her hand, and Loren heard the *clink* of coin.

"What is that?" hissed Loren. She looked up, frantically scanning for Gregor or one of his guards. But she could not see him, nor did any guard give her a second glance.

"A purse. The first in a long, fruitful career for the nine lands' next great thief."

She thrust it towards Loren with outstretched hands. Loren snatched the purse and threw it back. The bag slammed into Annis' chest, making her wince.

"Are you mad? I am your mother's guest. What would any honorable person think of me if I stole from her? And as for you, what daughter steals from her own mother?"

Annis' nostrils flared. "And you took nothing from your parents when you ran away from home, did you?"

Loren balked, unable to think of a reply.

"I thought as much," said Annis. "It is a fine thief who calls another thief dishonorable. This purse is a tiny thing, one from a chest of many. No one would notice it had gone, least of all Mother. How do you think you will make your way upon the road without even a penny in your pocket?"

"Your mother is kind and generous to me, and to you as well. What reason could you have to do this?"

"Because," said Annis, her eyes flashing. "I wanted to come with you. But now I think I may not wish to travel beside one so stupid."

The words might have stung, but Loren's mind leapt far away in an instant. She saw herself beneath the boughs of the Birchwood, Xain standing before her.

I want you to bring me with you.

That is what I feared, Xain had said. *No. I will not.*

How could she have been so foolish? Now she could see herself in Annis, too young by half, asking a favor she could not understand.

But no. There *was* a difference.

"My parents had turned my life to something scarcely worth living. Your mother tends to your every need, and has raised you to be no fool besides. We are nothing alike."

"We are more alike than you know," hissed Annis. "If I do not—"

A shout cut her off. Both their heads snapped towards the sound. Near the front of the caravan, Loren saw a bustle of sudden activity.

"What is that?" she murmured.

"An alarm," said Annis. "They have spotted someone on the road."

They jumped to their feet and ran. It took them only a moment to reach the front of the caravan where Damaris stood with Gregor looming beside her, blocking his lady from the road.

"Mother, what is it?" cried Annis. Struck by a thought, Loren looked for the purse of coins, but it had vanished.

"Riders," said Damaris. "Several of them, and led by a constable."

Loren quailed. "Is it . . .?" She could not finish.

"One from yesterday? I cannot tell. But we should not take any chances. Loren, come with me. Quickly."

Damaris hurried down the line of caravans. "You remember the compartment set in the floor of the wagons?" she said.

"Yes," panted Loren, breathless from fear. "I can hide there."

"Not the same one. Here."

Damaris stopped at the fourth wagon in the line. Loren vaulted into the back, squinting as her eyes adjusted to the darkness.

Now that she knew what to look for, she spotted the edges of the panel easily. Her fingers found the crack, and she heaved it upward. This compartment held no brown cloth packages, leaving her plenty of room to lie down. Grateful, she slid into the floor and pulled the panel back over herself.

It took forever before she heard the hooves upon the road. They grew louder and louder before pulling to a stop nearby.

"Who approaches?" Gregor's booming voice shook the wagon floor.

"The king's servants, about his business." Loren did not recognize the voice as either Corin or Bern. *Yet they might still be here,* she reminded herself.

"The road seems fairly thick with constables," came Damaris' clear voice. "Two visited us only yesterday."

"The same who sent us," came the new voice. "They seek a man and a girl, and said they saw the girl near your caravan."

"They told us the same," said Damaris. "But we told them we had seen nothing."

"I have heard the tale. But then I questioned them closely. For many merchants upon the road carry goods that give the king great displeasure. To hide them, such merchants might have panels and holes within their wagons. I asked my brother constables if they had searched for such concealment, and they said they had not. They sent me to see if such might be found."

Loren's throat went bone dry. Silence lingered outside the wagon.

The man spoke again at last. "What say you, my lady? Must my agents break your wagons apart plank by plank?"

Damaris hesitated only a moment before answering. "There is no need. The girl hides within that one. Come, and I will take you to her."

ELEVEN

"Surround the wagon!" The constable's thin, wheedling voice rang out in the still air. "Leave no gap for her to escape."

Loren feared she might vomit. If she had held any illusion of walking with Damaris outside the law, that dream had now gone. She must flee as fast as she could, before the searchers could surround the wagon.

She flung away the wooden panel that covered her. No one stood at the wagon's rear. She still had a chance.

Just as she tensed to run, a cry of alarm sounded from outside the wagon. It was Damaris.

"She has fled!" cried Damaris. "Where did she go? Gregor!"

"I know not, my lady," said the captain. "My guards stood vigilant."

"Vigilant as sleeping bears," snapped Damaris. "Find her, or it will go ill with all of you!"

Loren stood rooted to the wagon's floor. No one stood near her wagon. What game did Damaris think to play? Loren could not know, but she must place her faith in the merchant for the time being. Quick and quiet, she dropped back into the hidden space. Her fingers slid across the wood panel, and she winced as a splinter sank into her flesh. Silent as she could, she lowered it back into place.

She was not a moment too soon; within moments, the wagon shook under heavy feet. A man climbed inside. Loren heard shouts farther down the line: the agents of the King's law had split up, searching the wagons in ones and twos.

In a moment they would find Loren, and then all would converge upon her. Whatever Damaris planned, Loren hoped it would take place soon. The wood beneath her head shook with footsteps. Her breath came fast and ragged.

The man grunted and heaved. The wood panel flew up to reveal her. Not the constable, but one of his riders. A grey mustache sat atop old, weathered lips, and deep lines creased his face from cheeks to eyes. Those eyes squinted at her for a moment, and then widened.

The man's chest erupted in a spray of blood, twelve fingers of steel protruding from his breastbone.

Loren screamed.

The man gurgled and sagged. His lifeblood sprayed forth, dousing Loren's cloak. As he fell she saw Gregor behind him. The giant's eyes shone cold and baleful, like the blue flame of an ancient king's funeral pyre. His boot lashed out, kicking the man towards the front of the wagon.

Outside she could hear the sounds of ringing steel and terrified voices crying out in death. The wagon's canvas could not mute the screams. Loren feared she would hear them as long as she lived.

Loren leapt up and threw off her cloak. Blood had soaked through it in places, and she could feel it pressing upon her skin. She stumbled past Gregor, who did not move a muscle.

She lost her footing on the wagon's edge and crashed to the ground on her shoulder. Pain lanced through her chest. She scarcely noticed it as she rolled over onto her stomach and retched. The previous night's salted meat came up, thick and chunky and smelling of bile. She vomited until her stomach could give no more, and then she lay unmoving, except for her heaving chest.

Loren had seen death before. No one went forever without accidents. She had seen people crushed by falling oaks, or wasting away from infection after a wayward axe took a finger. But never had she seen a man murdered in cold blood, stabbed through the back.

The sounds of death subsided. Gregor's guards had won before their foes knew a battle was afoot. A half-dozen corpses littered the ground.

Soft footsteps drew Loren's gaze upward. Damaris loomed. Her dark eyes found Loren's green ones.

"Whose blood stains your tunic?"

Loren looked down at herself and saw the crimson streaks.

"Why would . . . they were *king's* soldiers!" Loren tried to stand, but wobbly knees soon made her think better of it.

"Aye, and with noses far too keen."

"They would not have killed me! They did only their duty!"

Damaris' brow crinkled for a moment, and then she shook her head softly. "Oh, simple child. You think too highly of your worth if you think I played this hand for you. You are an amusing companion, but I do not risk the law's wrath for amusement only."

Loren slowly gained her feet. Gregor appeared by his lady's side in the space of a blink. His blade lay bare and blood-soaked. Loren swayed backwards to lean against the wagon. A quiet, persistent voice screamed in the back of her mind, growing ever louder. Soon she could make out the words: *Mennet, Nightblade, Mennet, Nightblade, Mennet, Nightblade, you fool.*

"For what, then?" said Loren. "For your hidden panels and your packages of brown cloth? What do you judge worth these lives—the lives of people you did not know, who may leave widows or orphans behind?"

Damaris rolled her eyes. In that gesture Loren saw a wealth of dismissal, a wide ocean of scorn and embarrassment. "The nine lands make widows and orphans of us all in the end. The wretched and woeful are the rule, and joyous folk the exception. Not needlessly do we spill blood, I said—but I did not say we feared to, or had not before."

Loren blanched. "What of me, then? Do you mean to send me to the dark forest with them?"

Damaris shrugged. "Why should I?"

Loren did not know what madness seized her, but she needed to know the manner and meaning of what had happened. "I have seen this." She gestured around at the corpses, though she was unable to look at them. "How could you let me live, fearing that I might reveal today's deeds?"

"Do you mean to?" Rather than fear or anger, Damaris displayed only faint amusement.

Loren said nothing.

Damaris nodded as if an answer had been given. "Your wisdom is, again, a welcome surprise. If you think you could report this to the King's law and escape your own justice, you are sorely mistaken. These people died, in part, to keep my cargo safe. But, too, they died to protect you in your flight from the constables. You would face the block for that, and find your own way to the darkness below apace. None who walk shaded from the law may withstand its burning light."

Loren shuddered to hear the ghost of her own thoughts on the merchant's tongue.

"Now, come," Damaris continued. "I tire of this argument and its lack of purpose. You will help rid the ground of this . . . mess. Gregor will instruct you."

Loren's knees grew weak. "Me? I do not . . . I could not."

"Oh, not alone," said Damaris. "Gregor's guards will manage the bulk of it. But you will help and learn something of value. Who knows but that you will need to dispose of a mess or two yourself one day? You will find it no worthless skill."

Words of denial leapt to Loren's mind. *Nightblade did not murder.* Nor would she. But those words died under Damaris' steely glare. Instead, Loren bowed her head. And when Gregor summoned his guards and set them to drag the corpses off, Loren walked beside them.

She watched the lifeless heads bouncing against the ground. The constable's face pinched thin and reedy, reminding Loren of a squirrel. A thin, pathetic mustache clung to his upper lip—and that lip sat drowned in blood, probably summoned by the man's dying coughs. His torso lay open, and slimy ropes trailed behind him in the dirt. The others wore simple clothes, no uniforms. One of Gregor's men, too, had been killed. The bodies numbered eight in all.

They were all dragged into the woods. Loren felt grateful she did not have to help with that. But once safely ensconced in the trees, the giant's guards set about with shovels and made Loren work as well. The summer sun soon brought on a stench, and she retched twice more before they finished. The bodies they covered with loose dirt and a blanket of leaves, but only after they had stripped the corpses of any coin. Other valuables they left in place; it seemed that the family Yerrin held themselves higher than grave robbers, at least.

Just before Loren had covered the last corpse, the thin clipping of hoofbeats rang out through the tall trunks. She looked up to see Damaris atop her brown steed. Gregor went to her side and took the reins as his lady dismounted. Damaris made her way to Loren. She had something under her arm.

"Come now, and try this on. I think you will find it your size. It will serve you well, and costs more than a forester's daughter might earn in a lifetime."

She pulled out the thing beneath her arm and unfurled it. A black cloak fluttered in the afternoon breeze. Had Loren not been bone-weary with gravedigging and soul-sick from the rotting bodies, she might have gone breathless. The cloak fairly shone with fine cloth, and it shimmered in the sun. Each fold caught a ray of light and absorbed it, never appearing brighter but only growing darker. Its cowl stretched long, able to draw down almost to the wearer's chin.

Loren stood immobile. Damaris waited for a moment, and then stepped forwards to drape the cloak around Loren's shoulders. Coming around front again, she drew the cowl up. The cloak rested on Loren's shoulders like a cloud, the cowl at once warm and pleasantly airy. She felt a light breeze kiss the back of her neck.

Now I am cloaked in shadow, thought Loren. *Like Mennet, but with blood on my hands.*

"There," said Damaris. "It fits as though I had cut it for you myself. And you can hide that needle at your waist again."

Loren's cheek filled with red, and her hand leapt to the dagger. She had forgotten it utterly.

Just at the corner of her vision, Loren saw Gregor. The captain looked poised to leap at a moment's notice. But she knew he would not be able to move fast enough. Loren could draw the dagger and lay Damaris' throat open before Gregor could take his first step.

But she would not. *Nightblade does not murder.* That was the only victory she could take from today, and she would not lose her grip upon it.

Damaris relaxed. Her hand rose without warning, the backs of her fingers trailing against Loren's cheek. Loren looked into the merchant's eyes in wonder. Steel still showed there, it was true, but Loren saw something else: a keen affection, a softening just around the pupils that spoke of concern.

"Do you think I enjoyed what happened?" said Damaris. "You wrong me. One must do what one must. You will know this, too, if you spend much longer in this world. You will understand, and mayhap see me as wise instead of monstrous."

If you spend much longer in this world, Loren thought. She felt she might lose her gorge again and pictured vomit splashing across Damaris' pretty leather boots.

Damaris gave her a final gentle pat on the cheek. "Do not trouble yourself overmuch with this. Let it flow over and through you, occupying your thoughts as it must, and then let it run away."

She turned and went back to her horse, mounting and riding off swiftly. Loren turned to the men behind her. The graves lay filled and blanketed with leaves. She stared at the turned earth with a vacant stare, imagining the dead eyes that lay beneath it.

She dropped her shovel and turned for the caravan. Her cloak of shadows rippled in her wake.

TWELVE

From that moment on, Loren watched for an opportunity to escape. But Gregor hounded her like a shadow, never out of sight. It seemed that Damaris did not trust Loren after all, despite her kind manner.

Loren's only solitude came when she went to the woods to make water. Then Gregor let her leave his sight. The first time, she kept going into the woods, hoping to fade away and leave him behind. But she had only gone a few paces when she saw one of Gregor's guards between the trunks, eyes fixed upon her.

They traveled south through the day, and Loren's mind raced to determine what Damaris could want from her. She could think of nothing.

Once they stopped for the night, Annis appeared as if from nowhere. Her manner seemed airy, light, unreal. "Unpleasant, that business this morning. Would you not say?"

Loren paid the question no mind, hoping to ignore the girl altogether.

"Still, we made good time," Annis went on. "And at least you need not fear my mother turning you in to the constables for a bounty. I think we have well moved beyond such distrust."

Loren looked over her shoulder. Gregor still stood nearby. He did not react to her gaze, keeping his stony eyes trained forwards.

"What do you want?" Loren hissed.

"Want? Why, whatever do you mean?"

"Leave me alone," said Loren, putting as much venom in her tone as she could. "I wish nothing to do with you."

Loren stalked off into the night, looking for a place to lay her head. Mercifully, Annis let her go. At last Loren found a spot on the open ground, with guards in plain sight but at a distance, and laid her head upon a mound of dirt. It took her a long while before she could fall asleep, and during the night she woke often to terrifying dreams of a sword in her chest.

The next day turned bleak, with heavy grey clouds covering the sky like a blanket.

Unusual weather for summer, thought Loren. The thought came dead and hollow, from a distant part of her mind. A forester's daughter should heed the change in weather, but she could not find it in herself to care.

Annis left her alone as they traveled, but after another day's slow journey the girl reappeared. This time she simply sat without invitation or request, plopping down beside the tidy fire.

Loren wanted to snap at her, to shout, to tell her to get away, but she dared not. What if Annis took insult? Would Damaris have Loren killed and dragged off to the woods, to join the constable in feeding the forest floor?

So Loren listened as Annis chattered nonsensically about this and that and the roads she had traveled since leaving the High King's Seat. Before long, Loren wanted to shake the girl until her silly head came off.

The evening wore on and on, and still Annis showed no signs of slowing her speech. As the sun's last light faded on the horizon and Loren thought of sleep, Annis scooted closer and grasped her wrist with a smile.

"Might you tell me another tale of Mennet? He sounded a wondrous man, and I would wager you know more of him than just what you told me."

Loren hesitated. She had no wish to tell a story, but anything seemed preferable to listening to Annis' babbling. And mayhap a story of Mennet would calm Loren's mind. She felt ragged after a day of looking over her shoulder, wondering always if each moment might be her last.

Loren knew one thing above all else: she must escape, and as soon as possible. Damaris must have something planned for her, and Loren had no wish to learn of the scheme. She would find some escape, and meanwhile she must bide her time.

The fire had burned low. Pushing up to her knees and finding more wood for the flame, Loren thought at last of a tale.

"Shall I tell you of the time Mennet bent iron with cloth?"

Annis looked at her askance. "You must jest. Cloth cannot best iron."

Loren fanned the flames, watching as the orange glow painted Annis' chubby features. "But best it he did. One day Mennet found himself within a king's dungeon. The king knew of Mennet's cloak of shadow, and thus he bade his jailer to line every bit of the wall with torches. Without darkness to hide him, Mennet's escape seemed hopeless."

Annis sat forwards. "They trapped Mennet?"

"Trapped, yes, but not for long. Mennet had many years ahead of him as the greatest thief in the land, and he would not let a Wizard King stay him."

Mayhap Loren imagined it, but she thought a sharp breeze gusted. The tongues of flame danced for the moment. Both girls shuddered.

"A Wizard King?" said Annis, her voice cracking.

"Yes, they still ruled in those days, many years and more before Andriana the Fearless outlawed them." Loren reached into her bag to gather her supper.

"But how could Mennet hope to stand against a Wizard King? They held a dark power, or so my tutors have taught me."

"They taught you well, but a dark power is nothing next to the power of darkness itself. And so they kept Mennet bathed in light. He inspected every corner of his cell, but the iron bars held firm. He could find no loose stone or crumbling mortar to aid his escape."

Annis remained perfectly quiet, only leaning back to wrap her arms around her knees. Loren paused for a moment to let the words sink in before she went on.

"The Wizard King laughed to see Mennet search so earnestly for a way out. At last Mennet grew thirsty and begged a pitcher of water. The Wizard King—"

"What was his name?"

Loren frowned. "Whose?"

"The Wizard King."

"He was . . ." Loren thought hard, but not for the life of her could she remember. "Bracken told me once, but I cannot recall."

"Why did the Wizard King not just kill Mennet? Why hold him prisoner, if he did not mean to kill him? And if he meant to kill him, why not do so at once?"

Loren gave an exasperated snort. "If he killed him, how could he go on to become the most famed thief in all the land?"

Annis folded her arms, stubborn. "Why would the Wizard King care about that? He should have killed him. *I* would have killed him."

Loren saw Damaris standing there above the corpses by the wagons. Fear formed like a white-hot stone in her gut. Yes, Annis might have killed Mennet. The apple rarely fell far from the roots of its tree.

She pressed on. "The Wizard King granted Mennet's request. His guards fetched a pitcher of water and a wooden cup to drink with. Mennet drank a deep gulp of the water and curled up in the corner of his cell, wrapping his arms around himself as though taken by a chill. The Wizard King soon left, bored by his new plaything.

"Once he was alone, Mennet rose in silence. He pulled the tunic from his back and tied it around two of the iron bars that held him in his cell. Then he took one of his boots, made from hard leather, and pushed it through the tunic. He seized both sides of the boot and twisted as hard as he could. Round and round he turned the boot, until the tunic strained at the iron bars. The fabric stretched, but it did not break. Finally the iron bars bent under the strain, just enough for Mennet to slip through. He donned his tunic again and slipped out the door."

Annis sat dumbfounded. "Can cloth truly bend iron this way?"

"Would I lie to you?" A small smile played across Loren's lips. *Yes. Yes, I would and I have.* She felt no obligation to tell Annis everything. Let the girl feel the frustration of hearing a bad tale.

Annis shook her head. "No. I cannot believe it. Else how could any prison hold its captives?"

Loren shrugged. "Believe it or not, as you will. I tell only an old tale."

"What value has an old tale without a kernel of the truth? What else are stories for?" Annis folded her arms, pouting.

Loren had tired of her little performance. "I am sorry to have disappointed you. But now I must away. I have had much water as I walked, and it begs leave of my company."

"I shall accompany you," said Annis, leaping to her feet.

"You? What happened to refined society, where we must hide our bodies away?"

Annis shrugged. "It grows dark. And we may take turns."

Loren grimaced, but she could do nothing. Together they tramped towards the trees, Gregor shadowing their footsteps. Once they had passed between the first two trunks, Annis turned to look at the captain.

"You have come far enough," she said.

Gregor did not blink. "Your lady mother commands me, Annis. Not you."

"And what will my mother think, if I tell her that you leered at me like a lecher when I went to relieve myself?"

Gregor did not reply, or move a muscle. But when Annis turned and walked on, he followed a bit farther back. When they stopped, he fell out of sight. But he did not fool Loren—she knew Gregor's men lurked all around them. She gave a grumbling sigh and prepared to do her business.

"We must speak, and quickly," hissed Annis. "And for the love of decency, do not do that while I stand here."

Her urgent tone drew Loren's attention. "What must we speak of?"

"You are in danger as long as you stay here."

Loren snorted a grim laugh. "You bring me no news. Your mother seems to see little value in any life, much less my own."

Annis' eyes grew hard. "I believe my mother keeps you here as a distraction."

"For what?"

"I have heard her speak with Gretchen in the carriage. If questioned, my mother will tell the city guard that yesterday's constable pursued you north along the road. But if that should fail, they will likely search our wagons. Then Mother will change her tune. I think she means to trade you in exchange for safe passage into the city."

Loren swallowed hard. It hurt her throat. "Why tell me?"

"Do you think I resemble my mother?" whispered Annis, glaring at her. "She has fed many men to the underworld, ever since I was a babe. I was raised to think it normal. Then one day, I realized the truth: that murder was wrong, and outside the King's law. My mother only escapes justice thanks to the depth of our coffers. I have sought escape from her ever since."

Loren could say nothing to that. She knew something of the desperation to escape home.

Annis looked into her eyes. A stern, set expression crossed the girl's features. "Will you do it, then? If I help you escape, will you take me with you?"

Loren nodded. "I will. I swear it."

THIRTEEN

As they traveled on the next morning, Damaris emerged from her carriage.

"Loren."

As soon as she heard the merchant's clear voice, Loren's heart leapt into her throat. She pictured Annis' face glowing blue in the moonslight. Had it all been a ruse? Mayhap Annis had told her mother everything, and now Damaris summoned Loren for judgement.

But no. If they meant to kill her, they could have done that last night. Gregor could have ended her in an instant at any time. While Loren still lived, she must keep hope. So she quickened her pace to join the merchant.

Today, Damaris wore a gown of light green. It hung slimmer than her average garb, though that by no means rendered it plain. Elegant designs like spiderwebs wound up and down its length, some in gold thread and some in light pink, interlocking to create a varied palette of color. Her hair clung to the top of her head in tight braids, worked into a wide bun.

But the merchant's beauty no longer impressed Loren, for she had seen what lay beneath it. Only a fool saw a bear trap wrapped in velvet and still desired to run their hand along it.

As Loren came to her, Damaris took the edge of the black cloak. She ran her fingers along its trim, an eerie smile playing on her lips.

"It suits you very well. Do you enjoy it?"

Loren chose her words carefully. "I have often dreamed of a cloak just like it." That was true enough. In Loren's dreams, Nightblade always wore a cloak of fine black cloth.

"It will serve well for riding, as well as foot travel," said Damaris. "Gregor, bring my horse."

That took Loren aback. What did Damaris play at? She mocked Loren for objecting to the constable's death, and then gave her a fine cloak. She put Loren under guard like a common criminal, and then continued her riding lessons.

"My lady is too kind," said Loren, hoping Damaris could hear the wryness in her voice. But Damaris only nodded and stepped aside.

This time Loren mounted more easily and sat loose, hands firm on the saddle horn. Gregor mounted his own steed and came forwards to take the reins from his lady.

Thus we walk down the road together, as pretty a picture as one could imagine, thought Loren. *The captain, the merchant, and the forester's daughter.* It sounded like the name of a song, but Loren could not smile at the thought. Even being on horseback again could not improve her mood. Damaris had poisoned that dream.

"That dagger at your belt," said Damaris. "A fine make, is it not? Gregor, you know of such things."

Gregor did not bother glancing at it. "A fine make indeed, my lady."

"I confess my curiosity as to how you came by it," said Damaris. "An heirloom, mayhap, passed down from nobler days of your family?"

Loren shrugged. "I see only a knife, my lady."

"Oh, no," said Damaris. "No, not only that. To the wise and trained eye, that dagger holds more words than a tome. It speaks of breeding, of artistry. If I did not know better, I would say you had taken it from a corpse—" she gave Loren a sharp glance at that "—but of course we have seen how abhorrent you find such things."

"It came from my parents," said Loren, her voice cool, nonchalant. "Where they came by it, I never knew. But when I left home, it passed into my hands. I made a vow to use it honorably."

She put a small bite in the last word, hoping to anger Damaris with the dig. But if the merchant noticed, she gave no sign. "But that is even more curious. How came simple foresters by such a fine thing? Mayhap my guess of grave robbery falls near the mark, though it may not have been you who did the robbing."

Now came Loren's turn to feel the bite of words well chosen. Her cheeks flushed, and she found herself surprised by her anger. What did she care for insults delivered to her parents? In her fifteen years she had harbored far worse thoughts about them in private.

"Oh, do not take such offense," said Damaris, tossing her head. "I jest. And even if your parents acquired the dagger through . . . less than savory means, what of it? I do not know the tale of how my forebears came by their wealth, but I doubt that book is free of darker chapters."

"Is that why you act the way you do, my lady? Are you only following in the footsteps of your ancestors?"

"Do any of us do any different?"

"I will never be like my parents."

"So have all children said throughout history. But if they only considered things clearly, they might not see their parents as villains after all. Take Annis, for example. She does not approve of many things I do to ensure her safety. Did she tell you?"

Loren felt suddenly glad for years of experience lying to her parents. Not a muscle in her face twitched. "No. She seemed quite cheerful, in fact, after . . . after what happened."

"A farce she puts on to hide her disgust, I fear," said Damaris. "Yet I would go to any length for her future, to depths twice as dark as you can imagine."

"You did it to protect her, then? Would the constable have killed a little girl if he found your cargo?" Loren could not quite keep the bitterness from her voice.

Damaris shrugged. Loren had the urge to kick her. "They would have spared her. But safety means more than survival; true safety lies only in plenty, and sometimes not even there. Do you know how long the nine lands have had a High King?"

Loren frowned at the unexpected change in topic. She thought hard. "Two thousands of years."

"Thirteen hundreds," said Damaris. "And the kingdoms have changed mightily in that time. The men who laid the rules of election and first drew our borders would not recognize the lands you and I walk today. Nine royal families there are now, but only one of those families existed when the High King first took his seat, and even that one cannot trace its lineage straight back to Roth. But do you know how long my family has dealt in our . . . unique brand of goods?"

Loren did not wish to seem foolish by answering wrong, so she remained silent.

"Twenty-six hundreds of years. We are the oldest family in the nine lands. Vast is our wealth and extensive our power. Kings claim the right to rule, but their right has only ever come from coin. Coin that my family, and others like ours, control. Even as a lesser scion of my house, I may yet have the ear of anyone in the nine lands, save for the High King herself, if I so desire."

Loren's body had grown tense. She forced herself to relax and move with the horse. What manner of people had she fallen in with?

"Do you know that there has never been a Merchant's War?" said Damaris, again shifting subjects as swiftly as the wind. "Neither in name, nor in practice. Wars are brutal, messy things, far below our station. Yet kings insist upon fighting them. We are only too happy to lend them the coin to do so. But while we do not go to war, that does not mean we have forgotten the benefit of a swift killing. What death we deal occurs in darkness and silence, the bodies quickly buried and even more quickly forgotten. Many know of it. None acknowledge it. As long as it remains well out of sight, most would sooner ignore it. Thus it has always been, and thus it will always be. Do you understand?"

Loren nodded quickly atop the horse, now more frightened than ever. "I do, my lady."

"I doubt it. But one day, you might."

Loren knew it would be better to still her tongue, but she could not avoid one question. "My lady, why do you tell me all this?"

"Because," said Damaris, "I see precious things in your eyes, child. So much fear and anger, and yet so much wonder. You have suffered greatly, and yet you still believe the world can hold something other than suffering. Who has not felt the same? Girls such as yourself are like pure white eagles found in the woods; rarer than Elves and twice as sacred, treasures we must preserve at all costs."

The flowery words floated in Loren's mind like a dream. She remembered Annis' words from the night before and tried to find her senses. Damaris sought to flatter her so she could be more easily deceived. She would not fall prey to such a simple scheme.

And as she thought on them, Damaris' words touched off a thought in Loren's mind.

Damaris clucked her tongue. "Come, try trotting again."

Gregor spurred his horse and tugged on Loren's reins. Both beasts erupted into motion and trotted off together, Loren clinging to the mount's neck and glancing every so often at the sword on Gregor's belt.

That is the truth of this world, she thought. *Not flowery words, but a large man with a blade at his waist.*

FOURTEEN

THE FINAL MORNING DAWNED, THE DAY UPON WHICH they would reach the walls of Cabrus. Loren woke earlier than normal, when the sky held only a faint grey with no trace of pink.

She looked up and, for once, she did not see Gregor standing nearby. The giant *did* sleep, then. She rose and took a hesitant step away from the caravan. A guard solidified from the darkness to watch her.

She could not shake a persistent feeling between excitement and apprehension. Today her journey with the caravan would end in one of three ways: Loren would escape, the constables would take her prisoner, or someone would kill her.

Kill me.

The thought that she could die today did not cause her nearly as much worry as she thought it might. After witnessing eight men murdered, death seemed common now, a trite thing, almost too often done.

Gregor appeared, and the other guard vanished into the diminishing darkness. Soon after that, Annis emerged from her carriage. She stretched and yawned noisily in the early light, her eyes sparkling as they fell upon Loren.

"Good morn! We reach Cabrus today."

"So I have been told." Loren had decided the day before that she must maintain an air of sullen silence and resentment around Annis. Gregor must not suspect the girls of plotting together. Annis, for her part, seemed to understand, for she wore the same chipper, vacant smile she had worn the day the constable's men had died.

"Come," said Annis. "Let us visit the woods before we set off. You may not see them again for a while, I fear, and you have spent your life among trees."

"I suppose." Loren laid the waterskin in her travel sack and slung it over her shoulder. The sack now bulged with fresh provisions. The waterskin sloshed full and noisy, refilled from the caravan's stores.

Annis kept up her chatter as they came under the boughs, pink light now bathing her upturned face and somewhat squashed nose. After a time, she turned to Gregor. "I need my privacy."

He nodded slowly and gestured at Loren. "Very well. Come with me, girl."

"Not from her," said Annis. "We are maidens both. Besides, dawn rises—she must need to relieve herself."

Loren shrugged, giving Gregor a dead-eyed stare. "I suppose."

Gregor backed off, looking none too pleased. Annis pretended to squat, and Loren joined her.

"Our time runs short," said Annis, her voice a low whisper. "Today we must escape."

"I have an idea."

Annis blinked in surprise. "Truly? Tell me."

"If I can distract Gregor and his men, can you acquire one of your mother's brown cloth packages?"

Annis blanched. "Mayhap I can, but why?"

"Damaris told me that the world runs smoothly as long as no one must face the deeds of her and her kind. I plan to turn things rough."

Annis shook her head. "If I am caught . . ."

"I can provide ample distraction. Can you do it?"

"I can." Annis did not sound pleased.

"Good. Come, then. Let us return, for we must act before the caravan moves on."

They made their way back. In only a moment, they spotted Gregor through the trees. He watched them with an expression that Loren could not read. But he said nothing, and followed silently.

Once they neared the road again, Annis bid Loren farewell and headed off on some pretense of preparing her carriage. That left Loren and Gregor alone. Loren increased her pace, making for the third caravan from the end—the only one she knew for certain held the packages of brown cloth.

"Where are you going?" said Gregor.

Without meeting his eyes, Loren said, "Oh, nowhere of consequence. Tell me, when did you learn swordsmanship?"

Gregor did not answer.

"Come, now. Surely no harm can come from my knowing. Were you as old as me? Younger? Older?"

Gregor sniffed. "Younger. I began my training as a boy of ten summers."

"Ten!" Loren allowed shock to spread across her face. "Then you have the advantage. I greatly desire to learn how to protect myself. Could you teach me?"

Gregor did not answer.

Loren spotted a guard near the wagon, standing near its head. She made for him quickly, her pace just below a run. "If I wish to catch up, I must begin immediately. Do you think you can teach me what you know today, before we reach the walls of the city?"

"I trained for years," said Gregor, and now Loren could hear an undercurrent of exasperation.

"But I do not *have* years to waste on such an endeavor. We must speed the process."

The guard noticed them at last, looking up in confusion. Without warning, Loren sprang forwards and dragged his sword from its scabbard. The man shouted in alarm, but Loren danced away on the balls of her feet. The sword felt much, much heavier than she had expected.

"How do you manage such a thing? I can scarcely lift the blade!"

"Drop it," said Gregor. His hand shot to his own sword, and his face drew together in a scowl.

The guard came after her, arms outstretched, but Loren turned and ran away a few steps.

"I mean no harm! I wish only to learn!"

She must not appear a threat. Loren had no desire to end this day on the end of Gregor's blade. She danced down the line of wagons, waving the sword in the air in what she hoped passed for an imitation of a true fighter. "Come! Teach me the intricacies of parry and thrust, the elegant dance of death!"

She let her feet tangle beneath her and send her crashing to the ground, though she was careful not to land on the blade. The guard leapt forwards, but Loren shot to her feet and just out of reach. It *was* a dance, she realized, though her partner seemed unwilling. She took a fighter's pose, one arm behind her and the sword held forwards.

"Now, how does one manage the thrust?" She tried it, and the guard cried out as he fell back. He stumbled over his heels, barely managing to keep his footing.

"If you do not drop that weapon—" said Gregor.

"You will take it from me? I welcome it! Come, teach me the way they taught you as a boy!"

All the while, her voice took on a high, strident pitch. Guards up and down the line of wagons came closer, drawn by the commotion. She saw many of them smiling, amused by her ungainly swings. Best of all, Gregor still did not draw his steel. No one could see a danger in her wild flailing.

Again the guard came forwards, and again Loren fled, drawing him farther from the wagons.

Now no one stood close by. A flash of purple told her that Annis had slipped inside one of them.

"Come, Sir Lord Captain Commander King! Teach me! You will not find a more willing student." Loren faced off against Gregor from ten paces away and swung the sword in two interlocking circles. "Meet me with a riposte, if you can, or whatever it is that you call it."

She glanced over her shoulder to see if any guards approached from behind, and was surprised to find Damaris. The merchant stood near her carriage at the head of the line, her eyes fixed intently on Loren. Her face broke into a small smile.

"Your lady laughs at you," said Loren. "You should defend your honor." The other guard lunged again, and she spun clear at the last moment. The movement nearly made her drop the sword, but she rescued it before it fell.

But at last she had chosen her words unwisely. She heard the sharp *hiss* of steel and turned to see Gregor's sword in his fist.

Squaring her shoulders, Loren smiled. "At last! Do you mean to teach me, master?" She leapt aside to avoid another attempt by the guard to recover his weapon. Her foot lashed out to entangle his, sending him crashing to the dirt. "I warn you, I will not go easy on you."

Gregor advanced upon her with measured, resolute steps. "I have warned you. Your fool's tongue will not spare you."

In his glare she saw hate and fury, the first true emotions she had seen in him since first she came to the caravan. But over his shoulder, she saw another flash of purple cloth with gold brocade, this time moving away from the wagon. Loren had done her job. She dropped the sword, and it sank point-first into the ground.

"Very well," she said hastily. "If you do not mean to teach me, I shall press upon you no further."

Gregor did not answer, nor did he stop. Loren scarcely had time to think, *He truly means to kill me* before the air whistled with the passage of his blade. She dropped to the ground and rolled away as it cut through the air where her head had been.

"Gregor!"

Damaris' sharp voice cracked like a whip. Gregor froze as he stood above her, and his eyes snapped to his lady. Three deep breaths he took, while Loren waited on her belly.

"She makes you look a fool, and you allow it to anger you? Do you act upon the whim of a girl not yet come to womanhood?"

I have, too! She held the thought, knowing that to voice it might mean death.

Gregor returned his sword to its scabbard in a single fluid motion and bowed to Damaris, his face once again an emotionless mask. "Of course not, my lady. I only acted because I thought her a threat."

"This one? A threat?" Damaris scoffed. "Return to your duties. All of you."

The other guards drifted away and back to their posts. Loren heard more than a few chuckle as they went. Her eyes rose to meet Gregor's. She could not mistake the fire that burned within him. Loren knew she could no longer consider herself safe in his presence. But with any luck, she need not worry after today.

"Thank you for the lesson, master," she said softly.

Gregor turned and stalked off without a word. Loren rose and went to find Annis.

FIFTEEN

THEY SPOTTED THE WALLS OF CABRUS AS THE SUN hung low in the sky, bathing Loren's right side in a soft orange glow. Nerves made her blood roil, and she hunched her shoulders a bit lower.

She walked near the carriages, in plain sight of both Damaris and Annis and under Gregor's baleful glare. As the walls loomed taller, Damaris' carriage swerved left to draw near to her. The merchant disembarked and walked beside Loren.

"You will stay safe if you remain unnoticed," she said. "They will not recognize you in your new cloak. Keep the hood drawn about your face, and we will pass through the gate without incident."

"Yes, my lady. And thank you." Loren had to force earnestness into her voice.

Damaris nodded and returned to her carriage. Just behind it, Gregor glared at Loren from horseback. She stuck her tongue out at him.

She let her eyes rove to the second carriage and saw Annis peeking out from the door's window. The girl looked terrified, and Loren's own fears rose to fever pitch. But she must rely on Annis now—she had no time to turn from her course or plan a new one.

They drew closer still. And then as she scanned the wall, Loren's heart sank into her boots.

There before the gate stood Corin and Bern. Loren recognized them at once, the one short and broad, the other tall and slender but no less muscular. On instinct she ducked her head, dutifully studying her feet. Her steps wandered right as if by accident, drifting closer to Damaris' carriage.

"My lady!" she whispered. "They are here!"

Damaris looked out from her window. "Who, child?"

"The constables. The ones who pursued me."

Damaris leaned out to look ahead. "My eyes are not what they used to be. The two before the gate?"

"With the red leather pauldrons, aye."

Damaris pursed her lips for a moment. "This complicates things. Still, we should have nothing to fear. Fall behind Annis' carriage, and let me confer with Gregor."

Loren did as commanded, though she could almost feel Damaris' hidden intent. Annis looked out her window as Loren walked by.

"What is wrong?"

"The constables," said Loren. "Those who pursued me. They are here."

"What for? I thought they wanted the wizard, not you."

"They must have had little luck finding him, and have decided to guard the road against me instead."

"Then Mother will place you into their hands for certain."

"Not if we carry out our plan. Are you ready?"

"How does one ready for this?" said Annis. "But yes."

The carriage door swung open, and Annis came out to walk beside Loren. Her face seemed pale somehow under its dark coloring, and her eyes flitted about.

"You look nervous," said Loren in a murmur.

"I *am* nervous!"

"But you must not show it. Come, tell me of the High King's Seat. Speak as you often do when we walk."

Annis thought for a moment, her mouth hanging open, and then shook her head. "I cannot. I can scarcely remember what the place looks like. All my thoughts reside here, now, and I am not overjoyed at our chances."

Loren thought her heart might hammer through her chest. If Annis lost her nerve, Loren was finished. The merchant's daughter would carry on, but Loren would find herself in the hands of the constables.

"You must not lose heart," said Loren. "Without me, how long before you have another chance to escape? What if they discover your mother in that time? They will cast your family down and throw you in chains or the stocks. Do you think your age will save you? And meanwhile you will bear witness to betrayal and death, powerless to stop it."

Without answering, Annis clutched a bulge at her side under her cloak, the bulge of a package wrapped in brown cloth.

"That is better," said Loren, hoping she spoke the truth. "Come now. Courage."

Just then, Gregor pulled up to walk beside them. The walls stood dangerously close now, and Loren felt far too exposed under the eyes of Corin and Bern. The captain spoke without looking at her.

"My lady commands you to walk by her daughter's carriage. You will pose as her lady in waiting."

"But I will be in plain sight," said Loren. "The constables will recognize me for certain."

Gregor glared at her. "I bring my lady's orders, not an opportunity for debate. The carriage. Now."

Loren swallowed hard and let Annis guide her to the carriage. But Annis did not climb aboard again, electing to walk instead.

The caravan halted before the gate. There, only ten paces away, stood the constables who had pursued Loren for days. Behind them stood several guards, with more posted along the wall. Loren thought of the arrow Bern had loosed at her and could not suppress a shudder. She peered at the constables from within her cowl, desperate not to show her face.

"Well met again," said Corin. "What news from the road?"

"Precious little," said Damaris, leaning out to speak from her carriage window. "And in the city?"

"Little as well," said Corin. "Tell me: where is our brother constable? We sent him north to meet you, for he thought that mayhap we had not questioned you as closely as we might."

"We met him upon the road," said Damaris. "He put us to the search, and when he found nothing, he rode away north."

Corin and Bern traded glances. Then Bern said, "Why would he ride north, and not south to inform us?"

Damaris dismissed him with a laugh. "You ask me? What could I know of his aims and intent?"

"Mayhap he never reached you," said Bern, his voice a low growl. "Or mayhap he did, and took coin to leave."

Loren felt a presence and looked up to see Gregor looming behind her. She stood within easy reach of his long arms, and she pictured them leaping out to wrap her in a death embrace.

"Your men must tarnish easily, if you so quickly suspect bribery," said Damaris.

Bern acted as if she had not spoken. "Or mayhap he lies in a cold ditch somewhere along the road, a concern to you no longer."

Damaris scoffed again. "Do you think I would raise my hand against the King's law?"

"It runs in your blood," spat Bern. Corin raised his hands and tried to calm his partner, but the taller constable would not subside. "Tell us where he is, or I swear I will put you to the question."

"You would threaten a friend to the crown?" Damaris spoke lightly, as though she asked after the constable's family.

"My partner speaks hastily, my lady," said Corin. "We have had no luck finding the wizard, and the search wears us both thin."

Bern ignored him. "Friend to the crown?" he snapped. "What have you ever done to earn that title, you leech?"

"Why, I have brought you both a mighty gift," said Damaris.

Loren felt a shifting behind her, and she knew the moment had arrived. "Annis, now!" she cried.

She leapt forwards and felt the tail end of her cloak slip through Gregor's grasping fingers. Annis drew back her arm and let fly. The package of brown cloth flew through the air. For a moment Loren feared it would fall short of its target, but Annis had a surprisingly strong arm. The package landed perfectly between Damaris' carriage and the constables, bursting open upon the ground. Loren caught a flash of glistening black as a cluster of obsidian crystals spilled across the ground.

A moment's pregnant silence stretched. Then many things happened at once.

The constables cried out in unison and drew their blades, as did the men behind them. Atop the wall, a guard blew a horn. The men on the ground rushed Damaris' carriage, and Gregor's guards surged forwards to meet them. The air rang with the clash of steel. Gregor screamed in fury and charged the constables, forgetting Loren and Annis for the moment.

Loren seized Annis' hand in hers and ran for the girl's carriage. The dagger leapt into her hand before she could think to draw it, and she slashed at the leather binding the lead horse to its harness. The driver cried out in alarm, but Loren ignored him. Clashing steel made the horse whinny in fright, and it nearly bolted. Loren jumped back, but Annis pressed forwards. She took the harness in her hands like reins and put a hand on the horse's neck, whispering soothing words.

The driver started to climb down from his perch. Loren vaulted towards him, her dagger held forwards. She thrust it at the space between his legs, and the man yelped as he flew back to his seat.

"Stay where you are! Next time I strike true." It was a lie, but the man believed her and did not move again.

The horse had calmed. Loren flung herself onto its back and leaned down to drag Annis up in front, where her long years of riding would help most. Annis kicked her heels into the horse's flanks. Loren nearly pitched off the back, stopping herself only by clutching the girl's body with both hands.

The horse swerved at first, heading straight for the fighting. Loren screamed wordlessly, and Annis dragged the reins to the right. At the last moment they turned aside, passing the men who swirled in battle around Damaris' carriage.

Gregor turned to stare in astonishment. They passed close enough for Loren to lash out with her boot. His nose crunched under the sole, and he fell.

They fled as fast as they could. Behind them, Loren heard Damaris' voice erupt in rage and anguish as her daughter sped away from her forever.

"We will ride around the city!" said Loren, shouting over the hoofbeats and grunting after every other word. Riding a horse hurt even more without a saddle. "Then stay on the road south and make for the next one. Or mayhap we will hide in woods nearby while we think of where to go."

"We cannot," said Annis. "It is too far to the next city on one horse. Mother will catch us for certain. And they say bandits roam these woods."

"We cannot enter the city," said Loren, aghast.

"We must. We shall come in by another gate, before word has had time to spread. Easier to hide among a thousand people than ten thousand trees, or so I have heard. We will hide until we find secure passage from the city. I have brought coin."

She dug into a pocket and pulled out a purse, placing it in Loren's hand, and then dug out another and jingled it between her fingers. She glanced at Loren over her shoulder, and an impish grin spread across her features.

"And that is not all. Look."

She dug within her pocket again and withdrew a second package wrapped in brown cloth.

Loren's breath hissed between her teeth. "I fear you have stolen something far more dear than coin."

"If others value it so highly, that is to our advantage."

"And here I meant to be the thief. You take to it most naturally."

Annis laughed, and they rode on.

Soon the horse had carried them to another gate, this one on the south and west side of the city. Many people crowded this avenue, unlike the King's road that had lain empty. Annis skillfully guided the horse into line between two wagons, one loaded high with hay, the other filled with caged chickens.

"Cabrus has a large district where the people are poor and the constables lax in their patrols," said Annis, speaking quietly now. "We will find an inn there, the sort where the master does not ask too many questions. Then we will seek out some traveler or trader who means to leave the city and buy our passage with him."

"Whom can we trust? Anyone who hears of your mother will turn us over for the reward she will surely bring."

Annis bit her lower lip. "I had not thought of that. But no matter. We will think of something."

They passed through the gate without incident. The guards waved them through after one look at Annis' fine dress and Loren's black cloak. Only one guard gave a curious look at the horse's lack of saddle, but she gave no remark. Loren realized with some surprise that the guards thought her a girl of noble birth. That felt curious.

Once inside, Loren dismounted and walked beside the horse, relieved not to feel the creature's spine slapping between her legs any longer. Though at first she glanced over her shoulder and peered doubtfully around every corner, soon her gaze drew up and around to stare at the city.

Loren knew she had visited Cabrus once as a child, but only because adults had told her of it. She could remember nothing of the place. Now she could not imagine how people lived here. Buildings pressed against each other, some sharing walls. Some rose only a single level, while others had second floors that overhung the street. Loren yelped and dodged as someone emptied a pot out a window into the street beside her. A wave of stench a moment later told her it had been a chamber pot.

"Is this the poor district?" she said, tugging on Annis' dress.

"This? No, of course not." Annis looked down at Loren from the horse, nonplussed.

"But then why—"

Loren could not finish her thought, for strong hands seized her from behind. One gripped her left hand, and the other seized her right shoulder.

"Greetings, Loren of the family Nelda," hissed Bern's cruel voice in her ear.

Loren had no time to think. She acted upon the first thought to cross her mind. She reached out and slapped the horse's rump as hard as she could. The beast whinnied and tore off, speeding down the cobbled street and out of sight.

"After it!" cried Bern. Several men in leather armor pursued the horse down the street. Bern whirled Loren around, and she saw Corin standing there with several others.

"Welcome to Cabrus." Corin's eyes were grim. "You have much to answer for."

SIXTEEN

Loren slipped, her boots scrabbling on the cobblestones as she almost pitched to the ground. Bern tightened his vise-like grip on her shoulder, and she winced with pain.

"Keep your feet, lest we chop them off," he growled.

Fear scattered her thoughts. How had the constables found her so quickly? Where would they take her? The unfairness of it cut her to the bone. It was Xain they pursued, and Xain who should be in their clutches now.

"I do not know where the wizard is," she pleaded. "Let me go. I have done nothing."

Bern did not reply. Loren looked to Corin. The shorter constable's eyes met hers for a moment. His glare seemed resolute, but not so hateful as Bern's. If she would find leniency with either of them, it would be with Corin.

"I am only a forester's daughter. What do you want from me?"

Corin's mouth turned down. "We have questions. You would do well to answer them honestly."

"I have told you, I know nothing!"

They answered her only with silence. She searched the streets around her for succor, halfway hoping that Annis might return with some plan for her rescue. But Loren had sent Annis' horse running, and in her heart of hearts she did not expect the girl to return.

Nothing about the city seemed familiar. Loren had only vague childhood memories of large buildings and winding streets. Now the buildings seemed smaller, but the streets no less confusing. After the first few turns round street corners, Loren had swiftly lost all sense of direction. There seemed no rhyme or reason to the place, the roads as varied and directionless as gaps between trees. It made her feel that she was in a strange and unknown forest, her woodcraft useless.

Only a few men accompanied her: Corin, Bern, and two more. The other constables had chased after Annis in her headlong flight. Loren hoped she might face no further punishment for aiding the girl's escape, but she would have done it again. Annis deserved a life free from her mother, at least.

Thoughts of Damaris piqued her curiosity. "What happened to the merchant? Is she slain?"

Bern snorted, his voice growing crueler. "She is within the city. In fact, she greatly desires to speak with you when she may."

Shock overcame Loren's fear. "What? But her men attacked you."

"Mayhap you should not have fled, then." Bern's fingers tightened again, and Loren knew her skin would bruise. "Once you left, she halted the fighting and claimed the magestones were your property."

"The . . . what?" said Loren, utterly lost. *Magestones* was a foreign word to her.

"We could not gainsay her without you there to defend yourself," said Corin. "Though that may not have mattered in the end. The family of Yerrin has a long reach, and their influence can be felt even behind the walls of Cabrus."

"I would have had their heads, and well justified," said Bern. "But that blame goes to you, girl."

"I do not even know what the things were! Search Damaris' wagons. You will find plenty more, I assure you."

"Not now," said Corin. "As she spoke, the mayor's envoy arrived with a writ of passage. Her wagons have no doubt been cleared, their cargo well hid."

"And all thanks to you," said Bern.

Loren felt sick. Annis' actions should have cast the King's justice towards Damaris, freeing Loren to find safe passage to other lands. But it seemed she had aided the merchant's crimes after all, and earned Bern's ire in doing so.

She was trapped, just as surely as when she traveled with the caravan. And without Annis or any other ally, her escape seemed even less likely than before.

The constables paused for a moment as a line of carriages proceeded through an intersection. Loren's eyes flitted back and forth, seeking an opportunity. Bern must have sensed it, for his grip tightened again. Loren whimpered as stabbing pain shot through her shoulder. "You are hurting me."

"Not near as deep as I would like."

Corin scowled. "If she will be put to the question, then leave it for the mayor's men. It is not our place."

"Nor is it our place to lose the wizard's trail, nor allow smugglers of magestones to wander unmolested, and yet we have done both. I for one am tired of duties unfulfilled. And lest you forget, this one sent us on a wild chase through the Birchwood while she escaped with our quarry."

Corin's frown deepened, but he spoke no further. The carriages passed, and they went on.

Loren's feet, long used to dirt and grass underfoot, soon wearied on the cobblestones. She stumbled more and more. Each time, Bern jerked her upright. Soon she cried out, and each time Corin's mood grew darker. But just as she thought he might speak again, they stopped.

Above them loomed a building at least ten paces tall. Loren saw three rows of windows stretching across its width. She marveled at the sight. Nowhere in the Birchwood had she ever seen a building with so much as a second floor. Then she looked closer at the top row of windows and saw the thick steel bars that crossed them. A jail, then.

Two guards stood at the front door, and in their hands they held halberds, tall and gleaming. As Bern drew close, one of the guards stepped forwards to place his halberd across the entryway.

"Hold," he said. "What is this?"

"A prisoner for the cells. I am Constable Bern, and this is my companion, Corin. We come from Garsec on the king's business. Let us pass, for we have another runaway to pursue."

"The cells are full," said the guard. "We have no room."

Bern's face grew uglier. "Then take off some pickpocket's hand and set them loose. Our business is urgent."

The guard drew up straighter, though still shorter than Bern, and his eyes hardened. "I take no orders from you. The master at arms has commanded that no more prisoners be brought here. Try the guardhouse in the eastern district."

"A walk that would cost us the rest of the day," said Bern. "We have no time."

"My orders stand," said the guard stubbornly.

"Where is your master at arms?" said Corin, adopting a diplomatic tone. "Mayhap we could speak with him and convey the urgency of our mission."

The guard's eyes flitted to the broader constable. "His quarters are upstairs. Though I doubt his mind will change, even for constables who claim to be on the king's business."

Bern stiffened, but Corin put a placating hand on his shoulder. "We will attempt it in any case. I will go."

"No," snapped Bern. "I will have words, and when I am through he will wish he had never held up the King's justice. Take the girl."

Loren found herself shoved into Corin's grip, too quickly to capitalize on the situation. Bern took one of the other constables and disappeared within the building. Corin guided her to the side of the doorway. If she would ever have a chance to sway his mind, it would be now.

"Constable Corin," she began. "I swear to you under the sky, I played no part in any scheme of the wizard's. He abandoned me as soon as we left the Birchwood."

Corin's face only grew more stern. "And before? When you sent us chasing shadows? When you stole supplies to place in the wizard's hands? You played no part in that, did you?"

Loren's face grew hot. "I . . . I did not know what crimes he may have committed."

"Yet you knew we pursued him. You will face the King's justice for that, if nothing else. Now silence yourself while we find a place to keep you—for the time being."

"And what then? I cannot imagine I will enjoy the comforts of a roof and daily bread forever."

"We shall see," said Corin.

"We should ready her for the cell, sir," said the other constable, the one who had accompanied them through the city streets. "Take her weapons and such."

Corin grunted assent. While the other constable took her arm, Corin knelt at Loren's feet and squeezed her boots. Beneath the leather he felt her hunting knife, and his fingers plunged within to withdraw it. He stood and grasped her bow, prying it off her—but gently, so the string did not break.

"Is that all? It will go better for you if you speak the truth."

Loren thought for a moment of withholding the dagger. But he would only search her anyway, and lies would not help to sway his mood. "There is a dagger at my waist," she said.

Corin nodded and threw back her cloak—and froze.

His grim face became a mask of shock. Loren stared at him, eyes wide, unsure of what to do.

"Sir?" said the constable at her arm.

Corin seemed to recover himself. "That is enough here. Get up and see what is taking Constable Bern so long."

The constable looked at Loren with a frown. "But sir . . ."

"You have an order, constable," said Corin, his voice suddenly gruff. "Obey it."

The man left with a final doubtful look at Loren.

Under the gaze of the guard at the door, Corin seized Loren's arm and marched her around the corner to a narrow alley, pushing her into its mouth.

"Your dagger," he whispered, glancing over his shoulder as though the High King herself might hear. "I wish I had seen it earlier. Much trouble might have been prevented."

Loren swallowed, her thoughts spinning. She had no idea what he meant, but he had sent away his only companion to speak with her alone. That had to mean something, and she must choose her reply carefully.

"How was I to know I should reveal it to you?"

Corin shook his head quickly. "Of course. I did not mean you were at fault. Only I would have done a great many things differently. This was not your intention, was it? Do . . . do *they* require you to be placed within the prison?"

They. The constable's emphasis on the word had been unmistakable. Who were *they?* Loren knew only that it must have something to do with her dagger.

"They do not," she said quickly. "I must remain free. To carry out *their* work. And," Loren added, struck by inspiration, "to continue my pursuit of the wizard."

Corin's eyes flooded with relief. "Then I do not abandon my duty by releasing you. Find him, then, and bring him to their justice. Though I wish it were the king's, I think he will find yours less to his liking."

"Indeed," said Loren, her heart racing. Could this mean what she thought?

"Go, then." Corin glanced over his shoulder one last time. He shoved the hunting knife and bow into Loren's hands. She hastily returned them to their places. "I shall make it look as though you overcame me. And when you return to your masters, tell *them* I helped you."

"I will," said Loren, in an earnest tone she did not have to feign. "And I promise you, Constable Corin, *they* will be grateful."

She turned with a whirl of her black cloak and started down the alley. But a thought seized her, and she turned back one last time.

"Constable," she said. "Where did the girl's mother go? The merchant Damaris?"

Corin's lips pressed tightly together. "The Wyrmwing Inn, in the north of Cabrus. But if I may advise my lady, I would warn you away from that place. Her guards will seek you out most eagerly, and they do not share our mutual . . . respect . . . for your masters."

"Your advice is well given and well heeded, Constable Corin. Fare thee well."

She turned and vanished into the alley with a flutter of black cloth.

SEVENTEEN

Loren ran until she could no longer see the jail towering above the neighboring buildings, and then ran a short while more. Once she felt safely away from the place, she found a narrow gap between two buildings and slipped inside, doubling over to catch her breath. The air reeked of human refuse and rang with the sounds of shouting men and crying children. Loren decided she rather hated the city.

She must find Annis. Mayhap the girl had abandoned Loren to the constables, or mayhap she had planned to return and rescue her. But Loren must give her the benefit of the doubt, and not just for honor's sake. Loren knew precious little about Cabrus or the lands beyond, and Annis seemed wise in all the ways Loren was not.

Her eyes raked the narrow alley, wondering which way to proceed. Her absent mind sent fingers brushing her dagger's hilt. At the feel of its leather, her attention snapped to it.

What was this thing she carried upon her hip, that could enspell a constable into abandoning his duty? Who were *they,* the unknown masters Corin had spoken of? The dagger seemed more useful now, but altogether more dangerous. For anyone powerful enough to sway a constable must surely have enemies just as powerful.

But whatever Corin knew of the dagger, not everyone shared the knowledge. Damaris had seen it, but had granted it no special significance. This was some shadowed knowledge, then, some great secret that surrounded the thing. Loren wondered if she would ever learn the truth.

For now, she must think only of finding Annis. Loren drew her cloak closer, covering the dagger against curious, knowing eyes. Then she emerged from the alley and into the street, wandering south and east away from the jail.

Before long her stomach spoke, so she found a bakery and bought a roll with two pennies from the purse Annis had given her. She ate idly, losing herself in the streets, eyes traveling everywhere. In her forest she had had a keen sense of direction, but that proved useless here. She had to stop every little while to observe the sun and ensure she maintained a southeasterly course. Every building seemed new and confusingly different, and yet just like all the others.

Then she saw something that *was* familiar—red leather armor. A pair of constables emerged from a door along the street, and Loren's heart froze. But just as she readied herself to flee for the nearest alley, the men burst into raucous laughter and threw their arms about each other. Together they stumbled off down the street, and from inside the building Loren heard many loud voices raised in laughter and song.

A tavern. Loren sighed with relief and resolved to keep a warier eye.

Soon Loren found herself coming under the gaze of many passersby. Some eyes took in the length of her fine black cloak, while others fixed upon the bow at her back. Fine clothing and simple weapons—these were an oddity, and many seemed to remark upon them. Loren kept her head down and her eyes averted. She did not wish for tales of a green-eyed girl in a fine black cloak to reach the constables. It would not do to rely very heavily on Corin's protection.

Eventually the curious eyes grew too heavy. Loren ducked down an alley, feeling better as her wariness abated.

She thought of removing the cloak and stowing it in her travel sack. But that might worsen things considerably. Loren had well noted that she looked different from most in Cabrus. She had seen complexions of all hues, but few as pale as hers. And not once had she seen eyes of green.

No, she must retain the cloak, though it brought its own kind of attention. She could find a simpler one later, but she had seen no clothiers yet, and she did not know where to look for one.

Loren walked farther down the alley to find a surprise. Where she thought it ended, instead it split both left and right. Both directions proceeded behind the buildings for many paces before turning once more.

Mayhap she could make her way through the city's shadows, then. Annis had even said something about hiding in the city's poorer parts when they entered. If Annis still walked free, she would likely seek the dark corners behind buildings as well.

So Loren followed the alleys, keeping to the shadows of taverns and houses. She had to cross unsavory puddles and gingerly sidestep piles of refuse, but at least she avoided most eyes. Every so often she saw desolate beggars and cripples, all of them curled up in corners. Some eyed her with interest, and one or two rose, but Loren flashed her dagger, and they vanished. That gave her a thrill, and she felt her confidence growing.

Soon she made a game of leaping from darkness to darkness, avoiding the sunlight at all costs. Loren fancied that she looked a bit like Mennet dancing with his shadows. When a beggar would look up at the sound of her footsteps, she would dart to the nearest doorway and shroud herself in blackness until they looked away.

After a while she tired of the game. It brought her no closer to Annis. The next time Loren saw a beggar, instead of dancing by she walked right up to the woman.

The beggar seemed impossibly old, her face holding more wrinkles than space in between. Still, her shriveled eyes glinted bright within their sockets, and those eyes tilted up sharply at Loren's approach. Loren kept an easy look on her face, but her hand hovered, ready for the dagger.

"Well met, friend," said Loren. "Mayhap you could help me."

"Mayhap not as well, for I have no friends." The woman had a voice like an iron pot flung down a rocky slope. "It depends on what help ye seek, and what gifts ye have for those who aid ye out o' the goodness o' their hearts."

Loren smiled and reached to her belt. From her purse she pulled a silver penny. But when the woman held forth grubby hands to claim it, Loren danced it back on her fingertips—a trick she had learned from Bracken long ago.

"Now then," said Loren. "Where would one go to find more like you, and worse besides?"

The old woman's lips drew back in a sneer. Loren nearly flinched at the sight of her old and well-browned teeth. "Ye are headed the right way a'ready. Keep your feet pointed south and east, and ye will find the scumsucking backside of this place soon enough."

"Thank you." Loren flipped the coin into the air, and the beggar woman caught it deftly, shoving it up her sleeve. Loren pulled another from her purse. "Another thing. I seek a young girl, mayhap one running from constables. She stands as high as my chest, with skin like the night and a fine purple dress. Have you seen her?"

The old woman shrugged. "See all kinds, I do, and not just here. Oft time I make for the streets, where folk are plentiful and their coins more so. I seen plenty like what ye say along the street. Young nobles' daughters love to flounce about on their pretty ponies with steel-clad guards close by, just to remind the rest of us how fat their bellies are."

Loren could not hide her disappointment. Still, she flipped the coin. It, too, disappeared into the old woman's sleeve. "Very well. May your day be bountiful."

"It shall," said the woman, with a curious leer.

Loren felt a heavy blow against her back. She cried out and bounced against the wall beside the old woman, crashing to the ground on hands and knees. Another heavy blow struck her ribs, and she flipped to her back. A young man, skinny as a sapling but wiry with muscle, fell atop her. His grasping fingers seized her wrist as she went for the dagger, while his other hand groped at her purse.

"Younglings do not do well to flash around so much silver," said the old woman, looking down at Loren with vicious amusement. "They get all kinds of eyes on them what they do not want. We would just as soon not open you up, girl. Give us what else ye may."

Atop her, the young man gave a mad laugh as his fingers wrapped around the coin purse. But if he thought Loren a helpless young maid far from help and home, he thought wrong. Not for nothing had Chet forever refused to wrestle with her after his third try.

The man held her dagger hand, but he had neglected the other. Loren clapped it against his ear. He released her wrist, howling, and Loren slapped his other ear. He tumbled off her and hunched over his knees, glaring with hate.

Loren gained her feet, ready when he came again. She took his first punch on her shoulder and sank her fist into his gut. His breath left in a *whoof,* acrid and foul, and she struck him again just left of his temple. He fell back again, blinking hard.

Then a knife flashed into his palm.

Loren's eyes widened, and he came after her. It was all she could do to avoid his wild slashing. As she ducked and stepped back at the same time, her boot landed on her cloak and sent her crashing to the ground. She recovered and rose just in time, his blade slicing the air where she had lain.

"Hold!" she cried, though she knew it a mad request. He did not mean to scare her—he meant to slit her throat and take the purse from her cooling corpse. Still, she tried again while scrabbling for her dagger. "Hold!"

She heard her only reply in the old woman's cackle.

But just as her fingers closed on the dagger's hilt, from the shadows of a doorway stepped another figure. Its fist lashed forth to mash into the young man's face, and Loren saw the gleam of a metal gauntlet. The guttersnipe crumpled like a puppet with cut strings. Loren looked for the old woman—but she had gone, vanishing into the twists of the alley.

Loren's rescuer stood with his back to her. She could see only a red cloak thrown over broad shoulders, above which a shock of grey hair spoke of age. But as he turned around, Loren was surprised to find light blue eyes set in a face free from a beard, and almost free of wrinkles. Not as young as she, but mayhap not much older than Xain. Still, she could not deny the heavy wisdom that weighed in his eyes. The man had a face that Bracken would have called "a grandfather's soul in his grandson's head."

Her fingers relaxed on the hilt of her dagger and emerged from her cloak.

Those old eyes caught the movement. He studied her for a moment, as though he were thinking what to say, and then spoke in a soothing voice.

"Did his blade kiss you?"

Loren shook her head. "No. I am no stranger to knife fights."

She was, but thought it might not be wise to admit. This man could be a thief as well, and if so, he seemed more capable than the guttersnipe.

He smiled at her words, and she wondered if he heard the lie inside them. But all he said was, "Indeed."

Silence stretched for a distance that neared awkward. Loren studied the man while pretending to look anywhere else. He stood of average height, but something in his composure made him appear much taller. Loren felt herself a small child in his presence. Under his dark red cloak he wore a shirt and sleeves of chain, as well as gauntlets of gleaming steel that folded over themselves. Some strange symbol clasped the cloak at his throat: three vertical rods bound by a ring, like a shock of wheat, and wings sprouting from either side. Loren had never seen anything like it. His hair he wore close-cropped, and no trace of stubble dusted his chin.

Loren realized how long she had inspected him and cleared her throat, trying to think of what to say. At last she said, "Thank you for your assistance, though I could have bested him. I am fortunate, I suppose, that you ensured it."

"Fortunate, yes," said the man, his voice holding a trace of amusement. "Though my presence was no happenstance. I saw you quite some time ago, skulking from shadow to shadow. I hazarded a guess that you might be a stranger to these streets, and deemed it prudent to follow you in case you should find them less hospitable than you might wish."

Loren thought of that, and what a fool she must have looked to this imposing man. She straightened. "If you thought me in true danger, you need not have troubled yourself." She nudged the man on the ground with the toe of her boot. "This one would have found me a pricklier foe than I look."

"Of that I have no doubt," said the man, inclining his head and taking a step back. "I know I may take my leave in assurance of your safety, now that you have had a taste of Cabrus' streets and alleys."

"Very well then," said Loren, strangely sad to see him go.

He nodded, turning it into a half-bow, and walked away. But just as he reached the corner and prepared to round it, he paused. After a moment he turned back, his blue eyes squinting slightly.

"How long since you arrived in the city, if I may ask?"

Loren shrugged. "One loses track."

"Indeed." He could put such hidden meaning in that simple word. "I am seeking a man. Mayhap you have seen him. Not overly tall, but neither is he short. Of just about your height, in fact. His hair falls in waves, and his eyes are a pale grey-brown. He may have worn a blue coat."

His description of Xain was so perfect that Loren could not help herself; she stood flabbergasted, her mouth falling open in shock. Too late she tried to hide her reaction, and her teeth clicked as they shut.

He stiffened. "You have seen him?"

"Never," said Loren. "I only wondered what sort of fool would walk about in a bright blue coat. If I *had* seen him, he would be lighter a coin purse, I can assure you."

He took a step forwards, and Loren tensed—but he moved only out of eagerness, and made no move to grip a weapon or attack. "It is most urgent that I find this man. I would offer a mighty reward for any information that led to his location." He drew back his red cloak to show his belt, and Loren saw two fat purses hanging there. But she also saw a sword.

Almost she felt tempted, but something held her back. Loren knew nothing of this man or his intentions, and whatever Xain had done, he had not earned her betrayal.

So she shrugged and raised her eyebrows. "Gladly will I take your purse if it weighs so heavily at your belt, but I fear you would gain nothing from the purchase. I'll admit an urge to lie and give you worthless information. But I'll not cheat a man who tried to save my life, needless though his aid might have been."

The man studied her a long moment, and Loren felt bare beneath his piercing gaze. "I do not seek to harm the wizard," he said in an even voice. "I ask you to remember that. If, by some chance, you should *discover* something about him, I would beg that you find me. While I remain in the city, you may find me at the Wyrmwing Inn."

He turned and left.

EIGHTEEN

LOREN'S HEART FLUTTERED. DAMARIS, TOO, HAD taken a room at the Wyrmwing. Were they in league? She supposed not, for then the man in the red cloak would have had Loren's description.

It did not matter. She had no desire to seek the place out. And now she stood in much the same straits as when Corin released her. She had to find Annis, and still had little idea where to look.

She turned her feet south and east again, making her way as best she could through the city's alleys. Now she observed the beggars with a wary eye, avoiding them where she could. When she had to pass one, she sank a hand into her cloak and placed it on the dagger. Whether they saw a threat in the gesture or for some other reason, she always passed unmolested.

Soon the alleys grew sparse, the streets more plentiful, and the difference between them diminished. Before long Loren found herself walking on crowded avenues covered with more filth than she had found even in the alleys.

This must be the area Annis spoke of, she thought. But when she found a wide square to gain some sense of direction, still she could not see the city wall. If anything, she felt more lost than when she began her search.

If I walked in Annis' shoes, what would I do?

As a child used to wealth and raised into plenty, she might try to find an inn. Then again, she might find no inn to meet her standards. She might shed her wealthy clothing for beggar's rags to blend in, but then again she might find such rags too louse-ridden and threadbare.

In truth, Loren knew little of what Annis might do. How could she know the mind of a girl brought up into wealth and privilege? Other than fleeing their families, they had nothing in common.

Loren felt a nagging in the back of her mind. She was attracting curious looks again. In this district, her fine cloak stood out like a crow in a blue sky. Whatever course she decided on, it had to be better than standing here looking lost.

She chose a direction and struck out, walking as though with purpose. Though the streets might be overrun with the poor and the unfortunate, they were nearly empty of constables. She saw only one, leaning against a wall to whisper in the ear of a woman whose skirt rode high. Loren looked hastily away. Even she knew the purpose of such a conversation as that. She did not bother to hide her face as she passed, and the constable's eyes never diverted from their goal.

Long and longer she wandered, up and down streets, into squares and alleys until the sun drew behind the tops of the taller buildings. Loren watched it with mounting anxiety. She did not desire to wander these streets come sundown. That meant she must find an inn for the night, but how could she know which one to choose, one where she might still live come morning? She could not help but think that Annis would know what to do.

When her stomach growled again in protest, she stopped at a tavern to order a stew. Above the door hung a sign that showed a princess dancing with a boar. Letters were scrawled beneath it. An old and stooped man passed, and Loren seized his arm before pointing up at the sign.

"Grandfather—how does the sign read?"

He barely glanced at it before pursing his lips. "I never learned my letters neither, but I know its name. The Princess Pig."

Inside, she paid extra to keep the bowl and wooden spoon, and she carried the stew with her into the street. She did not wish to pause her search when Annis might wander by at any moment.

She had neared the end of the bowl when a street urchin appeared, massive eyes imploring her from a gaunt face. The boy did not look older than ten summers.

"Have you any to spare, please?" he said in a tiny voice. He rubbed the back of a hand across his swarthy forehead, which only served to smear dirt across it.

Loren's appetite vanished. The stew had grown cool anyway.

"Here. Keep the bowl. You can use it to collect alms."

The boy's eyes, impossibly wide already, grew even larger. "Oh, mercy, my lady," he gasped. "Thank you, thank you."

Before Loren could stop him, he lunged forwards and wrapped her in a hug. The poor child's head scarcely reached her chest, and his arms felt like thin wooden rods as they pressed into her back.

"That is enough," Loren said, trying to sound gruff. "Be off with you before I take it back."

The boy nodded vigorously and turned to scamper away. Loren could not stop a small smile as she turned away from him. But then some instinct seized her. Something was odd. Different.

Loren slammed a hand against her hip to find her coin purse gone. A pair of frayed strings hung from her belt.

She whirled to see the boy's tiny form retreating between the tavern and a tanner's shop next door. "Stop!" she cried.

The boy turned for the space of a blink. He smiled with his tongue poking through his lips, and then he turned and sprinted away.

"Does no one in this city keep their thieving hands to themselves?" cried Loren, and chased after him. She rounded the corner so fast she nearly skidded to a fall. Only luck stopped her, letting her bounce off the wall instead and keep running.

The boy fled like a rabbit, any trace of frailty or weakness gone. His bare, filthy feet pounded across the stones. He spun once as he ran, flinging the empty bowl at Loren. She barely got a hand up in time, and the bowl *cracked* off her forearm.

This boy was fast, but years of hunting with Chet, running for hours through the forest to reach the best grounds, had given Loren an endurance unmatched by any in her village. Every time he reached the gap between two buildings and dodged through, Loren seemed to have gained a little ground. The boy noticed, as well, for his occasional looks over his shoulder slowly took on an air of fear. Her blood boiled. How dare this boy steal from her? She was the Nightblade.

He soon changed tack, using size to his advantage. He found narrow gaps in wooden fences and stone walls and leapt through like a rabbit. But the boy could find nothing too narrow for Loren. Though she sometimes paused to preserve her bow, always she made up the distance in the next long sprint from building to building. As she drew nearer, Loren felt a grin spread across her face.

"You run a pretty race, little rabbit, but this wolf will catch you!"

The boy answered by increasing his pace. He diverted course suddenly, running straight for a wall that had a tall wooden gutter affixed to it. He seized the gutter in his hands, propped his feet against it, and shimmied up like a bear cub climbing a sapling.

On the nearer wall, the building had two rows of windows with wooden sills. Loren leapt for the first windowsill. Her fingers gripped its wooden texture as easily as a tree branch, and she vaulted up to seize the next one. She pulled hard and pushed up with her feet, leaping to seize the shingle roof with her fingertips before hauling herself up.

The roof sloped gently upward. She ran up and reached the peak just as the boy scaled it. He barely had time to look up in surprise before Loren took him in a flying tackle, slamming him hard into the shingles.

The boy cried out, more from fear than pain, and tried to squirm away beneath her. But Loren wrapped one arm around his torso and used it to flip him face down. She caught his neck in the crook of her elbow.

"You would do well to stop," she growled in his ear. "There was no better wrestler than I in my village."

The boy went tense and still below her, panting heavily. Then the fight left him all at once, and he went limp.

"Now," said Loren. "Where is my purse?"

The boy said nothing, but she spied a bit of brown cloth poking out from between his tightly curled fingers. She freed one hand and snatched it, trying to pry his fingers open. A bit of his spirit returned, and he gripped the purse more tightly. Loren slammed his hand onto the shingles and he cried out, letting go with a whimper.

She snatched the purse and pushed up, rolling away to inspect her prize. The boy had cut the strings, which hung in frayed tatters. Still, they were long enough to retie around her belt, and she took a moment to do so. All the while she kept a careful eye on the boy. As soon as she removed herself from him, he leapt up into a crouch, looking like a cornered rat. But as Loren made no further move, gradually his narrowed eyes softened.

Once she finished retying the purse, Loren got to her feet. The boy recoiled, ready for a fight. But Loren only dusted herself off and flapped her hands as if shooing a cat.

"Go on, then. Off with you. Begone."

The boy studied her carefully. "You mean you do not want to fight?"

Loren scoffed. "Fight one such as you? I would break you in half, and for what? You are only a little boy, and the worst thief I have ever seen."

The boy finally released his crouch, standing as tall as his diminutive frame would allow. "A bad thief? Never! I steal a thousand and one purses each day, and never have I ever been caught, excepting only you. And there is nary a one better in Cabrus when it comes to rooftops." He glanced at the gutter he had climbed and then eyed Loren ruefully. "Well . . . excepting only you, I suppose."

Loren laughed at him. "A thousand and one purses every day? Then you must be the wealthiest man in the nine lands. How could you even count them all?"

"I know my numbers better than a wizard," the boy boasted. "And my letters as well. I could have been a scholar if I had been born in a noble house, and a wiser man you would never have seen."

Loren rolled her eyes. She had never learned to read, and might have been impressed by his boasts if she had thought there might be even a crumb of truth to them.

"Very well, master scholar. Or was it wizard? Or thief? Consider me honored to be in your presence. Now, remove yourself from mine before I give you a beating you will not soon forget."

He scowled, trying to look fierce. But his dirt-browned face with its fawn's eyes only looked the more ridiculous. "Why do you withhold yourself? I can take it. I have grown up fighting, and many know to fear my fists. You are a stranger to this city, clearly, if you have never heard the tale." He raised his hands to demonstrate, waving them back and forth as though he might throw a punch.

Loren seized a wrist and used it to spin him around before she caught his feet with her ankle. She lowered him gently to the roof, rather than letting him crash down, and then put a foot on his throat to hold him there. He lay there for a moment, blinking as though unsure quite what had happened.

"Oh, I can see the strength of your fists most clearly. How could I have thought to challenge such a mighty warrior?"

"I *am* mighty!" he said, hitting her boot with his free fist. "I am Auntie's favorite! She always says so!"

"I do not know your aunt, but she seems a poor judge of fighting skill." Loren let him go.

"Not *my* aunt," said the boy, rising. He rolled his eyes as though she were an idiot. "Auntie. She runs us. Me and the children, I mean. At least until I am of age to take over, for as I have said, I am the most fearsome pickpocket in Cabrus."

His words drew Loren's interest. "This Auntie you speak of. You say she commands you? You and the other . . . children?"

The boy nodded emphatically. "Aye, the most feared thieves' guild in all the nine lands."

"And you all pick pockets? Cut purses?"

He shook his head. "Only the smallest, like me. Everyone thinks we are too young to be a threat. The bigger boys, Auntie has them do the heavy work. Steal from wagons, taverns and inns, jobs of that sort."

Loren's pulse began to race, and an idea formed in her mind. The boy surely exaggerated, but she had heard tales of thieves' guilds from Bracken. The old man had said that gangs of pickpockets and burglars roamed the underbelly of every great city in the nine lands. They knew the alleys better than anyone. Thieves delved into the cracks and corners and crevices that no one else dared explore. What better way to find Annis?

And failing that, where better to begin her new life as Nightblade? She could not remain in Cabrus by herself forever, but what if she had a dozen or more companions to help her stay hidden?

Her mind made up, she drew up and placed her hands on her hips, eyes hardening as she fixed the boy with a stern glare. Despite his bravado, he quailed a bit.

"Do you have a name, boy?"

"Only the best," he said, lifting his chin. "Gem, they call me, for I am a jewel among dirt."

"Well, Gem," said Loren. "I think you had best take me to this Auntie of yours."

NINETEEN

LOREN HAD FEARED SHE MIGHT HAVE TO CONVINCE Gem, but he agreed to take her quite easily. *Mayhap too easily,* she thought. As Loren followed him through the city streets, she kept one careful hand near her coin purse and the other near her dagger. She would not be made a fool of twice.

But no danger presented itself. If anything, Gem took quite well to her, mayhap because she had not beaten him as he feared. Soon after they began their walk through the streets, he began to speak, and once he started Loren thought he might never stop. It reminded her of Annis, and she felt a twinge of sadness.

"Auntie will quite like you, I am certain," said Gem. "You with your fine cloak and climbing. They are quite useful things. Though you should not expect her to enjoy your eyes."

Loren looked at him askance. "My eyes?"

"Green," said Gem, as though that were the only explanation needed. When Loren looked at him without understanding, he sighed. "Folk remember green eyes. You do not want anyone to remember you. No one remembers me," he said proudly.

Loren nearly gave that a snide answer, but decided to let it pass.

Their path wound north and west, and for a moment she feared they aimed for the district where Corin had released her. But it was not long before Gem swerved suddenly left, ducking through a hole in a fence where a board had been removed.

Loren followed him to find a small yard floored by dirt and straw instead of cobblestones. It was empty save for the two of them, but a smell lingered on the air that told her this place had once held many pigs. The building attached to the yard lay empty, its back door fallen from iron hinges and lying on the ground. No one looked to have lived here for quite some time.

"Where are we?" Loren's nerves prickled at the possibility of a trap.

"This is Auntie's place." Gem walked to the gaping back door, leaned his head in, and cried, "Fresh blood!"

After a few silent breaths, Loren heard the quiet pitter-patter of feet.

Then they came.

From every crack and corner, children poured like the sudden onset of a flood. Some spilled through gaps in the fence, others from the doorway and windows of the house. A few even climbed down off the roof. Soon dozens of children filled the yard, all more than a head shorter than Loren, all small and starved-looking. Their wide eyes mirrored Gem's as he stared up at her.

"Er . . . hello." Loren thought she ought to be frightened, but she could see no threat in their wan eyes. "Which of you is Auntie?"

"None of these," scoffed Gem. "She—"

"She is here."

The voice came from the house. There in the door's frame stood a woman. And a true woman she was—Loren immediately felt gawky and childish. Auntie wore a tunic with short sleeves that did not reach her elbows, over which she had donned a pale green vest that clung tightly to her supple frame. Her arms bore olive skin, with fine-fingered hands free from grime or calluses. Loren curled her own fingers into her palms, for they felt suddenly peasant-like.

Auntie's eyes captured her the most. They were of a light hazel, unremarkable in itself, but their intelligence dazzled the mind. They flitted back and forth, up and down, always assessing her surroundings, observing everything. Loren suddenly felt underdressed. She grew even more self-conscious at the sight of Auntie's face: slender with high cheekbones, long, entrancing eyelashes, and framed by hair cut almost as short as a man's. Her hair was dyed so blonde as to be almost white, except near the scalp where it darkened towards black. Loren had never seen anything like it, or like Auntie herself.

"Well, do not gawk forever, girl, lest I think you wish to marry me."

Loren's eyes widened and quickly turned away as her cheeks flushed full crimson. "My apologies, my la—er . . ."

"Just Auntie. None of that 'lady' nonsense. Ladies are who we steal from, and quite well, too." She lifted her hands to brush against the front of her vest, displaying its fine pattern. "It is how I gain such niceties and keep the children fed."

Loren did not know what to say, and so elected to remain silent. But Auntie spoke no further word, and Loren realized that she bore the burden of introducing herself.

She bowed low. "I am Loren, of the family Nelda. I thought . . . I had hoped you might help me. And, mayhap, entertain my company, at least for a little while."

"I hardly see how I could help you if I did not," said Auntie with a wry twist to her mouth. "Presence is oft required for assistance, unless one is paid to go away. I know many a bard who plays worse than they are capable for just such a purpose. But come, tell me: what do you require? You seem a capable girl, and unless I miss my guess you are well acquainted with that bow on your back. And mayhap the knives at your belt and in your boot."

Loren gave a little gasp and glanced down. Her cloak still kept the dagger hidden. And the knife in her boot remained invisible, for the leather was too thick to show a bulge.

"It is the way you hold yourself." Auntie pushed off from the door frame and came out into the yard. The children parted before her like water in a pool, even closing in behind her to complete the effect. Auntie walked in a slow half-circle to stand behind

Loren. She placed one gentle hand on Loren's left wrist, the other on the right of her waist. "This hip juts out slightly. That might be a stance of rest, but this hand you hold a bit farther from your body than the other. It is ready to leap to the hip and draw forth the knife." She released Loren and came around in front of her again.

Loren swallowed. "And the one in my boot?"

Auntie smiled warmly. "I have never known a forester who did not carry a knife there. Those who wander the woods for long hours cannot keep their tools in drawers and cabinets like us city folk."

The answer left Loren with even more questions—how had Auntie known she came from the forest? She had to swallow again before she could continue. "As for your question. I seek a girl within the city. I thought . . . you might . . ."

"That the children and I would have eyes in all quarters, and that we might help you find her?" finished Auntie. "Aye, that is as may be. And what of the other thing? You spoke of keeping company for a time."

Loren looked around her uneasily. The idea seemed suddenly ridiculous, surrounded by these children who had grown up lifting coins from unwary victims. "I thought mayhap you could use a willing hand. Though now that I stand before you, I see you have many to spare."

But Auntie stepped forwards and took Loren's hands in her own, raising them to her chest. The smile she gave Loren held such secret promise that Loren felt utterly entranced.

"Willing hands are never in enough supply here. Especially when attached to one who, unless I am mistaken, has traveled far and done much using them. I love my children after all . . . but sometimes a woman grown serves better."

Loren swallowed once more. "Does that mean you will have me? I will learn all you can teach, as quickly as I might. You will find me an excellent worker and a quick study—"

Auntie cut her off by drawing her hands away and letting Loren's fall limp to her sides. A sad little smile dusted her lips. "Ah, that it were so simple. But, Loren of the family Nelda, you must understand something. I am mother to these children in all but blood. My first duty is to them always. I hold myself the sole caretaker of their well-being."

"Of course," said Loren, looking at the urchins that surrounded them.

"Then you know I cannot simply accept any person who offers to serve us. First you must prove that you will help the family, and not make yourself a drain upon us."

"I would never," said Loren, shaking her head quickly.

Again, that small smile. "I believe you. But if belief were food, none of my little ones would ever go hungry again. And so I must beg a task of you. A small something to prove yourself. A token of faith, a proof of skill, and something to fill the bellies of my children."

Loren's heart raced, and she smiled. "I think you mean to tell me that someone's purse sits over-fat, and I must lighten it for them."

Auntie grinned. "I knew you for a clever girl. Just so. And if you fetch this thing for me, you may consider yourself my . . . well, not my daughter, for you and I are near of age. But family nonetheless. My children and I will spare no trouble in helping you find your friend."

Loren could not remove her smile. An auspicious start, indeed. Her first task as a thief, other than what she had stolen from her village.

"Only point the way, and I will do as you ask."

Auntie smiled. "I thought you might."

TWENTY

GEM LED HER THROUGH THE STREETS AS LIGHT faded from the sky. All around them, torches sprang to life as the townspeople readied themselves for the approaching night.

The woman you seek spends her time near the northern gate, Auntie had told her. *She often frequents the square outside the Bottomless Mug, or the common room of the tavern itself. But if you are wise, you will not approach her within the building. Too many eyes.*

Loren felt her heart grow heavier with each step that drew her closer to her destination. Her excitement had evaporated the longer Auntie went on.

The northern gate? Loren had asked, thinking of the constables' station, which lay between the northern gate and the western.

Yes, Auntie had said, thin eyebrows arching. *Is that a problem?*

Loren had forced herself to look carefree, shrugging her indifference. *Nothing I cannot overcome. Go on.* But her heart sank lower with every moment.

You will find her in a pink gown, and will know her by her long yellow curls. Darker than my hair, but not by much. She carries a purse at all times. I need it.

And so Loren had struck out with Gem as her guide. With every step, she had to convince herself to take another, resisting an ever stronger urge to flee. Mayhap she could find Annis on her own after all.

But then the two of you would be alone, she thought. *And you would be on the run, rather than a thief learning her craft.*

Loren pressed on.

As they drew farther and farther west, Loren pulled Gem aside. "It may be that some near our destination seek me out," she said, choosing her words carefully. "If there is any way forwards that will hide us best from prying eyes, let us take it."

Gem pursed his lips. "What manner of someone? Constables, or elsewise?"

Loren thought of Gregor and his guards. "We would do well to avoid both sorts."

Gem's eyes widened slightly. "Beset on all sides, are you? Very well. I suggest the roofs. Not far from here, we may find a route that will take us all the way west with hardly a heel on a cobblestone."

Loren followed eagerly as Gem turned their course due north. They ducked into alleys that grew ever more narrow and dark, until Loren felt the press of the walls on either side.

To take her mind from their ominous surroundings, she asked a question that had sat with her for some time. "Did your mother name you Gem? I have never met someone with that name."

Gem shrugged without turning to look. "I know not what my mother named me. Jarmo was the first name I ever knew. But when I found Auntie, I chose my own. Who has ever heard of a thief called Jarmo?"

Loren had never heard of a thief called Gem, either, but she did not tell him that.

Soon Gem brought her to a low building. Its roof reached so near the ground, Loren could almost touch it from tiptoe. She boosted Gem to reach it and then made use of a nearby barrel to pull herself up. Gem led her on, up one side and down the other to where the next building's roof sat only a pace away. Loren leapt the gap easily and followed him to the next.

Gem had spoken truly: the rooftops ran in an almost uninterrupted path west. Every so often the wide gap of a street blocked their progress, and Gem led her either north or south to circumvent it. Only once did he lead her back to the ground. Then they ran across several streets in a mad dash, Loren looking in all directions for any sign of the constables or Damaris' men.

On the roofs she felt herself relax, and even allowed herself to enjoy the night air as stars emerged above. The press of the city seemed far away. She could imagine that the soft shingles underfoot were the natural rise and fall of the forest floor. Easily she ignored the sounds of the people below, and focused instead on the moons. They, at least, had not changed, though everything else around her was different. And between them, Loren still saw fiery

Dorren making his way across the sky, and from him drew comfort.

When Gem called a halt to their journey, it seemed almost too soon. Loren crawled with him to the roof's edge. Together they sidled along the shingles until they could peek down at the people below.

Night made the crowd sparse, but still a fair few walked in the torchlight. Among them she saw a few constables in their red leather armor, but they scattered far enough to avoid if she were careful.

Her eyes fixed on a figure in a pink gown with golden curls spilling from her head.

"There!" she whispered, pointing.

"I see her," said Gem. "What now?"

Loren inspected the square further. There sat the Bottomless Mug, a noisy establishment through whose windows firelight poured to bathe the street below. The woman sat outside the glow, upon a bench placed in the square amid a cluster of grass and flowers. Other nightgoers passed by, some men in fine cloth inclining their head towards the woman. Loren realized that in the rush of explanation, she had never thought to ask the maiden's name.

"She sits unattended and alone. I can easily come upon her unawares."

"But the open space that surrounds her," said Gem. "The constables will catch you."

"They will not have time to react. Besides, I can outrun them. I will make for the roofs again." Let the constables try and follow her up here.

Gem frowned. "I do not like it. But I see no other choice. She does not look of a mind to move."

"Very well, then. Come, let us—duck!"

Loren shoved Gem's head into the shingles, and he gave a muted cry of protest. The woman's head had turned towards them, and Loren feared they were discovered. But as she cautiously raised her face from the shingles, she saw that the woman's gaze had simply wandered. Now she looked away again, oblivious. As Loren watched, the woman stood and made for a dark alley at the side of the Bottomless Mug.

"Fortune smiles," said Loren. "Come! Quickly!"

They rose and scuttled across the rooftop towards a gap above the alleyway. The woman in pink disappeared into the shadows below. Loren spotted a wooden gutter.

"Remain here. No need for both of us to risk ourselves. I will return shortly."

With that, Loren shimmied down the gutter like a squirrel. Her leather boots came down silent on the cobblestones, and without a moment's hesitation she ducked into the alley.

The woman in pink stood a few paces within, her back still turned to the alley's gaping mouth. The purse hung tantalizingly from her hip, dangling by thin strings. Loren stole forwards like a mouse, sliding her dagger from its sheath.

This was her first time cutting a purse, but she knew the idea of it. Grip the purse and slash the strings in one quick slice, and the quarry might never feel the tug. In a crowd she might have jostled the girl unawares to hide it, but this would have to do. And if the woman spotted her, what could she do? Pursue Loren in that gown?

Only a pace remained now. Loren held her breath, trying to still her heartbeat. Her hand reached out for the purse.

The woman whirled, her hand snapping shut on Loren's wrist. Loren nearly shrieked from fright as she met the girl's face.

Then the girl's eyes glowed, and her face began to change.

Before Loren's startled gaze, the girl's eyes turned from deep blue to light hazel. Her skin darkened, and her cheekbones shifted higher. Her hair seemed to shrink into her scalp, turning paler except at the roots, where it was black as night.

It lasted only moments, and then Auntie stood there in the pink gown, an iron hand clasped around Loren's wrist.

Loren's mind screamed a word: *weremage.*

"What an excellent presentation," said Auntie in a cool tone. "You have done exactly as you should."

As Loren tried to understand, she heard the clump of heavy boots behind her. Auntie's grip kept her from turning, so she had looked over her shoulder.

In the mouth of the alley appeared a tall, muscular constable with a cruel face. It was Bern. And behind him appeared another constable—not Corin, but a man she had never seen before, with naked steel in his hand.

"I must thank you for finding us," said Auntie over Loren's shoulder. "The reward for your capture will go *so* far towards filling the children's bellies."

In a flash, Auntie drew Loren's arm behind her back and pressed a knife to her throat. Bern smiled and took a slow step into the alley.

"We meet again, thief," said the constable. "It seems that with every encounter, the list of your crimes grows—"

Loren heard a shrill shriek above, and her eyes went skyward. Bern, too, looked up, just in time to get both of Gem's bare feet in his face. The pick-pocket landed full on the constable's head, slamming the man back into the wall of the building where he fell to the street, stunned.

Loren's mind reeled with shock, but she recovered faster than Auntie. Her free hand seized the weremage's wrist, dragging the dagger away from her throat as she threw her head backwards. She judged the blow well, for she felt Auntie's nose crumple against the back of her head. Blood spattered across the back of her cowl as she pulled away and Auntie hit the cobblestones. But as she fell, her hand wrapped around the tip of Loren's bow, and Loren heard the *twang* of the string snapping.

Loren looked down in horror. Auntie grasped furiously at her nose as she lay there, but her other hand wrapped around the bow. *My bow,* thought Loren. *Chet's bow.*

She could not risk retrieving it. She had no time. Almost Loren ran for the mouth of the alley, but then she saw the other constable standing there with his sword. Bern, too, rose from the ground, looking around as if dazed. Gem ran towards Loren, snatching her hand and dragging her farther from the square.

"Run!" he cried.

Loren needed no second urging. They hit the alley's end and cut left down a smaller one just as Loren heard the slap of boots behind them.

"The rooftops!" she shouted. Gem understood and led her around two sharp turns before they found a gutter to climb. Loren gripped the boy under his arms and flung him skyward, letting him grip the gutter just under the roof's edge. Then she launched herself up hand over foot, and in a moment she had gained the shingles.

"This way!" Gem ran south and leapt the gap to the next roof, Loren hot on his heels. Behind them she heard Bern's furious bellow.

On they ran, across another two roofs. Finally Loren seized Gem's arm and stopped him, looking back for a moment. Several men had made the climb far behind them.

"They do not share our skill," Loren said, exulting. "Look at how they scramble to—"

She heard the *hiss* of air a moment before an arrow whizzed by her face, so close it nearly passed through her hair.

"They mean to kill us!" screamed Gem. All the boy's bravado vanished in an instant, and he turned to flee.

Loren followed. "We must regain the street! We are easy targets!"

Gem heard her through his panic and slid to the roof's edge, launching into empty space. He bounced off the opposite wall before coming to a hard landing on the street. Loren descended more carefully, gripping the roof's edge before dropping to the ground.

They landed on a narrow street filled with people, some of them beggars staking a claim on the wealthy area, others men of questionable purpose moving about under cover of darkness. Many stared at Loren as she helped Gem to his feet. But the two of them must not have been all that unusual a sight, for all eyes soon turned away.

But Loren's gaze fixed on one man in particular. He seemed unaware of their presence, face almost hidden by his cowl, his shoulders stooped as if with great age. But Loren spied his face and the long dark curls that hung from his head. Her heart nearly stopped.

"Come!" She seized Gem and pulled him along. As she watched, the man ducked into the back door of an inn, dragging the door shut behind him. But just before it closed, Loren jammed her boot into the gap. She gripped the edge and flung it open, launching herself into the back room. The man recoiled in surprise as Loren closed the door behind her.

She turned to face the man, smiling in grim triumph. "Well met again, wizard."

Xain straightened, dragging the cowl back from his head as he scowled at her.

TWENTY-ONE

THEY STOOD IN A SMALL STOREROOM FILLED WITH the odds and ends required by any inn. A broom leaned in the corner, several buckets and washcloths stacked haphazardly beside it. Loren's nose caught the pungent odor of wood polish from shelved bottles above.

Xain scowled down at her, his grey-brown eyes flashing beneath dark brows drawn in anger. His glance slipped to Gem for a moment and then, dismissing the boy, focused on Loren again.

"What are you doing here?" he growled.

"Fleeing the constables and the cell they hold ready for me. I might ask you the same. Prudence would have sent you from Cabrus days ago."

"Prudence and convenience are not often bedfellows. Now, be off with you. I cannot take the risk of your company, nor should you be eager for mine."

Muffled shouts came through the heavy wooden door. Loren glanced over her shoulder, and the wizard's eyes flashed with fear as they followed her gaze.

"That will be them," murmured Gem.

"Who?" said Xain.

"Constables," said Loren. "They pursue us, and closely. You must hide us."

"I cannot be involved!" said Xain, his voice low and urgent. He looked towards the storeroom's opposite door, the one Loren knew must lead to the inn proper. "It is a hard enough task avoiding their clutches without caring for two children into the bargain."

"Mayhap I could have helped, had you not stolen away in the night like a craven."

"You were better off without me," said Xain. "I am hardly safe company."

Loren pointed towards the back door. "Yet I find myself beset regardless. Did you think if you left me, they would not hunt me down for information? I aided your escape!"

Xain's lips pressed tightly together, but Loren saw his eyes shift to guilt. His shoulders hunched as if in resistance, fighting the thought she could see creeping into his mind.

The shouts outside grew louder, and Loren heard the heavy tramp of boots. "Loren," whispered Gem. "Let us flee. This man will not help us."

"He will," said Loren, folding her arms as she glared at Xain. "Or I will open that door right now and throw him to the mercy of the King's law."

"You would not dare. They would take you as well."

"They will take me regardless! But if I give you to them, they may grant me leniency. Let us find out."

Loren turned and put a hand on the door as if to push it. Behind her she heard a sharp *crack,* and heat tickled the back of her neck. Slowly she rounded on Xain.

The wizard's eyes glowed white in their sockets, and the corners of his mouth sank into his cheeks as words of power spilled from his lips. Blue fire burned in both palms.

"Do not touch that door," he said.

"Hide us, then. Do not fear that your presence might burn us. I have had ample time to make other enemies, and I would suffer your fire before theirs under any sun or moons."

Xain blinked. The glow in his eyes vanished, and the fire died. "Very well, then. Come with me, and quickly!"

She needed no further urging, throwing her cowl down to hide her face as she followed him farther into the inn. Gem pressed close beside her. She drew the edge of her cloak about the boy, walking with her arm over his shoulders.

The door swung open to the murmur of voices in hushed conversation. A fire burned in the common room's far wall, throwing smoky orange light upon the floor. The glow did not seem to find all the corners, and within those dark places she saw the dark shapes of patrons. Firelight glinted on eyes that turned towards them and then drifted back down without interest.

Xain took them up a staircase to a landing that wound down a short hallway. He showed them to the third door on the left, and from his pocket he produced a key. Again he let them go first, closing the door behind them all.

A large window spanned the opposite wall, and several candles burned along tables within the room. Xain darted down the line, dousing them one by one with his fingers. Loren followed suit, proceeding in the other direction and licking her fingers before snuffing each wick. Xain left only one, which he moved to the center of the floor. He drew the curtains and sat before the small, flickering flame.

"That should be sufficient. Come, sit away from the window. They may walk the roofs."

But Loren did not obey immediately. Instead she went to the window and drew back the edge of the curtain. Two men in red leather armor walked the street below, but she could see no sign of Bern. The roofs, too, looked empty, but in night's shadow she could not have said for certain. Satisfied, she went to sit opposite Xain on the floor. Gem took his place beside her, folding his legs beneath him and placing a hand on each knee.

Now that she had a moment to think, Loren looked at the urchin in wonder. "You nearly threw away your life for mine tonight. What madness spurred you to attack the constable that way?"

Gem ducked his head suddenly, unwilling to meet her eyes. He shrugged and said in a sullen voice, "I did not want to see them take you. Would you rather I had?"

"Of course not. Only . . . I took you for Auntie's boy."

"Man," he corrected her. "And yes, I am. But I am beholden to no one, for I am no one's lackey. Auntie has cared after me for a long while, and yet never provided more than a meager living."

"You said she called you her favorite."

Gem looked askance out the window. "Oh, she has. But being her favorite can sometimes be a burden. And then at other times she calls me other things, things I might boast about less readily. When I saw how she betrayed you, it somehow struck me as wrong. I hardly thought at all."

"Why did you not tell me she was a weremage?"

"A *what?*" snapped Xain, who had contented himself with listening. His eyes snapped to sharp focus, and Loren found them piercing her.

"A weremage," said Loren, thinking he had not understood. "A skinchanger. A—"

"I know the word, girl, though you do not; they are called therianthropes. How have you run afoul of another wizard in the span of only a few short days?"

"Mayhap you would know, had you not been so quick to abandon my company," said Loren, feeling her blood run hot with anger.

Xain rolled his eyes and looked away. "Yet I must do the same again. I will keep you here for the night. Then you must be on your way. Hardly could I overstate the danger if you remain with me."

"It cannot be greater than what I have faced upon the road to reach you," said Loren.

"I am hungry," said Gem.

Xain's lip curled, but he leaned over to snatch a half-eaten bowl of stew from the table beside his bed—remnants, no doubt, of a meal earlier that day. He pushed it into Gem's eager hands, and the urchin eagerly dug in with bare fingers.

"What happened upon the road?" said Xain.

"The constables pursued me west, where I hid within a merchant's caravan. Afterwards, I fell into their company."

"A merchant's caravan? I came upon one such, and bought from them a horse."

Loren nodded. "They told me. And you were fortunate to leave when you did. Though I enjoyed their hospitality for a time, it soon became . . . less than sincere."

Xain cocked his head, so Loren told him everything: Damaris and Gregor and the constable's men, and the black rocks Annis had flung at the constables' feet. As she described them, Xain sucked a sharp breath through his teeth, and his eyes went wide. In the light of the candle, they turned from a light brown-grey to pale orange.

"You know of these stones?" she said. "Tell me, what are they?"

"Nothing you would understand," said Xain shortly. "A matter for wizards. Go on."

Loren told him of her capture, but she paused before speaking of Corin's reaction to her dagger. She could not have said why, but she thought it better to keep that a secret. Instead she told him that when Corin got her alone, she tripped him and sent him into a gutter, whereupon she fled.

Xain gave a grunt at that and raised his eyebrows. "You are full of more fight than you look."

She glanced at him, wondering if he knew more than he said. But his eyes focused on the candle flame burning bright before them.

When she had finished recounting her adventures, Loren pressed Xain for his own. "What have you found since your arrival in Cabrus? And why have you not left already? The constables seek you, and not for conversation."

"And there we find the problem. A heavy guard lies upon all the city's exits. I had to find a way of slipping through undetected."

Gem, who had remained silent while Loren told of her journey, piped up. "But you are a wizard. Why do you not snap your fingers and fly over the wall?"

Xain glared at the boy. "Magic is not what you have heard in Elf-tales, child. I could not fly so much as a chair over a city wall."

"What, then, do you plan?" said Loren.

"I have an associate. She has found a way out, but it does not leave until tomorrow night. Until then I must remain out of sight."

"Take us with you," said Loren.

Xain shook his head. "My associate procured passage for one. I can do nothing more. My pockets have bottoms, you know." Loren noticed for the first time that his sizable coin purse no longer hung at his belt.

"The carriage leaves regardless," said Loren. "What matter if you board alone or with companions?"

"When one traffics outside the King's law, one gets nothing for free," said Xain, shaking his head. "If you wish to board, you must pay your own way, and I doubt you can bring the price."

Fear gripped Loren's chest. Now that the constables sought her as well as the wizard, how could she think to leave the city without his help? And with Auntie out for her blood, how could she think to stay?

"Hear me, wizard. Were it not for you, I would still walk beneath the boughs of the Birchwood. I am grateful for your help, and I do not mean to return. But if you abandon me here, I will suffer a fate far worse than my father's cruel hands. As well you might have left me there to take my daily bruises, to live the rest of my life beaten and alone. Do not leave me to this crueler fate. Have you never known what it is to wander the world alone?"

She played a risky game by throwing herself upon his mercy, but well did Loren remember the wizard's face within the Birchwood when he saw the bruises upon her arms. If asked to wager, she would have said he once knew a life much like Loren's own.

Something in his eyes relaxed, an admission of defeat. "I will stow you aboard my carriage. But only if I have your word that you will leave me at the next city. No." He raised a hand to forestall her protest. "That is my only offer. You refuse to see the danger you court in my company. The constables do not seek to jail me. They will kill me if they can, and any who stand beside me."

Loren swallowed. "Bern has tried that with me already. I will risk it."

"Not while your life sits in my pocket. Promise me you will leave me in the next city, and I will vow to take you there."

Loren's shoulders sagged. But when one path led to a bottomless pit and the other a dangerous cliff, one must brave the climb. "Very well. I give you my word."

Only time will tell if I keep it, she thought. Thieves had earned no great reputation for honesty.

"Then on the morrow I must speak to my associate once more. He will not be pleased to have another two passengers."

Loren grimaced. "You had best make that three."

Xain's face went stony. "I can count, girl, and you overestimate your number."

Loren's mind raced. Xain would never agree to take the merchant's daughter if he thought her mother might pursue them. "I met another within the city. A distant cousin whose family I thought to stay with when I arrived. But her parents have perished from plague, and now she wanders the streets alone. I lost her in my flight, but I cannot leave her here. We are kin."

The wizard's eyes went from stone to steel. "Already you make me regret my decision. I cannot drag a gaggle of wayward geese across all the nine lands."

"She will be no trouble," Loren said quickly. "As quiet as a mouse, she is, and timid as well." No description could have been further from the truth, but it would buy time.

"Very well," said Xain. "Where is she? You would do well to fetch her, for if the carriage arrives early I mean to take it."

Loren looked at Gem uncertainly, and he shrugged at her. "I never even saw her," said the urchin. "I know not where she might wander."

"I cannot be seen on the streets looking for her. Too many eyes now know me within the walls." Loren turned to Xain. "How have you moved about the city, when you have had need to leave the inn?"

"I wrapped myself in rags and took the manner of a leper," said Xain. "Stumble in just the right way, and no one seeks to peer too closely beneath your hood."

"Then we must do the same." Loren looked longingly at the wool rug on the floor, but she forced her eyes away. "Come, Gem. Our night has not yet finished with us."

TWENTY-TWO

LOREN SENT GEM TO FETCH SOME OF THE WASHCLOTHS from the storeroom, and they wrapped the rags around their arms and hands so that hardly any skin showed. Their faces too they covered, and Loren winced at the musty, moldy smell of the cloth.

She had to leave her cloak, which pained her greatly. But the fine black cloth would easily be recognized, whether by the constables or Auntie's urchins. Instead she took Xain's dark brown mantle. It sat too large on her shoulders and hung nearly to her feet, but that only concealed her better. Her dagger she tucked under the cloak. As she did she studied Xain's face, anxious to see any reaction, mayhap something she had missed when he saw it in the Birchwood. But he spared the blade no second glance. Loren sighed, folding her black cloak up and placed it beneath Xain's bed with reverence.

"Take care of that," she said solemnly, her green eyes meeting his grey ones.

Xain only snorted. "What will happen to it in here? Do you expect someone to come and steal it?"

They left the inn through the same back door where they entered, and Xain showed them how to trip the latch from the outside. As they walked away, Loren had a thought and asked Gem the inn's name.

"The Elf's Purse," he said.

It sounded vaguely familiar, though she could not recall why.

Once the inn was out of sight, Gem stumbled beside her. She moved to catch him, but he batted her hands away. "No, you fool. We are lepers, or have you forgotten?"

Loren flushed, glad he could not see it beneath her rags. She adopted Gem's shuffle, even dragging one foot slightly to add to the effect. They kept to the edges of the street, leaning against buildings as if for support. It worked. Not many prowled the city this late at night, but any man or woman who saw them turned away in fear or headed in another other direction.

"All goes well so far," whispered Gem.

"Boastful words tempt fate. Passersby will grow less discerning in the slums."

Loren panicked the first time they saw a constable, but the woman avoided them just like anyone else. After that Loren walked a bit less fearfully. Gem led her down streets, avoiding alleys where they might catch a knife. The streets seemed almost well lit, for even when torchlight did not illuminate their way, both moons glowed full in the sky. At first she had feared to roam the city at night, but now it seemed no worse than the forest.

"Hold." Gem stepped back and pressed her into a doorway.

"What?" But then Loren saw them. Four large figures in armor, walking heavily down the street towards them. They stood tall and broad, and their eyes searched every corner.

One of them was Gregor.

Loren's blood chilled to ice at the sight of the giant caravan guard, and she ducked to avoid his gaze. Part of her knew she need not have worried; Gregor could not have picked out her green eyes by moonslight alone. Still, she quaked within her rags as he and his guards passed by.

They had to be hunting for Annis, the same as Loren. She could think of no other reason for Damaris' guards to wander the streets in darkness. That made tonight's mission more urgent than ever.

She readied herself to step out of the doorway and hurry down the street, away from Gregor, when she heard a soothing voice in the darkness—too close, just by her ear.

"Can you not find your own place to stand? I find myself overcrowded."

With a squeal she leapt out of the doorway, dragging Gem with her. Her hand flew into the folds of her heavy brown cloak to the hilt of her dagger.

Like Mennet stepping from shadow, out of the darkness appeared the man in the red cloak, the one who had rescued her from the cutpurse in the alley just after Corin let her go.

Loren stared with wide eyes, her mouth sliding open. Gem squirmed beside her, bringing her to her senses. She shoved him hard, pushing him farther behind her. Her fingers tightened on the dagger. "What are you doing here?"

"Why, nothing at all," said the man, cocking his head curiously. "No more than yourself."

"Why are you following me?"

"I am not. You only just arrived." He stepped forwards, and Loren almost drew. But he bent before her, looking over her shoulder to Gem. "Hello, child. What is your name?"

"Stay back," said Loren.

The man misunderstood her. "Your disease does not frighten me. If you wish, I can provide you with herbs that will ease your pain."

Loren realized that he did not recognize her. Enshrouded in rags, she looked no more familiar to him than any other ill-lucked beggar hobbling on limbs ridden with plague. He had not followed her after all.

She took two steps back, nearly bowling over poor Gem behind her. The boy struggled to emerge from behind her cloak. "Stop pushing me!" he said.

"Shush," said Loren. "We must take our leave."

"At least let me give the boy some food," said the man, his voice growing even more soothing. "I would guess he is your son? I am well-learned in arts of healing and of—"

He froze, and Loren saw his eyes light in recognition.

"Ah," he said. "The girl from the alley."

"Aye, and about my own business. As I said, we must be going. Good evening."

"I would guess, then, that your . . . illness, let us say, is not nearly so bad as you would make it seem."

Loren nodded. "And we have no need of your herbs, as you will understand."

"And food? Can I offer you nothing to fill your bellies?"

"I *am* quite hungry," said Gem.

Loren shushed him. "We have plenty to eat if we should wish it, and no desire to impose."

The man straightened and stood back, folding his arms. "Help me solve a riddle. What chance have we, two strangers who know each other not, to encounter each other twice upon these city streets within a day? One might call it remarkable."

"One might, and then go on with one's life, marveling at the wide wonders of the world," said Loren.

The man smiled. "I am not of a mind to so easily dismiss a mystery. I believe something draws us together, girl. I caught only a hint of it before, but now I see it clearly."

Despite herself, Loren felt curiosity prick the back of her mind. "What do you see?"

"You bear something. Some burden, or some mark, I am not sure. It draws us together. We cannot avoid it any more than we can avoid the rising sun."

Loren snorted, disappointed. "You speak of fate? I have never put much stock in the notion."

"Not fate," said the man. "Deep within, we are all like sunbeams and moonslight. Sometimes we are drawn to others like ourselves, those who bear a similar purpose. That to which we belong, we attract to ourselves. Have you never seen this to be true?"

Loren thought of her parents. "If it were, my life should have been much different."

"Mayhap it is, and you have yet to see it."

Her scorn slid down a slope towards anger. "I have seen plenty," she snarled. "And nothing that I belonged to, as you say."

Behind her, Gem shifted restlessly again. "What is he talking about, Loren?"

"Be *silent!"* said Loren, but it was too late. She saw the man smile gently.

"Loren," he said. "A name of the forests, and of victory. It suits you."

"How should you know?"

"Does it worry you that I have your name?" the man shrugged. "You may have mine, if you wish. I am Jordel, of the family Adair. Well met."

"Mayhap, and mayhap not," said Loren. "And in any case, we must be going. Good evening."

"Stop, I pray," said Jordel. "What do you seek so eagerly? Mayhap I can help."

Something in his voice held her. As before, she could sense that he meant her no harm. He had made no move to hurt them, and earlier he had likely saved her life. But Loren could not let herself forget that this man sought for Xain, her only path out of this city and away from Damaris.

So she shook her head. "Nothing that is any concern of yours. We dally too long. Good evening."

A small smile played at the edge of his mouth. "If you insist, Loren of the family Nelda. But unless

I miss my guess by a wide mark, we will indeed meet again."

Loren snorted and turned away, tugging Gem after her down the street. Only after a moment did she realize he had said her family name, though she had not given it to him. She spun around, but Jordel and his red cloak had vanished.

TWENTY-THREE

"Who was that man?"

"No one."

"What did he want?"

"Nothing."

"Why would you not talk to him?"

"Be silent."

Gem opened his mouth as if to ask yet another question, but finally closed it to stare sullenly at his feet. Loren heaved an inward sigh.

"We must find Annis quickly and return to the inn. I do not wish for any more chance encounters tonight."

"Why should you think we can find her? Among all the thousands within the walls, she will be like a single stalk of wheat in a field."

Loren had no answer, and so she said nothing. She knew her plan for a fool's errand, that even walking these streets could be a disaster. Before, she had needed Annis. The girl knew this sort of place well, and would have been an invaluable asset. But now, Xain would arrange for her passage from the city. Wisdom would seem to direct Loren to wait in the inn and steal away with Xain. But something within her would not let her abandon Annis to the city.

She made Gem show her through the streets and alleys of Cabrus' slums, avoiding the rooftops where he told her Auntie's children might be watching. She followed in his footsteps as he showed her the nooks and crannies, the dark corners that ran through the city like flowing veins.

All the while, Loren found it hard to remove thoughts of Jordel from her mind. The man had spoken true about the impossibility of their chance meetings, but that was not the only thing troubling her. How did he know her family name, and what about his talk of sunbeams and moonslight? Loren could not begin to understand it. She did not hold herself in especially high regard, but she knew herself for a clever girl. And while she might not bring loaves for the hungry and gold for the impoverished, neither did she engage in cruelty or wanton beatings of the weak and defenseless.

She thought it a cruel jape, then, to say she drew in only more things like her. Why did she deserve a lifetime of her father's cruel fists? Why did she deserve a forced marriage, being treated as a tool to gain her parents wealth?

Her thoughts wandered further, and she thought of the day she left home forever. Her meeting with Xain, and her swift readiness to step beyond the King's law. Her stealthy flight from the constables, and how even after her discovery she had escaped again by shadow and silence. Theft, too, had bought her escape from Damaris and the constables, and once inside the city walls, she had twice been robbed.

Framed by those thoughts, Jordel's words seemed to hold some merit. The moment Loren had stepped outside her known world, she had lived a life of darkness, secrets, and subterfuge, just as she had always dreamed.

Her thoughts were drifting. Loren forced her focus back to the matter at hand and quickened her pace, forcing Gem to hop-skip in front of her.

"It would be easier if we knew at least where to begin our search," he grumbled.

"It seems we have begun already. If morning comes and we have not found her, I will return to the inn, but I cannot abandon her lightly."

"You mean to search all *night,* then?" Gem rubbed his belly. "Oh, for my aching stomach. I wish you had told me, so that I might have filled it before we set out."

"You will live. Or mayhap not, and then we shall hold a great feast of mourning."

"Would you?" said Gem, doubtfully.

"No."

They stepped around the corner and nearly ran right into Gregor.

Loren spotted his face at the last moment, too late to keep herself from hitting his chest—but Gem's quicker reflexes saved her. He leapt back, pulling her with him by the arm. She jerked to a stop, sucking a frightened gasp between her teeth.

Gregor, for his part, barely glanced at them as Gem dragged her farther back. Only then did Loren remember her disguise.

"Be careful!" hissed Gem.

But as Loren opened her mouth to reply, she heard the murmured conversation of the caravan guards. One sounded frustrated, and she caught the words, ". . . the girl said Annis would be here."

Loren froze, and as Gem tried to pull her along again, she placed a hand on his arm to still him.

"Wait," she whispered. "We must follow them."

"Why? Is one of them your cousin? Otherwise I say give them a wide berth, for their swords look sharp."

"They know where Annis is. Or whereabout, anyway. Come."

She stole after them without waiting for Gem's reply. Who was the girl the guard had spoken of? It had to be Auntie—she had no qualms working with the constables; why should she hesitate to work with criminals and smugglers as Damaris had shown herself to be?

Gregor paused where the street spilled into an open square. Loren stumbled on a few more steps and leaned against the wall as though stopping to rest.

"What is it, sir?" said one of the guards.

"I see her," came Gregor's booming voice.

Loren's eyes widened. Without a word she motioned to Gem and waved him forwards. They entered the open street and continued, ignoring Gregor and his men as they passed.

"Is that her?" said the guard.

"Yes," said Gregor. "In the threadbare cloak. I know her walk."

"Many in this city may walk the same."

"No. She is of a height with Annis. It is her."

"Very well, let us—"

"Look more closely."

Loren followed Gregor's pointing figure. There in the square she saw the figure Gregor described. Annis' height, to be sure, but could it really be her in such a threadbare and worn-looking cloak? Patches lay upon it so thick and in so many hues, she might have wrapped a rainbow around herself.

Then Loren saw what Gregor had: a squadron of eight constables standing nearby, each with a hand on his broadsword. They stood in a loose circle, talking in the dim light of the moons. If Annis screamed when Gregor took her, the constables would likely intervene.

"What of them, sir?" said the guard. "I wager we may take them."

"No fighting," said Gregor. "The mistress left no doubt on that score. That constable, Bern, hounds her closely enough as it is. If we worsen the situation, she shall worsen ours considerably."

The guard nodded with a gulp.

As Loren and Gem brushed by Gregor and the guards, one withdrew his arm as if he had been bitten. Loren kept her head down, well hidden in her cowl. She picked up her pace, drawing nearer to Annis.

"That is her," she said to Gem. "Be ready. We shall have to run."

"Again?" grumbled Gem.

"Wait until we pass the constables."

Annis walked with slow, measured steps, for all the world like a girl on a nighttime stroll, though she kept her face down instead of raised to the stars. Loren slowed to avoid reaching her before passing the constables. She risked a languid glance over her shoulder, as though checking on Gem. Her eyes stole to Gregor and his men. The giant gestured at his men with short, clipped movements, and one of them stole off to vanish down a side alley. Loren did not like that. The other two remained with Gregor.

"They are splitting up," said Loren. "We must move quickly."

"Only say the word. They will soon learn who they dare to trifle with."

Loren rolled her eyes. "Now!"

She leapt forwards and seized Annis' arm, at the same time saying "It is I," in her ear. Annis tensed for a moment, but then slackened as she recognized Loren's voice. Loren shoved her into an alley, seized her wrist, and ran, Gem's bare feet slapping the stones at their heels. From the square behind them, Loren heard Gregor's wordless bellow to his men.

"How did you find me?" cried Annis.

"Later," said Loren. "Gregor and his men are close. I hope you wear shoes meant for running. Gem, lead us to the roofs."

"No good," he said. "Auntie's children. We must go below."

"What do you—" Loren began, but Gem seized her hand and dragged her along. In a moment she saw a hole in the street, cut into the cobblestones and leading to darkness beneath.

"Below," Gem repeated. "Come. We can all fit, but I would wager that giant and his lackeys cannot."

Annis pulled up short, yanking on Loren's hand and pulling them all to a stop. "I will not go in there!" she shrieked, panic in her voice.

"We must. They will find us too easily up here." Gem looked angrily at Loren. "Tell her."

"Come, Annis. It is only until we get away."

But Annis' face twitched in terror, and she took a fearful step back. "I will not! I will not climb into that tomb to die!"

"If you are afraid of mussing your pretty face—"

Loren silenced Gem with a cuff to the ear. "Annis, we have no choice. Come, please. I will not leave your side or let go your hand."

More shouts and the tramp of many feet echoed down a nearby street. From the sound of it, they were just round the corner, and Gregor had summoned the constables as well as his men. Annis looked towards the sound, her tongue running nervously along her lips. Then she nodded and stepped forwards.

Gem led the way, sliding down into the darkness before raising his hands. Loren made Annis go next, and the girl fell into Gem's arms with a frightened cry. Loren slipped in behind her, and not a moment too soon—above she heard more running, and as Loren looked up she saw shadows pass before the moonslight.

Annis threw herself to Loren's side, wrapping both arms around her. "Do not let me go," she said in a quavering voice. "You promised you would not."

"I will not," Loren assured her.

She looked around, blinking rapidly as her eyes adjusted to the gloom. After a time the sparse moonslight spilling through the opening was enough to see by. They stood in a stone tunnel in the bowels of the city, a thick sludge lining a channel cut into the center. It smelled worse than anything Loren had ever imagined.

Gem tugged at her sleeve. "Come. It is not far to the way above, and then we may walk beneath the sky again."

"Lead the way."

Gem set off along the stone walkway above the sludge, and Loren pulled Annis into the darkness.

TWENTY-FOUR

Annis remained so anxious that Loren feared the girl might shriek again and bring Gregor running at any moment. But the girl merely clung to Loren's arm, silent other than an occasional whimper.

"Why do you snivel so?" said Gem. "There is nothing to fear here, unless you are one of those girls who dreads rats."

"I do not," snapped Annis. Loren was glad, at least, to hear some spark in her tone. "Only I do not enjoy dark places, nor ones that keep me from the sky and open air."

They passed another hole leading above, and in its blue glow Gem eyed Loren. "Where did you find this one? She whimpers like a frightened pup."

"I told you," Loren muttered, "she—"

"You told me you were kin." Gem eyed Annis' dark skin and Loren's pale face. "I see that you take me for a fool, which is your folly. I have told you I might have been a scholar. And even a simpleton could see your claim is false."

"It is . . . a distant relation," Loren said, keenly aware how poor her excuse sounded. Gem scoffed and said nothing. To cover the awkward silence that followed, Loren turned back to Annis. "How have you fared since we parted? What did you do after you fled?"

"Mostly just that—I fled. First I rode heedless through the streets. Thank the sky that our friends the constables rode no horses. Once I had well quit them, I abandoned my steed and sought out dark alleyways to hide in. There I wandered for many hours, unsure what to do, until I determined to abandon my finery for these garments you see." She raised her arms, drawing wide the patchwork cloak draped over her shoulders. "I found a clothier who kept many such peasants' garments in his stores. He traded for my dress and some coin."

"Did you meet a woman named Auntie?" said Loren.

Annis only looked at her, expression blank.

"She is young, only a few years older than I, and a weremage. She had skin like potter's clay, but her hair glowed like wheat stalks in summer sun."

"That will not help," said Gem. "She might have looked like anything."

Loren blinked. He was right, of course.

"I met no one like any of that. I met no one at all. I sought only to hide, and to keep my face from being seen. Why would I seek anyone out?"

"Somehow they caught wind of you," said Loren. "Auntie and her children told Gregor where to find you."

"The clothier," said Gem. "I would wager he is one of Auntie's eyes. She has many such throughout the city, those she can count upon for a quick favor or a word of truth in her ear."

Loren gave a small growl of frustration. "Then how may we evade her?"

"The longer you remain, the slimmer your chances," said Gem with a shrug. "We must take passage, or she will kill us for certain."

"Kill us?" said Annis.

Gem stopped dead in the tunnel and turned to look at them, bathed in a halo of moonslight. "Of course, kill us. Do you think Auntie plays at some silly game? You, Loren, have now twice defied her. And you, O pretty merchant's daughter, may hope for some leniency, but like as not you will find none. Auntie knows a thousand dark holes just the right size for a body, and from which no one will ever recover you." He pointed at the rivulet of waste that ran by their feet.

"But I have done nothing to her," said Annis. "Why would she seek to harm me?"

Gem looked uneasily around. "Understand, Auntie seeks always for situations to improve our station. Anything that may gain her a few more coins for the children, or a week's leniency from the constables. But when she does not get her way . . . she angers swiftly."

Loren thought she saw him hide a shudder.

Annis clutched at Loren's arm, her terrified eyes sunken and hollow. "We must leave this cursed place, quickly! We are beset on all sides, Loren, and buried beneath the earth besides. I cannot take this dark coffin a moment longer. I cannot—"

Annis broke off, breathing so heavily that the air wheezed in her throat. The girl's legs buckled and pitched her to the stone, nearly throwing her into the stream of sewage. Loren grabbed her at the last moment and propped her up against the wall.

"Annis!" she cried. "What is it? What is wrong?"

"Hold," said Gem, pushing Loren aside. He grasped the back of Annis' neck and thrust her head towards the ground.

"What are you doing?" said Loren, trying to push him away.

But Gem held her off with an outstretched arm and gave her a look of such calm certainty that Loren felt herself paralyzed. Quickly the boy hooked a hand under Annis' knees, drawing them up to hold on either side of her head. He forced her head still farther down, and as he held her there Loren heard the girl's breath grow easier. Within a moment she slumped back against the wall, shaking, tears in her eyes, but calm again.

"Some children get the terrors when they first come to Auntie," explained Gem. "This is how we help them. I learned it early on. They say I could have been a medica, you know."

"They say you could have been many things," said Loren wryly. "But thank you." She scooted forwards on her knees, placing a soothing hand on the girl's shoulder. "Annis? Are you well enough to go on?"

Annis looked up at her, blinking away her tears. "I do not want to go on. I want to get out."

Gem grunted. "As well you should. We must move quickly, for I fear Auntie's children may soon draw near, if they have not already. They are never as plentiful in the sewer as they are upon the rooftops, but these passages are not unknown to them."

Together they helped Annis on her feet, and now Loren kept a steady hand on the younger girl's back, ready to support her. Gem pressed their pace hard, and before long he paused beneath another hole cut into the street. Loren knew not why this drainage differed from any other they had passed, but Gem pointed up with certainty.

Loren boosted him up first, for he was lightest. Once he peered around and waved them up, she seized Annis around her thighs, lifting her up and stretching as high as she could. Loren felt a moment's strange gratitude to her father—whatever he had given her in the way of bruises and beatings, she also owed him her height.

Gem seized Annis' wrists and dragged her up into the moonslight. With a small hop, Loren gripped the edges of the drainage, and a moment later she found herself under stars once again.

She could see nothing familiar. Gem set off down the alleyway, and Loren followed quickly. Annis' shoulders still shook slightly beneath Loren's hand, but the girl's relief at leaving the catacombs was almost palpable.

"The Elf's Purse lies only a few more buildings away," said Gem. "Soon we will be safe and—"

He stopped short, leaping back to push them all against the wall. "Curse everything," he snapped. "The place is watched."

"Watched?" said Loren. "By whom?"

"Auntie's children," said Gem, his voice low and ominous. "See for yourself."

Loren peeked around the corner, looking down the alley towards the inn's back door. "I see nothing," she whispered.

"Look at the roofs," said Gem. "And watch for the glint of eyes in shadow."

Loren looked again. There. Atop the roof of the building facing the Purse, she saw the small mound of a child's head. And in one corner where lurked a beggar, his head cradled in his hands, she caught the flash of moonslight on two orbs—the large eyes of a child.

She ducked back out of sight. "How? How could they know of Xain? And what would they want with him, in any case?"

"I do not think they seek the wizard," said Gem. "I believe they seek us. Some within the tavern saw us. One must have passed word to Auntie, and she sent her children to watch. She will never come for us in plain sight, but wait for us to leave and kill us in the shadows."

"How will we find our way back inside?" said Loren. "We must warn Xain. He is our only chance of leaving the city."

"If they watch the back door, the front will be doubly guarded. That leaves only a window." Gem pointed up.

Loren looked. In the second and third stories were windows like the one in Xain's room. It seemed an easy enough climb, but she glanced at Annis beside her.

Annis looked back at her, uncomprehending. "What?"

"How are you as a climber?"

Annis glanced up at the window, and her eyes widened in shock. She looked back at Loren. "Surely you jest."

Loren sighed. "Wait here, then. Gem, you stay with her."

"What will you do?" said the boy.

"Leave that to me."

The inn had rough walls, with many chunks of plaster having been torn free over the years. Not too high up, the plaster gave way to great wooden cross spars. Loren found a good place for her climb a few paces down the building's length. She looked up and down the alley for any observer, but saw only beggars lying oblivious.

Hand over foot she scaled the wall until her fingers found the lip of a wooden beam. But just as she began to pull herself up, plaster gave way beneath her right toe. Loren nearly pitched into the street, only saving herself by the skin of her fingertips. She winced as splinters dug into her flesh.

"Be careful!" said Gem.

"Be silent," growled Loren. She tried again, and this time managed to gain purchase on a windowsill. Cautiously she poked an eye above the ledge to look within the room.

She ducked down immediately, crimson rushing to her cheeks. The man and woman in that room would not take kindly to intrusion. Struggling to put the image from her mind, she sidled along the side of the building towards the next room, holding the bottom of the sill above her, and walking atop the window frames below. A wide gap of wall stretched to the next window, nearly two paces in length. Again thankful for her height, Loren stretched until she could just grab the sill before sidling along below the window.

This room lay empty. She pulled herself up, gripping the top of the window's frame as she stood on the bottom of it. Loren tried prying her fingers into the frame to pull the window open, but without success. She relented for a moment, reinforcing her grip on the windowsill as she studied the glass.

There. A lock at the top of the window held it shut. Loren dug for her dagger and drew it. The metal glinted strangely in the moonslight, throwing rays of blue into her eyes. She stared at it in wonder for a moment before coming to her senses. Slowly she slid into a half-crouch. With one swift movement she brought the pommel stone crashing against a single pane. Glass tinkled to the floor, too loud for her comfort. She snaked a hand in, careful not to cut herself on the shards, and tripped the latch.

As soon as she did, the bottom of the window swung outward and struck her hip. Almost she pitched out into empty space, but her hands lashed out and clung to the sill. Loren yanked herself to the building, clutching its side for a moment while she fought to catch her breath and still her racing heart.

"Are you all right?" came Gem's harsh whisper from below.

Loren looked down and nodded, and then placed a finger to her lips. In another moment she had slid into the room, where she went quickly to the bed. A blanket and sheet lay upon it, with another blanket folded on a table. Loren tied them into a line, thrice testing the knots to ensure their strength.

She returned to the window and threw her impromptu rope into the darkness. For security, she tied her end around one of the bed's legs before she leaned out into the darkness.

"All right," she whispered. "Come up, Annis."

Annis placed one hand on the blanket, and then another. She pulled, but her arms trembled, and she slumped back to her feet. "I am not a climber!"

Loren sighed. She had feared this. "All right, then. Do your best to hold on, will you?"

Loren braced her feet against the wall and wrapped both hands firmly around the blanket. Checking her grip again, she pulled as hard as she could. Hand over hand she tugged, and the blanket slid up the wall with aching slowness. A tense while passed before Annis' hands appeared at the windowsill and gripped it. Loren leaned out and hauled the girl in over the window frame, where she collapsed shaking on the floor.

Loren threw the rope of blankets back down. But before she could even think of hauling it up once more, Gem scrambled up and into the room. He landed lightly on the balls of his feet, glancing down at Annis with disdain.

"See?" he said. "Not so hard, is it?"

Annis glared up at him but said nothing.

TWENTY-FIVE

LOREN COILED THE BLANKET AND SHEETS UPON THE floor. She saw no use in trying to hide them; she could not repair the glass, and anyway they would be leaving the inn as soon as they could. She led her companions to the hallway and found the door to Xain's room. Three quick raps she gave at the door, and there came the scuffle of boots inside.

"Who is it?"

"Not the constables, certainly," whispered Loren.

The door cracked open. "Keep your jests muted. Would you alert all the kingdom that we hide from the law?"

She pushed the door open and stole inside, reaching up to peel away her rags. "No time for that now. The inn is guarded."

Gem and Annis followed her into the room. Xain's eyes fell upon Annis, and Loren saw an eyebrow raise. "This is your . . . cousin, is it?"

"Yes, this is she," said Loren. "Well removed, of course. On my mother's side."

"What kind of fool do you think I—" Xain stopped suddenly and leaned in closer, studying Annis' face. His eyes shot wide, and he straightened as he stepped back. "Darkness take us all! What madness is this?"

Loren raised her hands, trying to calm him. "She flees her mother, and if she is caught—"

"No!" snapped Xain. Then, seeming to remember that he was, in fact, in hiding, he glanced at the door and lowered his voice. "I took you into my care against my better judgement, but this would be the utmost folly. If you think I will smuggle away a child of the family Yerrin, you take me for a madman who seeks only his own demise."

"Please," said Loren. "We do not have time for this. I told you the inn is watched."

"I doubt it," said Xain. "Why would the constables place guard? They would come straight in, and their visit would be no pleasant one."

"Not the constables. The weremage. Or rather, her minions." Loren thought fast, and a lie came easily to her lips. "She has guards watch the place to ensure you do not leave. All while she fetches the constable to drag you from here by force."

Behind Xain, she saw Gem's hard look. The boy knew that for false. But Xain remained their best chance for escape, and she could not afford to lose it.

Her ploy worked. She saw Xain's face grow pale in light of his room's single candle. "How did they find me?" he mulled. "I took care to hide myself when I took to the streets."

"Auntie has eyes in all places," said Gem, stepping in to support Loren's story. "An agent of hers must have seen you."

"And we must leave, quickly, before they can do aught about it," said Loren. "But how, if the doors are guarded?"

Xain's eyes grew shifty. "There is a way. The reason I chose this inn. Come, follow me." He gave Annis one last despairing look, sighed, and shook his head.

After Loren collected her cloak from beneath the bed, Xain led them down the staircase. This time they did not draw so much as a passing glance from any in the common room. Loren studied the patrons carefully as she passed. One of these, she knew, had betrayed them to Auntie. She would have given much to know which one. But no eyes met hers, and she abandoned the search as Xain led them into another of the inn's back rooms.

There stood a fat man with a wide, grease-stained apron. Loren took him for the innkeeper; he had that sort of look, the portly good-natured face and clean-shaven chin. The man glanced up with surprise as they stormed into the room, giving the children a suspicious look before he looked to Xain.

"Good eve, Xain," said the innkeeper. "Looking for a meal?"

"Not at this hour, Bartin," said Xain, "though I thank you for your kind offer. I must leave your hospitality, and quite a bit sooner than I had intended."

Bartin's look hardened, and he nodded. "I see. My thanks for doing what you may to keep your troubles from my door. Not good for business, that sort of thing. I will leave you to it, then."

The innkeeper pulled down a sack of meal from a shelf and left the room. When the door clicked shut, Xain went to a panel set in the floor. He wrapped his hands around an iron handle and pulled up to reveal a stone staircase descending into darkness. An evil smell wafted up from below.

"No!" wailed Annis, backing away quickly. "Not again, I will not! Please, there must be another way."

Xain looked at her, brows furrowed in confusion. "There is no other way. This is how we must escape, or not at all. You see now the only reason I frequent the Elf's Purse. It is not for Bartin's ale, though bless him for that all the same. Now come, for we must put as much distance between ourselves and this place as we can before the constables arrive."

Loren went to Annis' side and put an arm around her shoulders. "I am still here," she said, keeping her voice warm. "I will not leave your side, just as I did not the last time. Come, Annis. It is this, or turn yourself back over to your mother."

Annis swallowed hard. "Please, Loren," she said, her voice pleading. "There must be another way. Let us escape through a window again, the way we came in."

"Enough of this," snapped Xain. "I am off. You may come, or not, as you will."

Putting action to his words, the wizard descended the steps and vanished into darkness. Loren heard him murmur, and with a sharp crackle, blue light erupted into his palm. He turned at the bottom of the steps, his eyes glowing white.

"What say you? I will not wait."

Loren put one firm hand on Annis' shoulder, and the other on her arm. It reminded her of how Bern had held her as he shoved her through the city. "Come now, Annis," she said quietly. "One step at a time."

Annis placed one foot on the top stair. Then another, and another. Foot by foot she descended into the sewer beside Loren. Once their heads were both below the floor, Gem stole in after them, waiting only a moment's time to draw the trap door shut behind them. Soon they had collected around Xain, who still stood bathed in his own blue magefire.

"Very well," said Xain. "I have another hiding place prepared. Follow quickly and quietly."

"Aye, and keep a careful eye," said Gem. "Auntie's children are no strangers down here."

The wizard nodded and set off, the others trailing in his wake. Loren kept a careful eye on Annis, who mostly kept her own eyes closed. The girl breathed heavily, though not with the same panic that had nearly crippled her earlier.

Xain paused at the first bend in the passageway and turned back to them. "The tunnel twists and turns most intricately. Do not lose sight of my magefire, and watch where you step. There are pits in the floor at times, the bottom of which you cannot see. Do not fall. If you lose yourself in the darkness, I cannot help you."

"And you think you can help them now?" came a familiar, haughty voice.

Xain's gaze snapped forwards. He growled and, with a gesture his blue magefire floated swiftly forwards. Soon its blue glow illuminated a figure in the darkness: Auntie.

She had abandoned her tunic for a leather jerkin. In it were set many loops of leather through which shone the gleaming blades of knives. Two more she held in her hands, strange weapons the likes of which Loren had never seen. Their handles wrapped around her fingers, and from the handles sprang the blades, like small triangles of gleaming steel. Her trousers, too, were tighter and less fancy, meant for fighting, for climbing, for slipping through the dead of night to slit a throat.

Loren saw something else, too: Auntie had brought more than the small urchins they had seen at the pigsty. Before her and beside her stood a small group of young men, ranging between Loren's age and Auntie's. All stood tall and wrapped thick with muscle, and each had some form of weapon. Loren saw cudgels, sharpened sticks to serve as spears, and even one with a sword broken nearly in half, its edge still sharp. Around these boys, Auntie's familiar crowd of children lurked at the edge of shadow, their wide eyes gleaming in the magelight.

"I thought little Jarmo might bring you down here," said Auntie, her voice a cool drawl. "Dear, young Jarmo. How could you do this to your poor, sweet Auntie? The purse you have kept from my hands would have fed so many of the children."

Gem quaked beside Loren and did not reply.

"But now I see you may have repaid your debt and brought double," Auntie continued, looking to where Annis quivered under Loren's hands. "That is the merchant's daughter, unless I miss my guess. We will be well paid for her return, I think. And if not . . . ah, well, there are so many places in this city for little girls to disappear."

Annis wailed. Loren squared her shoulders. "Leave us be! We have done nothing to you."

Auntie smiled, her features growing cruel. Her face in the blue light, turning to something monstrous. "Of course not, you little witch. But I do this not for you, and certainly not for the farce they call the King's justice. It is for the children." She splayed her hands wide within the hilts of her strange blades, indicating the dozens of urchins around them. "All my little children, with such wide mouths and empty bellies. All I do is for them."

From the gaggle of goslings came a low murmur: *Mother, Mother, Mother.*

Xain stepped forwards, summoning another ball of magefire in his left hand with whispered words. His right hand curled, and the flame before Auntie swelled in size.

"If you hold yourself their mother, begone and do not pursue us. I wish you no harm, but I will not hesitate to bring fire and thunder upon you if you refuse to leave us be."

Auntie cocked her head. "I think not. Children, these people keep coins from you. Take them."

The children rushed forwards, bare feet slapping on stones. Some leapt across the channel of refuse to circle around the sides. Behind them marched Auntie's young men, slapping cudgels into their palms.

"Run!" Xain waved his hand, and the magefire split into a wall of sapphire flame that receded before springing to new life in front of the children. They pulled up short, wide eyes and silent mouths visible above the dancing fire.

Loren led the way, dragging a wailing Annis behind her. They rounded a corner, and she heard a loud *snap* behind them. Loren glanced over her shoulder to see only darkness around the bend. "What happened to your flame?"

"It grows harder to control when I cannot see it," Xain growled. He pushed his second ball of magefire ahead down the passage, and brought another to life in his palm.

Ahead of them erupted a wave of small bodies, pouring from a side passage to block their path. Loren pulled up short, panic gripping her throat. Foes ahead and foes behind. They were trapped.

"This way!" cried Gem. He leapt across the river of waste, landing hard on a platform of stone. Xain followed, turning to wave his magefire in front of the children, who once again pulled to a stop, forced to wait for the fire to die before advancing.

Loren made to take the leap, but Annis clutched her arm. "I cannot! It is too far. I . . . I . . ."

She gripped the girl's shoulders. "Not now, Annis! Right now we must get away. Do you understand? Otherwise they will capture us, or worse."

"Jump!" cried Xain, keeping the magefire bright.

"I cannot," said Annis. "I can scarcely move . . . scarcely breathe . . ."

Loren reached out and clapped a hand on either shoulder. "I am sorry, Annis."

The girl only had time to look confused before Loren wrapped her fingers in the shoulders of her tunic and heaved. Annis flew through the air, wailing as she neared the stone walkway on the other side. Loren did not throw her far enough—her chest landed hard on the stone, but her lower half landed with a sickening splash in the river of waste. Loren thought the flow might sweep her away, but Gem wrapped his hands under the girl's shoulders and hauled her up onto the walkway.

Loren took two steps back, ready to leap. But just as she was about to take her first step forwards, she caught a flash of movement out of the corner of her eyes—a slim figure, flinging itself across the top of Xain's flames to fly at her from the darkness.

She whirled and ducked just as Auntie's blades sliced the air above her head. Without conscious effort on her part, her hand went to her dagger and pulled it forth. She backed away quickly as Auntie slashed twice more, waving the dagger before her like a torch, trying to stave off the woman's wild advance.

"Lie still and die, damn you!" snarled Auntie. Loren felt the passing wind of another headlong swipe. "What right do you have to enter my city?"

"I mean you no harm," said Loren, ducking another swing. "Leave us be, and we will never return."

"And me without even a penny for my little ones," said Auntie. "I think not."

"We have done nothing," said Loren.

Auntie paused, her eyes narrowing. Loren looked into her eyes, hoping against hope that she might see some leniency there. But it was only a trick—Auntie lunged again, and Loren barely raised the dagger for a warding stab. Auntie struck the blade with both of hers, and it went spinning from Loren's hand to the stone.

Loren cried out and made to reach for it, but Auntie scooped it up instead. She stepped back and dangled the dagger by its pommel stone from finger and thumb, the rest of her hand still wrapped around her own strange blade.

"Oh, this is a fine piece," said Auntie, taunting. "A pretty penny I would wager it cost you—unless you stole it. But no, no one who owned such a nice blade would let a wench like you place your grubby fingers upon it."

"Give it back!" cried Loren.

"Come!" said Xain across the way. His concentration wavered as he said it, and the flames flickered. The children pushed forwards, but Xain recovered and pushed the wall towards them again.

"You want your little carving knife? Come and claim it, if you dare."

Loren tensed, watching the movement of Auntie's fingers. Mayhap . . . if she could only move fast enough . . . she could dart in and snatch it from Auntie's grasp before the woman could react. Loren could move quickly. She knew she could.

Auntie saw the look in her eye. "Oh, come then, what good is the chase if—"

THWOOSSSH

A stream of foul, brown corruption erupted from the river of waste to engulf her. Auntie flew back along the stone walkway, followed by the torrent of waste.

Loren's eyes flew across the channel. Xain's eyes glowed brighter as one hand maintained the flames on his left, while with his right hand he guided the jet of filth like a hammer blow, knocking Auntie back into her waiting children. But he had relinquished his hold on the other wall of flame, and now the children rushed forwards unimpeded.

"Come!" cried Xain, one last time before he turned and vanished into the side passage where Gem waited.

The last flames blinked out.

Loren could spare only the briefest glance for Auntie, lying amidst her children, nearly drowned in the worst filth imaginable—and hand still clutching the dagger. Loren leapt away, wrapping a hand around Gem's and Annis' arms even as she landed. They all vanished down the passage, running for their lives through darkness and disgust.

TWENTY-SIX

THEY FLED THROUGH THE SEWER FOR SOME TIME, OR the rest of the night, or no time at all. Loren scarcely remembered it, for she could see only vague flashes of fire as Xain kept at bay the children who pursued them. Finally he—or mayhap Gem—led them to metal rungs set in the wall. They climbed into the open air just as dawn broke in the east.

Xain led them to a squat building caked with faded blue paint. He took them to a door set in the back wall where he knocked first three times, and then rapidly twice.

Gem must have noticed the somber look on Loren's face, for he leaned over and put a hand on her arm. "It was only a dagger. It was not worth your life. You will get another."

She nodded, but she wanted to shake the boy until his teeth rattled from his mouth. It had *not* been only a dagger. Somewhere on the road to Cabrus, the knife had become a part of her. It formed as much of Nightblade as Loren did herself.

A hatch in the door slid open, and a pair of wrinkled eyes peered out. "Who is this?"

"It is I, Markus," said Xain. "You cannot have forgotten my face in only a day."

"I did not mean you, boy. These ones." The eyes swept across Loren, Gem, and Annis, lingering on the latter a bit longer.

"They are friends," said Xain. "You may trust them."

The eyes squinted tighter for a moment. Then the hatch slid shut. A *clink* sounded from within, and the door swung open. Xain ushered them in before him.

Loren found herself in a small sitting room with a round wooden table and three chairs. Though her mind felt numb, she took in some details: a small fireplace in one wall, lazy smoke drifting up from embers; bits of leather hung by wooden soles ready for crafting; a bottle of something red sitting next to empty glasses upon the table.

The old man looked them over. He did not look precisely angry, Loren decided, but neither did he bear a look of welcome. Rather, he seemed the sort to think that everything might be a threat. Her eyes did not miss the dagger at his waist, or the knobbly fingers that curled and uncurled beside it.

"Markus, I must ask you a great service," said Xain.

"I thought I provided one already," said the old man. "Not everyone could get you a carriage so cheap."

"And I am grateful, you may believe it. But now I need more. These companions I must bring with me."

The man barked a short laugh that held neither humor nor incredulity. With a wave of his arm, he showed Xain to the table and offered him one of the chairs. The wizard threw himself down gratefully, his hands going to the red bottle without hesitation.

"You want to sit, girl?" It took Loren a moment to realize that Markus had spoken to her. "You other lot, make yourselves welcome on the floor. I can strike a fire if you have taken a chill." He looked Annis up and down. The girl had tried to scrub out the filth that soaked her dress, but she could not get it all. Markus' nose twitched. "And mayhap you would like fresh clothes as well."

Annis murmured thanks, and Markus shrilled a short whistle. A young girl appeared from the front of the house. For a moment she looked so thin, her eyes so wide, that Loren feared she might be one of Auntie's children. But this girl's dress seemed well-mended, if rather plain, and she did not bear that haunted, hungry look that all of Auntie's orphans wore like a cloak.

"Dearie, fetch this girl a dress. None of yours, they are far too small. One of your sister's. Quickly now."

The girl nodded and vanished. Markus turned back to Loren. "Sit. You look half dead."

Loren shrugged and went to the chair by Xain. The wizard had already poured and drained one glass. He filled another, and then a glass for Markus. A third he pushed towards Loren. "Here. Something for your courage."

Loren looked at the glass. She thought it held wine, but a wine darker and . . . *browner,* somehow, than she had ever seen. She had never tasted wine. It was common enough at festivals in the Birchwood, but her parents insisted she was too young. If Loren pressed the point, she knew what to expect from her father. And certainly her parents had never seen the value in spending coin on something so frivolous as drink.

Upon the night she left, in fact, she had planned to have her first sip. Her parents could no longer object—they sought to put her up for dowry, after all, and how could a man judge his future bride if he could not drink with her? But then had come Xain, and the constables, and she had left behind wine and festivals and her parents and Chet. Dear, dear Chet.

She looked at Xain and wondered: would she go back, if she could? Could she call herself happy here, now, in this place, when every waking moment seemed to be a flight from death or a fight for survival?

Then she thought of her father's face as she loosed the arrow into his leg. No. No, she would never return to that.

She placed the glass to her lips and took a healthy sip. It poured down her throat, burning like magefire. She almost coughed it back up, hacking and sputtering. But some part of her mind thought, *I could stand another.*

"Yes, good, is it not?" Markus' wrinkled lips split his pure white beard in a smile. "My own make of brandywine, and likely stronger than you are used to."

Loren gulped and sat up straighter. She raised the glass to her lips again. Knowing what to expect, the second swallow tasted better: sickly sweet, biting, and warm.

"A bit stronger, yes," said Loren. "But not a terrible vintage."

Markus gave her a final smile before he turned to Xain. "Well then, about your favor. I cannot put these children on your carriage."

"What?" Loren, Gem, and Annis spoke in unison.

Xain took another deep sip from his cup. "Go on, then. Why not?"

"I must pay my driver, as you know. His rates to move shoes are not so steep, but people fetch a heavier price. And you might think it is all the same moving one body or moving four. It is all one carriage, after all. But the constables catch you with one charge, mayhap they take a hand or a foot. Two, and they will take your tongue and kick you from the city for good. But four? It means the block, and you, and I, and most importantly *he*, know it."

"The constables want only me. And mayhap this one, but only because they think she helped me escape," said Xain, tossing his head at Loren. "The boy and the girl have done nothing wrong. They would be nothing more than passengers."

"They can ride on the driver's seat with my friend, then?" said Markus. He studied Xain's face as it fell. "As I thought. You are all of you running from something, and fleeing others outside the King's law is in many ways worse than running from constables. At least most constables will not slit your throat in the moonlight."

"How much would he need?" said Xain.

Markus' eyes grew crafty. "Well, I could not tell you without speaking to him. But let us say he would do it for . . ."

Their voices faded to murmurs in the back of Loren's mind. Her hand dropped to her belt where her dagger's sheath hung lonely. She stuck the edge of her thumb in its mouth, running it around the edge.

The dagger of power. The dagger that could master a constable's duty. The dagger her parents should never have owned, that had seemed as out of place in their kitchen as a dragon. Yes, just a hunk of fine metal wrapped in leather, Loren knew. But it was *hers*.

And she knew what she had to do.

She poured the rest of her glass down her throat, wincing as it burned in her chest and rushed to her head all at once. Then she pushed back her chair and stood, planting her fingers on the table before her. Xain and Markus stopped talking, looking up at her in surprise.

"I will not be going," she said.

Xain blinked. "You cannot mean to stay."

"Not for long. But Auntie has stolen something from me. I must take it back."

Xain looked over at Gem, and then at Annis. Both of them shrugged. "Have you lost your wits?"

"It is a matter of honor."

Xain barked a laugh. "Honor! Who cares for that? Do you think that thieving queen of infants will care for your honor when you come to her and ask for your dagger back?"

"I will beg for nothing," said Loren, surprised by her own fervor. "I will *take* it."

Xain shook his head, reached over, and snatched Loren's glass. "It seems hardly possible that you should be drunk already, and yet you must be."

"I am not," said Loren, though she *could* feel a slight wooziness settling in. "I will do this and meet you on the road."

Xain shook his head, poured another glass, and drained half of it. Loren saw Markus' mouth twist in annoyance. The wizard missed it, raising his glass to Loren and pointing one long, delicate finger.

"If you stay, you will die. The matter is that simple. Or mayhap you will find yourself in a constable's cell and put to the question. If that happens, they will know where to find *me.* So you see, more thoughts than concern for your safety spur my decision. I cannot let you stay."

"Let me? Who said I was yours to command?"

Xain frowned, his thick brows drawing together again. "No one. But I am, you will forgive me, wiser in this world than you have proven yourself to be."

"And yet we both find ourselves fleeing from constables. And in my case, because of you only. I will take no lessons in right and wrong and wisdom from a wizard outside the King's law."

Xain opened his mouth, but Markus put up a hand to forestall him. "Xain, she may have some merit. You cannot leave together in any case. Why not let her stay, and one of the others? I will find them passage in time."

"Time they do not have." Xain looked at Loren again and hesitated, as though he would say more if he could. Finally he stood from the table and made for the door. "Outside."

Loren followed, her mind a blur. She could not have said whether it came from the wine or Xain's mysterious look.

Outside, the sky grew ever lighter as the sun cleared the horizon at last. Xain closed the door behind them and paced the alley's width for a moment. When he stopped, it was to fix Loren with an angry glare and a pointed finger.

"What game do you play at, girl?"

"No game. Only I cannot abide the thought of Auntie keeping that dagger. It is mine. Part of me. I will take it back or die in the attempt."

"No," said Xain, swiping his hands in a single line, like a throat being cut. "You will die. You will find no 'or,' no chance for any other outcome. Who do you think you are, forest girl? One does not walk into a throne room and tell the king to relinquish her crown if one wishes to walk out again."

Loren's hands clenched at her sides. "You do not understand. That dagger . . . I need it. I need to learn what it means."

Xain looked mystified. "A dagger rarely has a meaning. What do you speak of?"

"Corin. You remember him. The shorter constable."

Xain nodded.

"When they caught me, Corin searched me and found the dagger. The moment he found it, he seemed a different person. He took me off alone, and once out of sight he let me go. He told me . . . he said to tell my masters that he had helped me."

Xain's mouth fell open. "Masters? What masters?"

"I know not. I know only that somehow, that dagger may stay even the King's law."

Xain's eyes darkened as though remembering some unwanted memory. Again he bowed and shook his head. "A matter of great interest, to be sure, but hardly a cause to throw your life away. The dagger could breathe gouts of flame and raise the dead, and yet now that it is in the therianthrope's grasp you will never see it again."

Loren gave an exasperated growl. "Speak like a common man—the *weremage*. And if I must die fighting her, so be it. At least it is my own choice."

That stopped Xain. Idly he turned and ran his hands down the smooth wooden doorframe. "You would risk everything for this?"

"And more," said Loren. "When a part of you is in danger, you must be willing to risk the rest of yourself to save it."

Xain rolled his eyes as he reached to open the door. "If you would convince me, do not speak with such childishly eager words."

Markus accepted the change easily enough. Then it came time to decide who would stay and who would go. Gem insisted on remaining by Loren's side, and she felt glad for it; Gem knew more about Cabrus and Auntie than Loren could ever hope to. Annis, too, wanted to stay, but Loren would not hear of it.

"You must away," she said. "Your mother hunts you most eagerly. You stand to lose much if she catches you."

"You stand to lose much more, if she should find you," said Annis, pouting. "Auntie is not the only one who wishes to have you in her grasp. My mother will not stop looking for you."

Loren smiled at that. "Indeed. But she will not catch me. She gave me the means for her own defeat." She swept the cloak up and across her face until only her eyes gleamed through a gap in the cloth.

Annis slapped her arm. "Do not be ridiculous. You must promise me—*promise,* you understand—that you will be careful."

"I promise, and willingly."

As Markus summoned the carriage driver, Annis changed to a fresh dress of muted grey. She and Xain wrapped themselves heavily in rags stained with shoe polish, gifts from Markus' refuse heap. They would pose as lepers one last time, hoping for constables to give them a wide berth as they left the city.

"We will ride south until sundown and find a place to wait," said Xain. "On the third night from this, we shall depart. I hope against wisdom that you will be leaving with us."

"I will be there if I can," said Loren. "If you do not see me, get Annis safely to the next city. Beyond that, I will not burden you with her."

"I will do as you ask." Xain turned and boarded the carriage.

Annis approached next. The girl's usual bluster had fled, and her lip quivered as she looked up at Loren.

"Will you not think upon it one last time, and come with us?" said Annis. "I promise, I will buy you a finer dagger than ever you have seen, if only you will leave this cursed city."

"I will see you two days hence. Spare no worries on my account."

Annis nodded, but she looked miserable. "Here, take this." She reached into her cloak and pulled forth her bulging purse. "In case you need it. I hope I shall not require it upon the road."

"Thank you." Loren only hoped that the coin would not find its way into Auntie's hands, pulled from her own cooling corpse. She stepped forwards, speaking quick and low. "Do you still bear a certain package? One of brown cloth?"

Annis' eyes flashed. "I do. It has not left my side since we escaped my mother."

"Take care of it," said Loren. "It may prove most useful. But whatever you do, do *not* tell Xain about it."

Annis looked at her curiously. "Why? What is it to him?"

She thought of the constables, and what they had said when they caught her. *Magestones,* they had called the black rocks.

"I do not yet know. Only I know he should not know you have it. Not yet, at any rate. Be safe."

She helped Annis board the carriage. The driver, an obese man with one eye, snapped the reins, and the carriage rolled off down the street.

"Now there goes your best chance of escaping this city," said Gem. "I say *your* best chance, of course, for it is well known that nothing can kill me."

"Well known indeed," said Loren. "Come, let us eat. We have a burglary to plan."

TWENTY-SEVEN

MARKUS FED THEM SMALL BOWLS OF GRUEL, SERVED in his cellar. He did not speak overmuch, nor did he linger after giving them their bowls. "If you remain in the city by nightfall, you may sleep here if you wish. Come here, to the cellar. I will have my granddaughter fetch you blankets, and open the door if you should knock."

He vanished before Loren could thank him.

"I find that one most strange," said Gem. "Why should a cobbler be in the smuggling business?"

"Will you keep your voice down?" said Loren, keeping hers to a murmur. "One should always respect one's host. And why should you expect a cobbler any less than any other? What profession *should* a smuggler find herself, to your mind?"

"Something . . . natural. Like a carpet maker. Or a brewer. Someone who makes big things, the kinds of things you can stuff a body in."

Loren shuddered. "A body living, or a corpse?"

"Either." Gem spooned up the last of his gruel, slurping noisily as it slid down his throat. The boy ate like three men twice his size. A symptom, Loren supposed, of rarely having enough to eat. Then he leaned back in his chair and fixed Loren with a hard stare.

"What is this all about to you, then?"

Loren swallowed her own spoonful, wincing at the slimy way it sat in her mouth. "What do you mean?"

"Oh, I heard what you said to Xain. But anyone in your place with half a stone's sense would flee this place if they had a chance—yet you have one, and here you remain. I cannot read the tale of it."

Loren scowled at the table. "A great thief cannot let others rob her and simply accept it. Who would respect her then?"

"And that is the other thing. Look at you. Tall. Strong. Not ugly, I suppose, though I have seen much prettier."

Loren glared at him.

Gem cleared his throat. "Well, erm, and you do not look like you have gone hungry more than a day in your life. So what brings you to Cabrus, seeking a pickpocket's life? Who goes about searching for a way outside the King's law?"

Loren scoffed. "You are one to talk. You have lived without it your whole life."

"No other opportunity presents itself to one such as me," said Gem. "If I have to lift a coin or slice the occasional purse string, well, that is what I must do. You, though—you could build yourself a little house in the forest by some river. I would wager you could live there fine, with someone to live with and all. Yet you come here with half the villains in the nine lands breathing down your neck, and you seek to lift purses you do not need."

"I would never take from those who had none to spare." Loren felt her temper rising, blood rushing to her face.

"Oh? What of the girl in the pink dress Auntie sent you after?"

"That was Auntie herself!"

"Aye, and you did not know it till you had your hands on her purse."

"She looked rich," Loren insisted. "Anyone who can afford a dress like that can stand to lose a purse of coins."

"Some might say the same about your cloak."

Loren's hand went to the black, velvety fabric, stroking it gently. "This was a gift," she said softly.

"Mayhap that pink dress was, too. Or mayhap she only bought that dress from coin that she earned. Earned doing things you would never do, that you would think were beneath you. I know many pretty youths with fine clothes who pay for those dresses with the coin of rich folk."

Loren pushed her bowl away and stood from the table. "It is time for us to go."

"I have an idea I like better," said Gem, rising as well. "Why do you not take those coins that Annis gave you, and the ones you had already, and buy us a horse so that we may leave this city forever? Find Annis and Xain upon the road, and together we will ride off to the outland kingdoms where they have never heard of Cabrus and we have never heard of them."

She slammed her hand down on the table. "I will not leave this alone! No one steals from me, especially not that simpering witch!"

Gem paused for a moment, letting hang her angry words and all the meaning beneath them. Loren came to herself and withdrew her hand.

"Where do we start?" she said.

"What are we looking for?"

"My dagger. Or Auntie, though not if I had my wish."

"She will have put it in the hidey hole."

They fetched more rags from Markus' workshop and wrapped themselves tight—neither Auntie nor her children had seen that trick the day before, and mayhap it would see them through again. Loren left her cloak in the cellar, folded neatly beneath the table.

She led the way up from the cellar and out the back door, but once they walked upon the street she let Gem walk in front. Sometimes he led her across streets, sometimes for a brief stint up a rain gutter and across rooftops that burned hot even through her boots. She could not imagine how he withstood the burning shingles, but then he had probably walked barefoot all his life. Other times their course dipped through the sewers, but never for too long. When they had to enter that dark place, Loren could feel her pulse thundering through her, every echoing noise like a slap at her ears that sent her jumping in fright.

The wandering course let her appreciate the three levels of the city, as she saw them. Most of those who lived in Cabrus only ever knew one: the streets and alleys, which probably held enough danger and darkness for the average person. But above stretched the roofs, Loren's favorite. There she was like a bird, looking down upon and scoffing at the petty lives of those beneath her feet. The sewers she liked least, and yet she saw their advantage. No one wanted to go there. Only those willing to brave the darkness and wretched smell would venture into the sewers, and thus one might traverse them unseen.

After a time Gem led her on a winding course through the drainage and waste. Oftentimes the tunnel branched in three or more directions, but Gem always chose his course without pause.

Loren saw that not all the tunnels channeled the city's waste and refuse. Some ran with water instead. She would not have drunk it, but it certainly smelled better than the other tunnels. Twice they came to long, sloping slides that descended farther into the city's underbelly. These always ran with water, and after Gem led the way, Loren flung herself down them with wild cries of delight. Wind rushed past her ears as she slid down, down, down into the darkness.

After the second slide, Gem paused at every intersection. He would sidle carefully up to the corner, poking an ear around it, followed by an eye. Once satisfied, he would lead the way forwards, but Loren took from his manner that they must not speak.

Here the daylight no longer came from holes in the street above. Instead, torches sat in plain iron sconces, casting a dim orange glow every ten paces or so. Darkness stretched between them, and twice

Loren stumbled over something in the blackness—what it was, she could not have said and did not wish to know.

"Let us take a torch," she whispered to Gem. "I cannot see a thing."

"Neither can they. Take fire with you, and you are a target. Light bounces in all directions." He shook his head at her and walked on. Loren stuck her tongue out at his back.

Ever onward they pressed, and ever slower Gem's footsteps became. Finally he stopped, at a place where two tunnels collided and split off in four directions. He waited for Loren to draw close and then motioned for her to lean down so he could whisper into her ear.

"The hidey hole awaits just round the next corner. It will be guarded. We cannot go too close."

"Let me see it," said Loren. "Then we may determine our course."

Gem nodded and stepped around the corner. Loren crept behind him, keeping close to the curved wall.

Another torch sat in the wall ten paces away. Gem edged forwards until his feet neared the reach of its light. He pointed to the tunnel's end, but Loren had already seen them. Two guards stood there, fifty paces away or more, at a joint where the tunnel split both left and right. In the wall opposite the split lay a small hallway, no more than six paces long, and at the end of that hallway stood a tall door made of wood.

"There," said Gem. "That is the hidey hole."

Loren looked it over. The wood seemed thick and strong, and she saw the gleam of a metal lock at the handle. The walls bore many torches, and their burning light made it hard to see much more detail from so far away.

"What does she keep in there?" said Loren.

"Anything special to her. Clothes. Souvenirs. Sometimes the big boys—those are two of them there—will steal something of unusual value, and she will stow it in the hidey hole. None of us are allowed down here, except the big boys she sends to guard it. I have only been here before because I am . . . well, I was . . ."

"Her favorite." Loren heard the twinge of pain in his voice and sought to reassure him by putting a comforting hand on his shoulder. He looked up at her but did not smile.

"That is it, then. What now?"

She pursed her lips. "Now we find a way to—"

A clanging screech tore through the tunnel. Loren's fingers tightened so hard on Gem's shoulder she feared she might draw blood.

The door to the hidey hole swung open, and Auntie emerged. One more boy she had with her, following at her heels like a massive dog.

"It is her!" said Gem. "We need to go!"

"Hold a moment."

"Why?"

Loren did not answer, but only watched. After the boy stepped out behind her, Auntie turned and closed the door. She pulled something from the neck of her tunic and fiddled with the handle a moment—*a key for that lock,* thought Loren—and then turned and walked down the short hallway leading out. The guards straightened their postures at Auntie's approach, like soldiers coming to attention.

Auntie stepped up to one of the guards, reaching up to wrap her arms around his neck. She yanked his head down and placed her mouth on his. Loren could not see at this distance, but she grimaced as she imagined details. Auntie stepped away, seized the other boy, and did the same. Neither boy wrapped his arms around her, nor did either let the kiss linger overlong.

"What . . . does she . . .?"

"Any boy has to kiss her when she wants it, and more besides." Gem's voice had grown suddenly small, so quiet that Loren could barely hear it. "If you do not, she will hurt you. You learn quick. Some of the boys like it all right, especially the other things she does. Most of us do not."

Loren looked at him sharply. Gem's gaze did not rise to meet hers.

Her throat felt suddenly dry, and Loren felt the slow-burning anger rise within her again—the rage she could never summon in the Birchwood, but which always seemed so near to her now.

Her attention returned to Auntie, fury now casting a red haze over her vision. The weremage walked forwards, leaving the two guards behind and coming down the tunnel with only the one she had had in the room.

Loren grabbed Gem's shoulder hard. He whirled with fearful eyes. Together they slunk back, utterly silent, and vanished behind the corner. Gem led her down the tunnel until they found a small alcove a pace deep.

"Here!" he said, his voice a sharp whisper.

"It is not big enough!"

"Trust me," said Gem, and he strode in. In a moment he vanished, ducking around a corner within the alcove. Loren blinked and followed him into the darkness. Within the alcove, she found that it curved away sharply to either side.

They huddled there together, hiding in the darkness with no other sound than the gently flowing water of the nearby channel. But soon Loren heard something else: soft, padded footsteps approaching.

She leaned out slightly, just the edge of her eye peeking around the corner. In a moment or two she saw her: Auntie, strolling idly by as though on an afternoon walk. The boy walked behind her, all height and muscle, bare arms looking like they could crush a skull between them. Mayhap they could.

Almost Loren listened to her inner voice, the voice that screamed for her to emerge, to *attack*, to leap upon Auntie and tear at the weremage until she lay bleeding in the sewer. But Auntie had her knives, and Loren had only her hunting blade.

And most importantly, Nightblade did not kill.

So Loren let them go. Just before the footsteps faded to silence, she heard Auntie's smooth, languid laugh drifting out of the darkness, chuckling at some remark of the boy's.

Loren turned back to Gem.

"I will take back what she stole. And mayhap not now, but one day, I will make her rue the moment she thought to cross either of us. How does that sound?"

Loren had never seen Gem's eyes wider.

"You will get no complaints from me," he said.

"Good. Let us start with my dagger. I have had an idea."

TWENTY-EIGHT

Gem was not overly enthusiastic about the plan. "They could catch me and gut me like a fish!" he said.

"You are only saying that because you are the one they will chase," said Loren. "But they will never catch you. I have heard and seen for myself how fast you can run."

Gem glared at her. "This is different, and you know it."

Loren put a hand on either of his shoulders and rocked him back and forth until he could not help a small smile. "Come now. You have proved to me already that Auntie had no better boy on the roofs. You have shown your worth in the sewers many times over. Do you really think they will be able to lay a hand upon you? Who knows this place better than you?"

"No one," said Gem reluctantly.

"As I thought. Come now. Destiny awaits. I am the one who must wait in plain sight for someone to sneak up behind me and slip a knife between my ribs."

Mollified, Gem stepped with her from the alcove and led her around the corner, back to the tunnel that led to the hidey hole.

In truth, Loren felt much less confidence than she showed Gem. It seemed a good plan, but she was a stranger here. She knew little, and only hoped that the gaps in her knowing would not cost the boy his life. She could not bear to think of that. But neither could she bear the thought of walking away.

They snuck back to the edge of the torchlight, the tunnel stretching long before them. Loren pointed to where a small plank bridge spanned the sewer's channel to the right of the guards.

"You will want to avoid that," she whispered. "They will cross more easily there. On the other side, they will be cautious."

Gem nodded. His eyes had grown large, and Loren could feel him tremble beneath her hand. She thought of speaking more words of encouragement, but that might only rekindle his doubts; she decided upon a gentle nudge instead.

"Go, master pickpocket. Remember: keep out of their reach until you are out of sight, and then disappear."

"Right," said Gem. "Very well. Here I go. Do not let this be for nothing."

He bounced on the balls of his feet twice, and then with a sharp cry he ran pell-mell down the tunnel towards the guards.

"Help! Help! They are coming!"

Both boys shot to attention at their posts, looking at each other and then Gem.

"Who is coming?" The guard's voice boomed low and resonant in the dank space.

"Constables!" said Gem. "We have been betrayed!"

The guards reached for the cudgels at their waists. But then one leaned forwards. "Wait a moment! Auntie is looking for you!"

"She is indeed," said Gem. He skidded to a stop at the end of the tunnel, hooked a left, and disappeared around the corner. With a cry of fury both guards gave chase, cudgels clutched in meaty fists.

It had been her idea, but still Loren marveled for a moment that it had worked. She stole down the tunnel and paused at the corner to peek around it. Torches stretched down the left-hand tunnel as far as she could see, but she saw no sign of Gem or the guards. She gathered herself, and then leapt across the channel in one quick jump. She did not hesitate, but darted into the small hallway that led to the hidey hole door.

There it stood, dark and imposing. The wood looked old, ancient even, but sound and without a trace of rot. Polish still covered its surface, and as Loren put a hand against it she found it dry as a bone, not damp as she would have expected. The door had no damage, save a grid of indents across its surface. She studied them, curious. They spaced perfectly across the wood, a mesh with six fingers between each point, from one wall to the other.

She threw one quick glance over her shoulder and then put a hand on its knob. It did not budge. Locked.

"Sky and stars." She kneeled to look at the lock. It was a massive thing, made from well-wrought iron that bore no rust. That was odd. Loren felt a prickling along the back of her neck. Could it be some form of enchantment, mayhap? Some firemage's spell to keep water from metal?

That was neither here nor there. Loren claimed no expertise with locks, but Bracken had taught her something about them, for in his tales, Mennet had had a belt of tools: small, intricate spikes and twisted prongs that could breach any door. She knew that a lock consisted of tumblers, little metal levers that one had to push in the right order to open. Bracken had once carried a big padlock in his pack and had let Loren toy around with it, using the end of his twisted knife. She had opened it once or twice, but only after much prodding and a great deal of time. And that lock had been a much larger, cruder affair than the one before her now.

Yet it did not appear that she had much choice. "Let us see what I remember."

Loren drew her hunting knife from her boot. It had a broader blade than Bracken's and did not twist as his had. She could fix that, mayhap. Thrusting the tip of it into the lock, she carefully pulled it to the side. The metal bent obligingly—almost too well, and Loren eased off for fear it might snap.

Now she had her poker. She inserted it into the lock, shoving a bit to make it fit, and felt around for the tumblers. The dagger *skritched* against the iron, and Loren became suddenly aware of how quiet the hallway had grown. Only trickling water sounded behind her. She looked over her shoulder again. She could see only the blinking torchlights stretching down the tunnel, yet she felt the presence of some unseen danger.

She turned back to the lock, and as she probed again she felt something give. A small piece of metal, hardly anything at all—but it had to be a tumbler. Loren heaved a great sigh and probed for another. Her knife scraped back and forth, seeking the things out.

Mayhap she had probed too far. Loren withdrew the knife slightly, almost to the entrance. With another *snik*, something gave. She nearly cried out in triumph.

SkreeeEEE

Loren looked up just in time to see the ceiling falling upon her. She had time only to drop to the ground and throw her hands over her head. Something snatched at the back of her shirt, dragging her forwards so that her head struck the door.

THOOM

The sound deafened her. But nothing struck her. No rocks or boulders crushed her.

Loren opened her eyes and raised her head. *So. That explains the indents.* A huge, spiked iron grate had swung down from the ceiling and slammed into the wooden door. Had Loren remained on her knees or, worse, been standing, she would now be impaled on a dozen jutting protrusions.

The bottom spikes had snatched at her clothing as the thing fell, and were now embedded in the door. Wincing from where her head had struck the wood, she tried tugging it free, but it would not move. Growling in disgust, she loosened the ties at her throat and freed herself from the cloak.

Now the grate stood between her and the door. But through its holes, Loren could still reach the lock, and the door opened inward. If she could get the thing open, mayhap she could lift the trap enough to slide beneath it. She bent to the task, slipping the tip of her hunting knife into the lock once more. But now the gate blocked her way, the grid making each movement awkward, blocking her arms as she sought to twist and turn them in her hunt for the tumblers. Loren gave another frustrated growl.

She must move the gate. Mayhap she could prop it up with something. She looked around but saw nothing. Very well, she would push it back to the ceiling. If it stuck, she would continue her picking. Now that she knew what to expect, if she tripped it again, she could get out of the way.

Loren wrapped her hands around the bottom of the grid and pulled upward.

SKREEEeeee

She dropped it like white-hot metal. They would hear her all across the nine lands, and the thing weighed so much that Loren doubted she could reach the ceiling with it. Frustrated, she knelt again and went for the lock with her knife.

"Loren!" A hand came down on her shoulder, yanking her back.

Loren screamed and whirled, slashing wildly with the knife. Gem cried out and tumbled backwards, crashing hard into the stone floor.

"Gem! What under the sky? I nearly killed you."

"You could not have cut me if you tried," said Gem, his nose in the air even as he found his feet.

"I came back to warn you—they are on their way. You must go."

"I have not got in."

Gem glanced at the door. "In or not, at any moment they will be upon us. We must fly before the chance to do so vanishes."

Loren gave the door another look. "If I could only . . . it is just in there, Gem! Do you know anything about locks?"

He tugged at her hand. "I told you, only the older boys learn that. We must go. I think one of them has gone for Auntie. Come. *Come!*"

Loren growled and followed him, running again into the sewer's gloom.

TWENTY-NINE

They found their way back to Markus' shop just before sundown. The cobbler's granddaughter let them in the back door without a word, and when they descended into the cellar two straw pallets waited for them. The blankets looked threadbare, and Loren saw no pillows, but still the pallets seemed like gift from a dream. She realized with a shock that she had not slept in more than a day—since the last morning she woke with Damaris' caravan on the road to Cabrus.

Without a word, she and Gem collapsed on the pallets. Sleep claimed her before she even smelled the straw.

Terror made a poor aid for sleep. Loren dreamed of fleeing through the streets of Cabrus while Gregor and Bern chased her on horseback and Damaris leapt across the rooftops. The merchant fired at her with bow and arrow, sending darts ricocheting against every wall, rebounding from the cobblestones, always just a fingerbreadth or two from the mark. Gregor and Bern swung their swords just above or beside her head, and Loren felt that they played with her, toying with her, like cats after a mouse.

She fell to her knees, lungs burning and heart threatening to burst through her chest. *Take me, then,* she cried in the dream. *Have done with it.*

They all smiled, but they did not advance. Instead, out of the shadows came Auntie, fingers wrapped around the hilts of her strange knives. A smile frosted her lips as she stepped forwards, and then her eyes glowed, and she changed to the woman in the pink dress, and then to Annis, to Loren's mother, her father.

He leapt forwards, knives swooping down to plunge into her chest.

Loren started awake on her pallet, and her heart would not still for a long while.

Gem snored mightily across the room. Pale light filtered in through a narrow crack in the wall, and from its color and angle she guessed that not an hour had passed since dawn. Down the stairs from the house above drifted the slow, lazy scent of bacon. She heard the *clunk* of tableware on wooden bowls.

She thought of nudging Gem awake to come with her, but the boy's face looked so placid, his mouth open and air roaring as he sucked it in through his nose. Loren could not bear to wake him, so she climbed the stairs alone.

Markus' eyes snapped to her as she emerged from the cellar stairway. "Good morn," he said.

Loren waited for him to ask after her success. He said nothing, but only returned to his meal.

She rubbed her stomach, which gurgled sudden and loud. Like a wraith from mist, Markus' granddaughter appeared out of what Loren guessed was the kitchen. In her hand the girl held a small wooden plate, and upon it were two thick and juicy rashers of bacon.

"I would not impose," said Loren, flustered.

The girl only smiled and pressed the plate forwards.

"Thank you," said Loren, taking it. "I fear my manners have been lax. What is your name?"

"Enough of that. Tend to your chores," said Markus. The girl vanished as quickly as she had appeared. Markus fixed Loren with a hard eye. "You will forgive me of course, but I keep from my grandchildren the names of those who pass through here. I have no knowledge of what you have or have not done, and I do not care to. If you come back through here with Xain, then you can meet her. Most come through once and never show their faces again, and most times that is the way I like it."

"Of course," said Loren in a small voice. She almost took the stool opposite Markus, but then thought better of it. Instead she turned and headed for the corner.

"Do not be ridiculous," said the cobbler gruffly. "Sit. You are not an animal, either."

"Thank you." She sat and picked up the first piece of bacon. It tasted so good, Loren thought she might faint.

"Have you not been eating?"

"Not well, or often, no."

"It shows."

Markus finished first, standing and vanishing through the door to his workshop. Once she had eaten, Loren returned to the cellar to fetch Gem.

The boy woke reluctantly, and only after Loren tried many times. Over and over he shot up, swearing he was awake. Then he would lapse back under the blanket and slip from consciousness once more. Finally Loren dragged him up and onto his feet. Fortunately he weighed no more than a bundle of sticks.

"Errm, what? I am awake."

"You look it," said Loren. "Now come."

"Why? The door is locked, and we have no chance of opening it. Why not just leave? We stayed, we fought, and from what my eyes have seen, we lost."

Loren glowered. He tried to meet her gaze with defiance, but in the end he only looked at his feet. They went upstairs, where Markus' granddaughter appeared again with a plate for Gem.

Her mind raced as he ate. *The problem is that he might be right.* She had not the first clue how they might find their way into Auntie's hidey hole, and thus no idea how to retrieve her dagger. Yet neither was she willing to give up, to slink through the city's gates with her tail between her legs.

"Tell me," she asked Gem. "You said the older boys, when they go to work the hard jobs, learn to work locks. They must use tools."

"Of course," said Gem, looking as though Loren had named the sky blue.

"Where do they get them? Mayhap we can fetch some of our own."

Gem shook his head emphatically. "No good. I would not know where to get them, but even if I did, those merchants sit in Auntie's pocket, and they would send her word before we left the shop."

"We could steal them."

Gem gave her a look of scorn. "Did you not hear me? I know not where to look. Besides, the boys have no doubt told Auntie about our escapade last night. Guards will line the sewer for leagues. You will not reach the door again, not now."

Loren felt helpless. All the boys they had seen in the sewers were as tall as she herself, or taller, and all of them strongly muscled besides. She would have wagered herself better in wrestling or boxing, and thought she might take one in a fight. But they would not come one at a time. Auntie owned many.

Why should the weremage wish to plague her so? Auntie had to know what it was to be alone in the world, seeking a place for oneself. She had found hers, caretaker of an army of children who would obey her without question. Why did she hate Loren with such fury?

A chilling notion struck her. "Gem," she said carefully. "Why does Auntie have only boys?"

Gem stopped chewing his food. He did not answer.

"Her fighters, I mean," said Loren. "The children are both boys and girls. But the older ones, the children who do the hard jobs, who fight for her. They are all boys."

Gem pushed his plate away. "The girls leave."

"Leave where?"

"I do not know." He picked at his fingernails. "Once they reach a certain age, they just . . . leave. Somewhere else."

"You never asked where?"

He cleared his throat and gnawed at his nails. "I knew one of them once, a girl named Tam. We were friends, or so I thought. One day she was no longer there. I asked Auntie about her, and she said Tam had gone, but she would not tell me where. After I asked too many times, she grew angry and asked me how would I like to join Tam, where no one would ever see either of us again. I said no, and she let it go. I asked no more after that."

Loren swallowed hard. "Do you think she—"

"I do not think about it at all, nor will I."

They sat in silence for a while after that. From Markus' workshop came the steady *plink, plink, plink* of a cobbler's hammer.

A thought struck Loren like a thunderclap. She raised her head, and her hands tensed on the table.

Gem must have seen it in her eyes. "What is it?"

"Jordel."

"The big man in the red cloak? What about him?"

"He said he would help us."

Gem pursed his lips. "He said something like that, yes, but I see this as far from his meaning."

"He can help."

"How?" said Gem, spreading his hands. "Will he storm the sewers alongside us, swinging a mighty sword? I do not see him as the type to cut down young men who have done him no harm, and I would not wish to see him again if he were."

"He . . . knows things. There is wisdom in him, and something else I do not understand. But you can hear it when he speaks, see it in the way he carries himself."

Gem's eyes widened. "You sound like some sunstruck beggar raving about kings in the sky."

Loren frowned. "I suppose you have a better notion?"

"Yes. As I have said before, and often. *Leave.* Flee from Cabrus, never to return."

Loren shook her head. "No. We must try this, at least, else I cannot live with myself. Come. We shall find him at the—"

She froze, her throat constricting. The Wyrmwing Inn, Jordel had said. Damaris, too, stayed at the Wyrmwing, and Loren knew she would not yet have left the city. Not without her daughter.

"What?" said Gem.

"Nothing. Only, we will have to wait for him to come to us. But finish quickly. The sooner we are off, the sooner our task will be done and we can leave this place behind."

They dressed as lepers again. Loren had grown to hate the rags, smearing shoe polish along her skin, smelling so strong they made her eyes water. She would have given much for clean rags, but lepers could not afford such.

It grew worse in the bright light of day. Summer grew near, and the city streets stank. The shoe polish baked on their skin, and Loren thought she might faint from the heat and smell of herself.

She told Gem to follow back alleys and side streets. She dared not risk the sewer again, and the roofs seemed too exposed. So he took her on the widest, most winding and hidden route he knew. Sometimes they snuck into basements that led into the bowels of other buildings before emerging upon the street again. Loren could not imagine how Gem had learned of all these secret ways, but then she thought of the Birchwood. To her mind came every hidden hollow, every secluded copse, all the secret ways and paths she knew through the woods that had been her home for so long. It was no different, she supposed, with Gem and his city.

They soon left the makers' district for the wealthier section of Cabrus. Crowds thinned, and Gem struggled more and more to keep them from wary eyes. Constables here would not take kindly to lepers wandering among the city folk. The wealthy had no taste for beggars and the diseased.

After they ducked down yet another dark alley to avoid a pair of women in red leather armor, Gem growled his frustration and kicked a broken bucket. "One cannot take two steps without bumping into the King's law. What I would not give to have the roofs again."

Loren considered it. Auntie could hardly expect them to come to this part of the city, where constables were plenty and Damaris' men lurked. Mayhap she would post fewer guards, or none at all. In any case, it seemed less risky than the army of constables that plagued the street. Gem spoke truly; their trip suffered immeasurable delay.

"Let us take the rooftops, then," said Loren. "And if fortune strike us down, at least it will strike swiftly."

Gem's face lit up. Together they shucked their lepers' rags. A low-hanging roof drooped above an obliging rain barrel, and within moments they had gained the shingles. Loren took a deep breath, free at last from the choking polish scent of the rags. A whiff of it still lingered and likely would for some time, but she felt as though she drank her first breath of clean air in years.

"Come," said Gem. "I will have us there in moments."

He darted away along the rooftop, laughing in the morning air. Loren grinned as she chased him, and for a time they made a game of it, Loren overtaking him before stopping to let him pass her. She would let Gem cross a few roofs, and then work hard at catching him again.

It ended all too soon, as Gem had said, and soon he pulled her to a stop at the edge of a roof three stories up. They sidled to the edge of it, Loren peering cautiously down. She did not fear heights—a forester's daughter spent too long in trees for that—but in the woods she had branches to grasp and break her fall. Here she saw only air between herself and the ground.

"There is the Wyrmwing." Gem pointed to a three-story structure, its walls purest, unmarred white, its roof painted green. Every bit of it bespoke wealth and luxury. Colorful banners draped its length, and its twin front doors hung wide, allowing air to flow freely within. Outside those doors stood two guards, both in light shirts of mail and armed with long blades.

"The finest inn in Cabrus," said Gem. "Or at least, no other will make the claim for fear of retribution from the Wyrmwing's owner. Darius is a hard man, and he does not take kindly to the less fortunate sullying his business."

"A fine place indeed. And now, we wait."

"For what?"

"For Jordel, of course."

They quickly found the roof's edge no comfortable resting place, for the shingles grew hot beneath them, and so they moved to another roof that lay in the shadow of a taller building. There they sat, always with one eye upon the Wyrmwing's front doors, and let the time pass.

As hours wore on, Loren grew increasingly fearful of discovery. Mayhap Auntie would not send her children here, but then again she might. Even if she sent a patrol to sweep the area once, they could not miss Loren and Gem sitting in plain sight. Her hope for Jordel's aid grew ever slimmer. Why should the man help them? Loren and Gem were nothing to him. At best, Loren served as a means to find Xain.

At last she convinced herself. She sat up from her slouch against the building's upper wall. "I think we remain too long. You might have been—"

"Hold," said Gem. "There."

Loren sat forwards, peering at the Wyrmwing's front doors. And through them stepped a tall man, taller than Loren herself, draped in a red cloak clasped with a strange symbol in silver.

THIRTY

"Come!" said Loren, pulling on Gem's arm. "Follow him!"

"What good will we do up here? We must find our way to the street."

"Very well, but quickly. If we lose sight of him, all the day's waiting will have been for naught."

"I think it will be in any case," grumbled Gem. "But very well. Come!"

They skidded along shingle and tile until they found a drainpipe. In her haste Loren slid too fast, and her hands burned against the iron. She winced and slowed herself, blowing on her hands as soon as she reached the ground.

"He went this way," said Gem, his voice now a low whisper.

They took many quick turns left and right, soon sliding through an alley that grew narrower with every step. When they reached its mouth, Loren poked a cautious head outside.

There he was, walking down the street towards where they stood. He seemed in no hurry, his steps slow and sure. Loren saw him approach two constables chatting by a low wall. One noticed him and nudged the other, and as Loren watched, they turned and *bowed* to him.

What manner of man was this?

She forced the thought away. "Pssst! Jordel!"

He stopped, his light blue eyes darting to where she hid in the shadows. Loren saw a spark of surprise, and then he made for them. So wide were his shoulders, she wondered if he would fit in the alley at all. He did, but it was a near thing.

"Loren," said Jordel. That voice, so soothing, so gentle. "And . . ." He gave a pointed look at Gem.

"Gem," said the boy. "Master pickpocket, scholar, and sometime medica."

"My honor, then," said Jordel, bowing his head. "What brings you here?"

"You seem surprised." Loren raised her chin. "When last we spoke, you thought our reunion fated."

A slow smile came over his face. "I said something to the effect, yes. But come now, tell me your business. Is it to do with Xain? Have you told him of me?"

Loren paused as a new thought struck her. Mayhap there was an even better way to assure Jordel's aid.

"I have," she lied. "He seems to think you might be worth trusting. But before he will meet you, we need something. Something stolen from me, quite important, that I must retrieve."

Jordel leaned against the wall and folded his arms. "I understand your concern, but I fear to tell you that I am no thief."

"That is obvious. You have neither the build nor the temperament for it," said Loren, trying to sound scornful. "And yet you seem to have some influence. Constables do not bow to every man in Cabrus."

"No, they do not. But how do you think that will help you?"

"That is for you to determine, if indeed you seek Xain," said Loren. "I can tell you where this thing is that was stolen from me. I can tell you who holds the key to its freedom. Can you not summon a squadron of constables, or mayhap some other men who will swing loyal swords in your name?"

The lines of Jordel's face set, resolute and somewhat sad. "Loren," he said slowly. "I fear that you ask for a favor beyond my power. I cannot help you in this, except mayhap to offer counsel."

"Counsel?" Loren stomped her foot. "What good is that? I do not need counsel. I need men with strong arms and loyal hearts. I am full to bursting with wit, but what good is that without the strength to back it?"

A spark flashed in Jordel's eyes, and to Loren's fury, he smirked. "With enough wit, the strength of an enemy is useless. That is a lesson I try to impart on all of my students. You say that some foe has stolen something from you. What do you still have that this enemy wants?"

Loren felt herself shrink. "Nothing I can give, for she wants only my blood."

Jordel's smile broadened, twisting with a crafty smirk. "Well then, why not give that?"

Loren snorted. "You must be renowned as a great teacher. If for a moment I fell into my foe's hands, it would be the end of me. The greatest fortune I could hope for would be a constable's cell. More likely I would find myself handed over to one who hates me even—"

She stopped. The whirling doubt in her mind subsided as she saw a new path stretch before her.

"I think the student has taken the lesson to heart," said Jordel.

"Thank you," murmured Loren. "Gem, let us be off. We have much to do."

"What?" said Gem. "Where?"

Jordel thrust out a hand, and Loren shook his wrist absentmindedly. Then she led Gem down the alley, looking back once to see Jordel silhouetted in its mouth. Though shadow covered his face, she thought she could see his smile.

"What madness has seized you? I feel as though the man whispered secret words only you could hear."

"In a manner of speaking, yes." Loren's thoughts settled, the plan clear in her mind. "We must busy ourselves. Quickly, find a constable."

"What?" Gem looked as though she had lost her mind.

"Never you mind," she said, exasperated.

She found an outlet and poked her head out. There. Four of them stood not far away, hands on swords as they waved off flies with mail-gloved hands.

"Now, you must go to them—" Loren began.

"What?" said Gem, his voice nearly a shriek.

"—you must go to them," she insisted, "and tell them this exactly: tell them you have seen the girl that Constable Bern searches for. Do you hear? Constable Bern. Tell them that she will be at Auntie's hideout tomorrow at the break of dawn, and they must inform Constable Bern immediately."

"I do not think many constables know of Auntie's hideout," said Gem doubtfully.

Loren cuffed him gently on the back of the head. "Of course not, fool. Explain to them where it is and what it looks like. Now, quickly. Go!"

She shoved Gem out of the alley and slid out of sight. She saw him stand there for a moment, frozen in uncertainty. Then he squared his shoulders and marched off towards the constables. She edged out just far enough to see the ghost of his image around the corner. The constables' eyes locked on him almost immediately, and almost his steps faltered. But he kept on, and soon stood before them, dwarfed by even the shortest. Loren saw his arms swing wide as he relayed her words, and the constables looked at each other with concern. Then one spoke gruffly, and Gem nodded. Finally he thrust out a hand. Three of the constables scowled, but the fourth barked a sharp laugh and pulled out a coin. With a sharp flick of the wrist, he flung it into Gem's chest. The boy caught the coin easily and turned, heading back towards Loren, who stepped out of sight.

Gem appeared in the alley moments later, flipping a silver penny in the air. "Done and done," he said, "and a coin for my troubles."

"We are hardly poor."

"It helped the story," said Gem airily. "What constable would believe a beggar boy unless he begged?"

Loren rolled her eyes. "Come, then. Now for the great gambit."

She strode with purpose through the alley, towards the open square near which they had met Jordel. Gem's steps slowed as they neared the alley mouth, but Loren pressed on.

"Loren—!" he whispered.

She stepped out into the open air. He squeaked, and she heard silence behind her as he thought of what to do. Then he jumped out and ran after her, bare feet slapping against the cobblestones.

"What are you doing?" he said—but he whispered, as though being quiet would hide him even though he walked in the open, under the burning sun.

"I hope I know," she admitted.

Straight to the front doors of the Wyrmwing she strode. The guards who stood there looked up at her approach, but she walked with such confidence and purpose that they glanced at each other, uncertain. Their moment's hesitation proved all Loren needed, and she marched straight through the front doors as though she owned the inn and every other building along the street. Gem whimpered audibly as she set foot on the sawdust sprinkled across the hardwood floor.

The whole of the Elf's Purse could have fit within the common room of this place. Loren scanned the tables as she walked. Many sat in the center of the room, level with her as she entered, but more ran along a raised walkway a pace off the ground that spanned the length of the walls. And at one such table she found what she sought.

She climbed the stairs and walked straight to the table where Damaris sat.

The merchant's startled gaze remained locked on Loren's face. Gregor stepped forwards as she approached, but Damaris raised a hand to stop him. Without a pause or a second thought, Loren threw herself into the chair opposite Damaris and leaned back, kicking her boots up to rest on the table. The shock of them rocked Damaris' goblet, tipping it over to send red wine spilling from table to floor.

"Greetings again, Damaris of the family Yerrin," said Loren. "I wager that we have much and more to discuss."

THIRTY-ONE

FOR SEVERAL TENSE MOMENTS, NO ONE MOVED. Damaris' piercing eyes remained impassive, and Loren became acutely aware of Gregor's hand resting on the hilt of his sword. Even the servers around the bar froze, all eyes upon the table's occupants. Though she tried to remain still, Loren's tongue snaked out and ran across her lips.

Damaris spoke first. "I will admit more than a little surprise at seeing you here, Loren of the family Nelda. I thought you had scurried off like a dog, tail between your legs. That was a disappointment, for I had thought so much more of you."

Loren felt a pressure at her elbow as Gem tugged on her sleeve. "Who is this?" the boy whispered.

"Be quiet, Gem." Loren gave a pointed glance at Gregor. "The adults are talking."

Damaris smirked, and Loren hoped the merchant's amusement would outmatch the captain's fury.

"You say there are words to be had," said Damaris. "Thus you seem to know what those words might be. Please, explain."

"I thought you might help me acquire something," said Loren. "Something stolen from me."

"Your dagger?" Loren flinched, and the merchant's smirk widened. "I noticed its absence the moment I saw you. And too, I wondered, where is the fine cloak I made you a gift of?"

"It rests in a safe place. I find that outside of shadows, it draws too much attention. I thank you for it nonetheless."

"My pleasure," said Damaris, inclining her head. "You deserve such and finer, and that is something I would say of few I have met in my travels. Wine?"

Loren nodded and removed her boots from the table. "Thank you."

Damaris waved at one of the servers in the room, who rushed to fetch an empty cup while Damaris righted her own and refilled it.

Loren's head felt light. Here she sat, talking with Damaris as if no animosity lay between them. She knew she played a dangerous game, riding upon the edge of a knife that could cleave her in two at a misstep. The merchant would not kill her while Annis' location remained unknown, but the longer the conversation continued, the more control Damaris would reclaim. Loren must move quickly.

"As you no doubt have guessed, there are two sides to the deal I offer," said Loren.

"Indeed," said Damaris. "I suppose that if I help you retrieve your fine weapon, you will return my daughter to me."

"Just so," said Loren.

"What?" said Gem, aghast. "Loren, Annis—"

"Gem, be *silent!"* snapped Loren. "Wait for me outside."

"No, I will be—"

"You will be outside. Go." Better to remove him before Damaris thought to take the boy hostage. Loren felt resolute in her course, but knew that his endangerment might make her waver.

Sullenly, the boy stalked to the front door of the inn and out, glancing back once at the threshold. The serving woman appeared with Loren's cup. But when she offered to fill it, Damaris waved her away, electing to pour it herself.

"It seems we aim to discuss matters of some delicacy," said Damaris. "Might we retire to my quarters? You may not mind, but I would rather our words did not reach the wrong ears."

Loren thought quickly. This could easily be a trap. But then, Damaris could not harm her in so public a place as this, could she? Even in one of the inn's room, screams would surely draw too much attention.

"Certainly," said Loren, taking a sip of wine and bringing the cup with her as she rose. Damaris put her own wine cup in Gregor's massive paw.

The merchant led her to the rear of the inn, where Loren saw a massive spiral staircase. The thing climbed through all four of the inn's floors. Every mahogany step fairly glowed with polish, and all edged by a bannister carved in an intricate pattern of leaves. For a moment it reminded Loren of the Birchwood, a thought that brought a surprising pang of longing.

Damaris led her to the top floor and strolled down a hallway with few doors. A final door stood at the hallway's end, and two of Gregor's men stood to either side of it, mail gleaming in the sun that streamed from a skylight above. They did not so much as glance at Loren.

"Here we are," said Damaris. The door swung open under her hand, revealing a room that stole Loren's breath.

The opposite wall opened to a balcony that stretched the width of the Wyrmwing. Loren had noted it from outside. Three separate doors opened to the balcony, each paned with clear glass and hung with lace curtains that wafted in the breeze. The room was almost all one unit, but at one end was a door that, she presumed, led to a bedroom.

Against that same wall, Loren noted with interest, sat a great chest that stood half as tall as Gregor. A great lock sealed it closed, a lock not fastened around iron rings, but worked into the wood itself like the lock of a door. From the fine silver that banded the chest and the gold inlay on its lid, Loren could guess what lay inside. If the room were a pile of dragon's gold, the chest looked a prize ruby whose luster outmatched all the rest of the hoard.

The place looked large enough to hold half a hundred, and mayhap more. Every bit of it had been built for comfort, with plush furniture of rich leather and fine cloth, decorated in patterns laced with gold. Loren had never imagined this level of opulence, or the life one must lead to grow accustomed to it.

"Let us sit here, where both the sun and wind may kiss us." Damaris waved her hand at two couches that curled almost around each other, with a small gap between either end and a sort of oval in the middle, holding a low table. The merchant led the way, draping herself lengthwise along the couch and placing her jug and wine cup upon the table. Loren followed suit, though she sat upright—*The better to run, if necessary,* she thought. She took another deep gulp of wine, and then thought that mayhap she should keep her head from growing muddled. She pushed the wine cup away.

"I find myself more curious with each revelation," said Damaris, returning to their conversation. "Why the sudden change of heart? You seemed eager enough to steal my child away from me. What, now, prompts you to return her?"

"You may choose to believe this or not, but Annis conceived our flight herself. She knew of my danger, yes, but she seemed most eager to escape from you."

"Your danger?" said Damaris, spreading her hands in confusion. "What danger was that?"

"That you intended to relinquish me to the constables. I know you see me as a foolish girl, but I have never been so foolish that I could not have seen your intent."

Damaris' eyes widened, and she leaned forwards with sudden intensity. "Oh, dear child," she said quietly. "Is that what all this mess has been about? You cannot think I meant to *leave* you in the hands of the King's law."

Loren blinked. "If not, then what did you intend by offering me up to them?"

"You would have landed in their cell, certainly," said Damaris. "But once you told them all you knew of the wizard Xain—and that is precious little, I wager—I would have ensured your release. Long is the arm of the King's law, they say, and yet the family Yerrin may reach farther."

Loren kept her face calm at the mention of Xain. Could she believe even a word of what the merchant said? She did not know. But whatever her inner thoughts, she could not hesitate now. She knew the course she must follow.

"Such words come easily now, when you know that if the constables took me, you might never see your daughter again," said Loren. "But the truth of your words is neither here nor there. Do you know of the weremage Auntie?"

"No, though her name fairly terrifies."

Loren allowed herself a small smile. "A jest of a name, yet the woman who holds it is fearsome and fell. It is she who has taken Annis and, even now, keeps her trapped below the city's streets. My dagger, too, she took."

"What is your thought, then? That we should break into this weremage's stronghold and rescue your blade, as well as my daughter?"

Loren shook her head. They must not proceed there without Auntie. If Loren stood alone when they entered the hidey hole and found Annis absent, all Damaris' attention and wrath would descend on her own head.

"The door to the room is locked and guarded," said Loren. "Your men may overcome the guards, but still the door will defeat us. Auntie holds the key. We must capture her."

Damaris leaned back, nodding. "And you know the way to do so, but you lack the means. Hence, my Gregor and his men. I understand."

"Just so," said Loren, nodding again.

Damaris let her eyes fall to her wine cup and ran her finger along its rim before taking another long, slow sip. Loren forgot her earlier decision, reached for her own wine, and drained it to the dregs.

"You know, I do respect you," said Damaris, her voice kind, gentle. "You have such spirit. And that wide-eyed innocence with which you face the world—it fills me with such longing. And yet, as would any loving parent, or mayhap a godsparent, I must tell you how foolish you are."

Loren found it hard to swallow. "Never let it be said that I turned down sage wisdom."

"First, you should never have acted against me. You leapt to broad conclusions about my mind and never thought to ask. This mess could have been avoided, over and done with already. Second, you should never have returned once you left. If you had had an ounce of sense, you would have run from Cabrus until your horses fell dead on the road, and then run on your own feet until they smeared blood in the dirt. Then, mayhap, crawled until your hands and knees were but bones."

Loren gulped. "Circumstances did not permit."

Damaris shook her head. "Oh, I know you thought it best at the time. But your third failing is greatest. Not only did you return to me, you placed yourself utterly within my mercy. You came with me here, alone, where I could kill you at any moment."

"You will never find Annis without me."

Damaris shook her head. "Nothing could keep me from finding my daughter. I will tear up every stone and street in this city to find her, and whether you live or lie a corpse will not change that outcome one whit."

Loren leapt from the couch. But Gregor moved faster, crossing the distance and intercepting her before she reached the door. His hand caught her wrist, and he twisted. She fell to the ground with a cry of pain.

Damaris stood above her. Gregor loomed. The merchant stared down, looking at Loren with a curious mix of detachment and fondness.

"I will not kill you, child."

Loren fought through the pain in her wrist. "Then why this attack? Call him off."

"It is important that you know your situation, and your station. Despite all that you seem to think, I still hold a certain . . . fondness for you. But remember this moment. Remember what I have said. Our paths align now. But if you stand in my way . . . well, not needlessly do we take lives. Not needlessly."

Gregor released her. Loren found her way to her feet, cradling her wrist.

"Now, what do you propose?" said Damaris.

"There is a house," said Loren. "An old, abandoned pigpen in the heart of the city. That is where Auntie hides herself. Tomorrow at dawn, constables will attack the place to find me, and Auntie will make her escape. That is where you will take her, and we will both gain what we want."

Damaris gave a slow nod. "Very well. Ready yourself for the morning, and we will see you upon the morrow."

She returned to her couch. Gregor remained unmoving, eyes burning as he glowered down at Loren. She turned and made for the door, hoping she had not made a terrible mistake.

THIRTY-TWO

THE NEXT MORNING FOUND LOREN HIDING IN A back alley behind Auntie's hideout. Grey slowly filled the dark sky, the sun still some distance below the horizon. All was quiet. Gem had already swept the rooftops; they were free from any of Auntie's children. Whatever suspicion the weremage held, she clearly did not expect a frontal attack.

Around her shoulders Loren wore her black cloak. Her fingers kept groping for the dagger at her waist, and she had to remind herself time and again that she would not find it there. Gem shifted from one foot to the other, rubbing his arms to keep warm. Gregor was there, a strange companion, and some few of his men. Many more filled the alleys and side streets in all directions. Before them sat the rickety wooden fence that rimmed the pigpen out back.

Damaris waited in the alley as well, standing far back behind her men, wrapped tightly in a cloak of sable. Puffs of mist erupted from the breath of everyone present, lending the air a smoky feel.

"Where are they?" growled Gregor. "Dawn nears."

"Be still," said Loren. "See there."

From the street by the hideout, a man approached with a torch. Beneath his brown cloak Loren saw the telltale sign of red leather armor. A constable, sent around back to catch any runaways. Little did he or his master Bern know how many children would flee upon their attack.

"Remember," Gregor said, turning to his guards. "Slay no guardsman. Any man who brings the King's justice upon us will be served up to it like a warm meal." His men made no reply, only tightening their grips on their sword hilts.

"They will attack soon," said Loren. "If they are already setting a boundary—"

The air split with a sharp cry from one street over. There came a great crash of wood splintering, the front door laid open with a single crashing blow.

Gregor did not wait, but charged from the alley's mouth. The constable before them could only gape before the captain's pommel crashed into his temple, laying him flat in the street. Two of Gregor's men seized the guardsman by arms and legs and flung him into a dark corner.

Like a rolling tide, children erupted into the night. Tens of them, dozens, all pouring through holes in the fence and into the streets. Their hunger-wide eyes grew larger at the sight of Gregor and his men rimming the house's yard. But the men ignored them, and the children melted into the vanishing darkness.

Fighting erupted in the streets. Loren saw two of Auntie's boys fighting a constable, and then she recognized the man as Bern. Though he was outnumbered, the constable's skill with a blade far outmatched the clumsy swings of his opponents and their clubs. With a sudden swipe, he sliced one's cudgel in half, and the boy fell back. Bern took the opportunity to lunge at the other, piercing him with three hands of steel. The boy collapsed, writhing and moaning on the ground as life spilled from his gut. The other boy fled, and Bern ran for the front of the house.

Loren thought she might be sick. She ducked farther into the alley, trying to shrink as small as possible. She forced her eyes upon the wooden fence again as children kept pouring through it.

A plank burst outward, and through the hole came a boy. Then another, and then a shapely woman in a fine green cloak. "There!" cried Loren.

Auntie turned at the sound just as Gregor and his men pounced. Both her boys quailed before the fighting men, but to Loren's relief the guards did not kill them. One fell before a crushing blow to the face; the other traded two parries with a sword before he dropped his cudgel and ran. Like a striking snake, Gregor seized Auntie's cloak as she tried to flee.

The weremage spun around, but she had changed. Her face had grown paler than Loren's, her hair in long red curls. Blue eyes flashed as she feigned a look of terror, falling to her knees and wailing for mercy. Confused, Gregor loosened his grip on her cloak. Like a flash Auntie fell back, out of his reach, and fled the street.

Loren gave a strangled cry of frustration and ran after her, ignoring Gem's frightened cry. "I told you she was a weremage, you fool!" she said as she passed Gregor. She did not wait for his reply, but followed the whipping green cloak as it rounded a corner.

The next street was empty. Footsteps echoed down a side alley, and Loren gave chase. But the alley, too, was vacant, and only a shadow passing on a far wall told her which way Auntie had gone. Gritting her teeth, Loren ran on.

Only after entering the narrow space between two buildings, far from Gregor's men and the torchlight of the streets, did Loren realize she had become separated from the rest. Just as the thought came, steel flashed out of the night. Loren fell back, ducking one swipe, but she cried out as she felt the kiss of a blade in her shoulder.

"Vile little witch!" snarled Auntie. "I will gut you and keep your heart with my treasures!" Her voice had grown to something frantic and mad, a shriek entirely unlike the seductive tones of their first meeting.

Her knives hissed again, and Loren backed away. Out of desperation she pulled her hunting knife from her boot, its twisted tip pathetic against Auntie's strange weapons.

"I sought not to harm you," said Loren, brandishing the knife. "I only wanted your help!"

Auntie pulled her knives to her sides, waiting like a serpent to strike. Loren saw her own blood upon one of them. "Why should I help you, sniveling child that you are? Any child of mine, fresh from the arms of his mother, knows more of the world than you. You are worthless to me! A grasping, mewling pup."

Auntie sidestepped, trying to circle and block Loren's path to escape. Loren took several hasty steps backwards. She must not let herself be trapped. With luck, Gregor would find them. *What an odd circumstance, to hope for succor from that brute,* she thought.

"You stole what was mine."

"Yours," spat Auntie. "The would-be thief has such grand notions of property. What is yours is what you can take!" At the last word she lunged, her blades passing a hair's breadth from the bridge of Loren's nose. Loren nearly fell as she tried to avoid them. "Now my children are lost in the night, without their mother, and so many of my boys lie dead in the street. Their blood is on your hands."

If Loren could only keep her talking . . .

"You mean to say your hands are clean? What do you do with the girls, Auntie? The girls you raise and profess your love for, naming yourself their mother? What happens to them when they come of age?"

Auntie smiled. Her face shifted for a moment, bones sliding around beneath it, as if her very soul stirred with her fury.

"Boys are useful to me. I can control them. I can make them love their mother. A girl is a pretty thing to have around, a beggar to tug on the heartstrings of any merchant. But a woman, who would force herself upon what is *mine?* They are useless to me. But come closer, and I will show you what I do with them."

Loren had nearly reached the mouth of the alley, and could see torchlight dancing at her vision's edge. Mayhap she could hope for a constable to see the fight and put an end to it.

As though she had had the same thought, Auntie attacked once more. But as Loren tried to dodge, the weremage released her hold on one knife, and the blade sped through the air towards Loren's head. Sheer luck saved her, for at last she tumbled backwards, wincing in pain at the cut in her shoulder. Auntie's blade tangled in the hood of her cloak, and the hilt came crashing into her forehead. She saw stars for a moment, reaching up to tug the knife free from the cloth that ensnared it. It came away from her vision just in time to see Auntie coming in for the kill, her remaining knife raised high in a curled fist.

Then the weremage's eyes focused above Loren, and she stopped. Loren heard heavy, running footsteps, and a sword swiped through the space before Auntie's frightened eyes. She stumbled back, as Loren had, and ran into the alley's mouth.

Gregor watched her go. Loren felt her heart sink into her gut with disappointment. The fight, and the deaths that came with it, had been for nothing.

Still, there might be some chance. "We must go to her hiding place. Mayhap she will return there, hopeful of protecting her treasures." Loren held up a hand for Gregor to help her up.

The captain stared down at her, his eyes a low, burning smolder. She became suddenly aware of the sword in his hand. The silence of the street stretched for an eternal moment.

"Gregor!"

Gregor's eyes snapped up, joining Loren's to find Damaris just up the street.

"What of the weremage?" she said.

"Escaped, my lady," said Gregor.

Damaris' lips pursed. "Escaped? You had her within your grasp. I hold you accountable."

"I apologize, my lady."

"We may still find her," said Loren. "If we go to her hiding place."

The merchant's gaze fell to Loren and considered it for a moment. "Very well. Make haste, then. And get up off the ground, child. You soil the cloak I gave you."

Loren gained her feet, dusted herself off, and went to Damaris. She did not want to look at Gregor, or see the hate that burned in his eyes.

THIRTY-THREE

Gregor's men gathered again near Auntie's hideout. As soon as Loren approached, Gem pounced from shadows, wrapping his arms around her waist.

"Thank the sky and stars! I thought I would find you again only as a corpse, or not at all."

"You could have come with me," said Loren, trying to sound gruff. She patted his head once before pushing him firmly away. "I might not have nearly died, then."

Gem drew himself up and placed his hands on his hips. "I am not so foolish as you. When a deadly foe seeks after my life, I do not pursue her into the darkness she calls home."

"Enough," snapped Damaris. "If you are right, Loren, we must make haste. Show us the way."

Loren waved a hand at Gem. "Here is our guide. Take us to the hidey hole, Gem."

Gem's eyes widened, and he looked around at them. "You wish to go there? But why? Auntie's boys—"

"Will flee or be destroyed." Damaris' eyes were iron, her voice like sharpened steel. "Lead us now, or join their lot."

Gem swallowed hard and looked at Loren. She gave him a nod. Their only chance at success lay with Damaris now, and the die was already cast.

Gem took them to a drainage hole, but Loren cuffed him lightly on the head. "How will these men crawl through that, simpleton?"

The boy rubbed his head and glared at her. "Am I at fault for their bloated size?"

"Take us another way," said Loren. "Have you forgotten our haste?"

Gem grumbled, but he did as she asked. They found an entrance like the one they had used to escape from Auntie the night Loren had lost her blade. Iron rungs set into the wall provided an easy way down, and the hole yawned wide enough for even Gregor's mighty shoulders. Loren had half thought the merchant might remain behind, but she climbed down just like the rest, hitching her dress up slightly to swish a few fingers from the filthy stone floor.

The moment their boots touched stone, Gregor's men pulled torches from the wall.

Gem said, "Torches will only let others see you the more easily."

"We are not cravens who fear to be seen," said Gregor. "Lead on."

Gem did. Again Loren soon grew lost amid the twists and turns, but the boy never wavered. Gregor remained close by Damaris' side, peering into the surrounding darkness with suspicion. Men flanked her to either side. But Damaris might have been on an evening stroll, or one of her horseback rides with Loren, for all the calm she displayed.

Before long they reached the intersection that led down to the hidey hole. Gem slowed before the corner and turned. "We are almost there. We will want to be quiet—"

Gregor grunted and pushed Gem aside with a sweep of his mighty arm. His men drew blades and marched around the corner, brandishing their steel in the torchlight. Loren helped Gem back to his feet and followed as quick as she could.

She rounded the corner in time to see Auntie's guards flee, terrified at the sight of men in armor coming at them out of the darkness. There lay the short hallway before the hidey hole, and beyond it the huge wooden door. But she saw no sign of Auntie.

"Where is she?" muttered Loren.

"With all the noise they are making, probably far away," whispered Gem.

Damaris' men did not slow. Two took up positions at the hallway's mouth, while others headed off to guard the closest intersections in every direction. Gregor himself moved down the hallway towards the door. Damaris waited halfway down. Loren paused at the hallway entrance, uncertain whether or not to proceed.

Gregor glared over his shoulder at Loren. "It is only a wooden door. We should have come here first." He tried the handle, but it did not move, so he turned and nodded to one of his men. "Break it down."

The guards at the hallway's entrance left their posts and went to the door. At Gregor's direction they backed up a pace and charged the door with their shoulders. Neither of them stood as tall or broad as Gregor, but still they brought a crushing weight against the door. It did not move. They moved back and tried again. And again. Five times they struck, and five times the door held.

One of the men rolled his shoulder, though he did not wince—Loren suspected Gregor did not cultivate weakness in his ranks. The guard turned to his captain with a look of bafflement. "It does not move, sir."

"I can see that," growled Gregor.

"No, I mean that it does not budge at all. Wood has some give, whether you can break it down or no. This has nothing. It might as well be a cavern's stone wall."

Loren half expected Gregor to yell at the man in anger, or mayhap strike him. But he stepped past without question, went to the door, and placed a hand against it. Then he furled a fist and sent it against the wood. He took two steps back and tried his own shoulder at the door. When he turned back to Damaris, he wore a dark expression.

"It is as he says, my lady. I suspect some sort of enchantment. I have seen a mindmage do something like this once. If it is so, only another mindmage can break it—or the key for the lock."

"And yet our little weasel of a weremage remains unfound," said Damaris. Though her words seemed harsh, Loren heard no trace of anger or frustration in her voice. She ran a hand up and down her neck, deep in thought. "I may know of a man—a mind-mage. But he is more than a day's ride from Cabrus, and if Annis is trapped within . . ."

Just then Loren heard a shout and a scuffle to her right. Turning to look, she saw two of Damaris' men thrashing and fighting some figure. A third man joined the fray and threw a fist. The figure jerked and fell still. The guards came forwards. As they emerged into the nearby torchlight, Loren saw skin of loam and hair like sunlight.

"That may not be necessary, my lady," said Loren. "Here comes our weremage."

Gregor's men hoisted Auntie up by her arms at the mouth of the hallway. Her eyes rolled wild in their sockets, piercing in their hate and mad as they glowed in the light of torches. They found Loren and focused with an impossible fury. Bones shifted beneath her skin.

"Hello, Auntie." Damaris stepped forwards while keeping well out of reach. "That is what you call yourself, is it not? I am Damaris, of the family Yerrin. Well met."

Auntie spat, but it went wide and flew past the merchant's shoulder. Damaris looked at the spittle upon the stone floor and raised an eyebrow. Then she lifted her head and spat directly in Auntie's eye. The weremage responded with a shriek of rage and a fresh bout of struggling.

Gregor's fist crashed into her face. Auntie's head snapped back, and she went limp. As she raised her eyes, still burning with anger and defiance, Loren saw that her nose had broken. But in a moment, the bones of her face shifted. Briefly she looked like someone else, someone with a sallow and pock-marked face, before she reverted to her normal visage. Her nose no longer bent at an odd angle.

Auntie's lips parted in a sardonic grin, and blood stained her teeth.

"It is my wish that we should avoid any more such unpleasantness," said Damaris. "Tell us how to open the door."

Auntie remained silent, and Loren thought she might try spitting again. But instead she chose to ignore Damaris, looking at Loren.

"Hello, girl," she said, her voice all silky smooth as it had been when they first met. "You know, of course, that no matter what happens here, I will find and gut you. No power on earth can stop me from leaving you bloodless and bloated, floating along the sewer's current until you spill into the river. I will cross the dark veil the wrong way just to haunt you in your dreams and lead you screaming off a rooftop. I curse it in every tongue of the nine lands."

Loren's heart chilled at the words, but she kept it from her face. "Another told me something similar, scarcely a week ago. I shot him with an arrow."

"That will not stop me." Auntie's eyes fell to Gem at Loren's side. "And you. The sorest waste of my life. The great traitor. I hope you sleep well thinking of all your brothers you killed today."

Gem shifted slightly to half hide behind Loren. "I killed no one," he mumbled.

"You brought it on them. And all for the traitorous wretch whose skirts you hide behind. Or mayhap you do more than that with her skirts? Does she love you, Gem? Treat you like your mother treats you?" The weremage ran her tongue along the length of her lips, smearing blood across them.

"You are not my mother," said Gem, his voice gaining a little strength, "and you never were."

"Enough," said Damaris. Gregor stepped forwards and hit Auntie again, this time in the chest. Loren heard something crack. Auntie screamed, and then turned it into a laugh, returning her gaze to the merchant with a predator's smile.

"Have your say, or kill me," said Auntie. "Only please, cease to bore me."

"You alone hold that power," said Damaris. "The door. How do we get in?"

Auntie shrugged. "It has been so long. I can scarce remember. My mind has never been a good one, and has only worsened with age. Though you look to have twice that problem."

Damaris rolled her eyes. "How clever. Search her. No, hit her again, and then search her."

Gregor sent an obliging fist into the weremage's face. Her head snapped back, and Loren feared her neck would break. But as she lolled forwards once more, Loren could see that she still breathed—though her eyes wandered in all directions, and she could not seem to see straight. A trickle of blood had erupted from one of her eye sockets, running gently down her cheek like a tear.

Without ceremony, Gregor drew a knife and sliced the strings that held Auntie's jerkin together and then cut through the top half of her tunic. The weremage winced when the knife brushed skin. Loren seized Gem and covered his eyes, but Gregor did not lay Auntie bare. Instead, he reached for something hanging on a chain around her neck and tugged. The chain snapped, and Gregor held up what Loren now saw to be an iron key.

"My lady," said Gregor.

"Well done." Damaris smiled. "Now, let us be done with this and away. I dislike the smell of this place."

Gregor turned to the hallway again. But then Loren remembered the trap falling from the ceiling above, and her pulse quickened. She stepped forwards, blocking the captain's path. "Wait, there is—"

Gregor batted her aside as he had Gem before. The crash of his hand on her chest felt like a warhammer. Loren stumbled to the side, and with a cry she fell into the water of the sewer's channel. She struggled to right herself, the cloak dragging her down, before she could free her arms and find the surface. She pulled herself to the edge of the channel, where Gem seized her arms.

"Are you all right?" He tried to pull her up, but an ant might as well have tried to lift a mountain.

"I told you we would brook no more interference," said Damaris, her voice light.

Loren ignored them both, struggling out of the water and leaping to her feet. She ran to the hallway where Gregor stood facing the door. Damaris gave a cry, and one of Gregor's men made a grab for her, but Loren twisted away from him and charged towards the captain. His hand rose, and the key twisted in the lock. It stuck, and he tried to pull it back out.

Snik.

SkreeeEEE

Loren flew through the air, her whole body crashing into the back of Gregor's knees. The captain bellowed as he went down, and at the same time the iron grate fell from the ceiling.

Loren felt Gregor's body jerk atop her, and then still.

THIRTY-FOUR

"No, no," whispered Loren. She pushed and squirmed, slithering out from beneath Gregor's heavy legs before fighting free and rising to her feet.

He lived. Spikes had punctured his shoulder in two places, but his head hung free from the grate, facing the hallway's mouth. His eyes twitched in pain, gritted teeth visible as his lips split in a grimace. All along his face, muscles spasmed in agony as he fought to contain a scream.

"Gregor!"

Damaris fell to her knees before him, holding his head in support. Her hands hovered over the spikes in his shoulder, at once seeking to hold him in comfort and afraid to touch the terrible wounds.

Loren seized the bottom of the grate and heaved as hard as she could. It remained as heavy as it had been before, and now Gregor's weight only added to it. Loren fought and struggled, gritting her teeth, until she feared her arms might tear from their sockets. A low, strangled groan escaped her.

"Stop!" Strong arms wrapped around her shoulders and dragged her back from the grate. Two guards pulled her back and away, one twisting her hand up behind her shoulder blades until she cried out.

"Release her, fools!" cried Damaris. Both guards froze. "She tries to save your captain while you do nothing! Help her!"

Their hands left Loren like she had grown fire-hot. Then, together, the three of them seized the iron grate and heaved. Gregor's resolve finally buckled as the spikes slid free, and a blasting roar of pain echoed through the sewer. From outside the hallway and out of sight, Loren heard Auntie's mad cackling laughter.

As the guards held the grate aloft, Loren released it and helped Damaris drag Gregor clear. They pulled the captain up against the sewer wall, leaning him against it where he panted in pain.

"Gregor," said Damaris, her voice verging on panic. "Are you all right?"

"I will survive, my lady," said Gregor. "I have suffered worse. Though mayhap we will not go riding for a week or two."

It was a weak jest, and Damaris gave it a weak laugh. Then she placed a hand on Loren's arm and met her eyes with gratitude. "He would have died without you."

Loren ducked her head, uncomfortable. "I wish for no one to be killed."

Damaris squeezed her arm. But Loren saw Gregor's eyes, and there was no trace of gratitude within them. She dropped her gaze.

"The key," said Loren. "Give it to me. I will open the door."

"It waits in the lock," said Gregor. "One of my men will open it."

"No, Gregor, let her. She knew of this trap, and tried to save you. Let us not risk another of our own, when one is here who knows this place."

Loren felt a flush creep up her neck and into her cheeks. Damaris spoke as if she were some authority on traps—*like a master thief,* she thought. Gregor's look only darkened, though he did hand over the key.

She stood and went to the two guards who still held the gate. A third had joined them, and she had to squeeze between them to bend beneath the grate. She glanced back over their shoulder at the guards. "Hold it until I have opened the door. Then try pushing it back into the ceiling. It may lock in place."

One of the men nodded, and Loren edged forwards until she stood before the lock. The key waited for her there, so she tried turning it. It twisted easily. But the door did not open, and when Loren tried to bring the key back to rest, she heard a *snik* within. That, then, was the trap's trigger. But how to open the door?

"Gem!" In a few moments, Loren heard the pad of bare feet behind her. She glanced back to see him on the other side of the grate.

"What do you want?" said Gem, looking nervously up at the guards.

"This key will not open the door. I hoped the greatest pickpocket in Cabrus, a scholar and sometime medica, might have a notion."

"I have heard of locks that have more than one layer. Try pushing it in farther."

Loren frowned, but she turned back to the lock and pushed on the key. To her surprise, it slid another fingerbreadth into the lock. She twisted, and it turned back in the other direction. But still, the door did not open.

Loren almost withdrew the key again, but then she froze. Very, very carefully, she took her hand from the key and slowly backed away, sliding out from under the grate.

"What is wrong?" said Damaris. "Why did it not open?"

"I am not sure. But I think there may be another trap in place. Have your men lower the grate."

The guards looked at Damaris. She gave them a sharp nod. Slowly, they lowered the grate until it rested on the door again.

"Everyone out of the hallway," said Loren. "Help him."

The men moved to lift Gregor, but he waved them off. Slowly he rose to his feet, though Loren saw a fresh trickle of blood stream from the gash in his shoulder beneath the chain mail. A red streak marked the stone wall where he had rested. Everyone backed out of the hallway and around the corner, where Gregor sank back to the ground.

Auntie waited there for them, a vicious grin plastered across her face. It widened when she saw Gregor. "Found my door sharper than you thought, eh? It serves you right for snooping where you are not wanted."

"Silence her," said Damaris. One of the guards struck Auntie again, and Damaris sighed. "Not like that. Gag her." Someone produced a strip of cloth, and they tied it tight around her mouth.

Loren took a step back into the hallway, but Gem put his hand on her arm. "What do you think you are doing?" he said, voice small and scared. "You cannot go in there alone."

Loren removed his hand. "If a trap awaits, the fewer people in danger, the better."

"But not *you.* Let one of these men do it."

Loren glanced at them. "I am smaller, and nimbler. If anyone can avoid another surprise, it will be me. I dodged the first one already."

"Let me do it," said Gem. "I am smaller still."

Loren gave him a little smile. "Not only a great pickpocket, but brave into the bargain. Thank you for your offer, but no. I could not bear it if anything happened to you."

That held truth, but Loren dared not tell him the rest: that she wanted to be first in the room, to seize her dagger and escape before Damaris realized that Annis did not wait behind the door.

Gem let her go at last with a final doubtful look. Loren approached the door slowly, each step harder than the last. Fear gripped her tight enough to weaken her limbs. If she guessed right, that another trap waited the withdrawal of this key, she had no way of knowing its nature.

The key poked out, tarnished and dirty. She placed her fingers upon it with effort. First, she tried pushing. The key did not move. She tried returning it to center, but it would not do that either.

With a slow, measured breath, she tried withdrawing the key. It gave, and she heard a *snik.*

Loren danced away on the balls of her feet, turning and running low for the mouth of the hallway. She hit the stones at the end of the passage, sliding and nearly falling into the watery channel. But she came to a stop just in time and, after neither sound nor attack followed, turned to look down the hallway again.

Nothing. Nothing had happened to the door.

Auntie's wild, muffled laughter brayed around the gag in her mouth.

"What? What is it?" said Damaris.

Loren felt her cheeks burn. Something to distract and delay a would-be thief, but not another trap. Auntie had only led Loren to make a fool of herself. She could withstand embarrassment easier than a spike through her body, but she did not have to like it.

She rose quickly to her feet and dusted herself off. "Nothing. I thought I heard something, that is all. I do not desire to find another iron grate falling upon my head."

"Well if it is nothing, then open the door," said Damaris, irritation sounding in her voice.

"Of course."

She returned to the door. The key still protruded, mocking her. Its rusty surface reminded her of the rot from a dying tree. Clearly it had not been cleaned in some time.

She sighed and tried turning the key again. It did not move. She returned it to the first position and turned it the other way. Nothing happened, except that she heard the *snik* that would have released the iron grate, had it not already been hanging down from the ceiling. Loren removed the key and tried the handle. Nothing.

She tried everything she could think of: pushing the key to the second position before turning it the other way; trying both directions from the first position; inserting the key upside down, trying to find a third position. Each attempt seemed more hopeless than the last.

Loren cursed and nearly flung the key at the floor. She had missed some trick, and from what she had seen of Auntie's madness, the weremage would not tell them no matter how stringently Gregor's men put her to the question.

Then a thought struck her. She looked again at the key in her hand. She saw the rust, so thick it pitted and bubbled the metal. Some of the rust had rubbed off on her thumb.

A smile spread across her face.

She stalked to the sewer passage and went to Auntie. The weremage grinned through her gag, hazel eyes cruel beneath a shock of white hair.

"The key is like you," said Loren. "A false face. The mask that hides the truth, too eye-catching and obvious to be ignored."

Auntie's smile faltered.

"Hold her," said Loren. Then she knelt and reached for Auntie's boot.

Auntie screamed and kicked out, narrowly missing Loren's ear. Another guard stepped in and seized her legs, holding her powerless and almost suspended in midair. Auntie thrashed and screamed, but they were too many and too strong.

Loren seized the right boot and pulled it off. "It is the way you hold yourself," she said. "One foot out and pointed. That might mark you as a dancer in a troupe, but when you speak you always keep your right foot hidden behind the other, so that the person before you cannot see." She reached into the boot and withdrew a silver key. It gleamed bright in the torchlight, every surface sparkling clean, its edges worn from constant use.

Damaris smiled. "A clever girl you continue to prove yourself, Loren of the family Nelda."

"Stay back a moment more," said Loren. "More dangers may await."

"As you say," said Damaris. Her eyes roved Auntie, who nearly frothed at the mouth with the madness of her struggle. "But I think we have discovered the witch's last trick."

Loren nodded. Damaris could believe that, so long as she did not follow Loren to the door—or see what lay beyond it.

Loren went back and inserted the key. It turned easily, once and in the right direction, and the door swung open under her touch.

"Did it work?" called Damaris.

"Indeed," said Loren. "A moment more. I will inspect the room beyond and ensure it is safe. Gem, your hand, please."

The boy came scampering down the hallway. Loren seized the bottom of the grate and hoisted it a pace above the floor up. Iron screamed on rock. Once she had it up, she tossed her head at it. "Take this. It is heavy, but you can hold it just long enough for me to get under." She leaned in a bit closer. "And back out."

His eyes widened, and he nodded silently. His thin hands wrapped around the iron, and she saw his wiry muscles springing to life beneath his hands.

Loren dropped to the ground and slithered forwards. She must be quick. Gem could not hold the thing forever, and Damaris would soon grow suspicious. Once past the doorframe, Loren rose to her feet once again.

Only the faintest torchlight penetrated the gloom of the hidey hole, and Loren's eyes took a moment to adjust. When they did, they took in rows of shelves that stretched from floor to ceiling. They ran the rim of a room that stretched more than eight paces wide in all directions, a perfect circle. In the center a round table lay piled high with gold of all types—coins, goblets, platters and other finery, as well as many, many purses that sat fat and bulging. Conquests of Auntie's children, Loren presumed, for all their strings were cut and frayed.

She whines endlessly about feeding her children, and yet here she has enough to feed an army, thought Loren.

On the shelves lay a thousand and more treasures Loren could not comprehend. She saw weapons, helmets, haphazard pieces of armor and shields, glass phials stopped with cork and many other things she did not recognize. Dust caked many of them, but others gleamed fresh and clean.

But the shelves faded from her mind as she saw her dagger resting upon the center table.

All her mind focused upon it, and at the same time she remembered Gem behind her. Loren ran for the table and scooped it up, sliding it back into its sheath, which still waited upon her belt. For good measure, she took the biggest purse of coins she could find, with strings long enough to tie at her waist. Then she ran for the entrance and dove to the ground, sliding out and onto the floor of the hallway past a struggling, red-faced Gem. The boy let go once Loren was clear, and the grate went crashing down.

"What was that?" said Damaris.

"Nothing," said Loren. "The place is safe."

Guards filed in immediately, seizing the grate and swinging it up. They stretched towards the ceiling and pushed the grate into place, where Loren heard a deep *click*. The men removed their hands, and the gate remained, held firm by the trap's mechanism.

Loren reached the hallway's end. She wanted to run before anyone could react. But Damaris stood close by, and Auntie behind her.

"Is she there?" said Damaris, eyes wide and hopeful.

Even as Loren grasped for the right thing to say, the voice of a guard came from the hallway. "There is no sign of Annis, my lady!"

Suddenly Loren's throat was bone dry. But Damaris only turned back to Auntie. She reached up and yanked the gag down so that it hung around Auntie's neck. "Where is she? Where is my daughter?"

Loren reached out and took Gem's arm, gently and without a sound. She took one step back. After a moment's confusion, he nodded and followed suit.

"Who cares?" said Auntie. "Probably dead in some alley somewhere, and a blessing to the nine lands."

Damaris did not scream at her, did not cry out. Instead she reached into the sleeve of her dress, and when her hand came out it held a dagger. The blade sank into Auntie's side, between the ribs and under the arm. Auntie gasped and tried to scream, but it came out as a thin wheeze.

"You can use your magic to heal yourself," said Damaris, withdrawing the dagger. Her words held truth, for Loren saw the wound sealing itself already. "I will test the limits of that magic, weremage. Tell me where my daughter is."

Loren took another step back, this one quicker. Too quick, for it caught Gregor's eye. He stared at her. She saw realization begin to dawn in his eyes.

Auntie gasped again, and her voice returned. "I have not seen your daughter in days. And the last I did, she was running about with *that* one." She tossed her head over Damaris' shoulder.

The merchant turned slowly, eyes fixing on Loren's. Her mask of cool, icy calm melted slowly away, and in her eyes Loren saw a fury and a fire more terrible than she had ever seen in the face of her father.

Loren seized Gem's arm and spun him around. One of Damaris' guards blinked in confusion as they dodged around him, and together they fled into blackness.

THIRTY-FIVE

Gem led her to the first drainage hole they found.

"It looks tall," he said, breathless.

Loren ignored him, seized him under the arms, and flung him to the edge of the drainage hole. Once he crawled out, she leapt to seize it herself. But he had been right, and Loren had misjudged the distance. Her fingers could find no purchase on the stone.

"Come on!" cried Gem, reaching down for her.

Loren heard shouts down the sewer behind her. She turned back for a moment to see a cluster of torchlights dancing down the passageway towards her.

"No time! Run! Vanish! I will not let them catch me."

Without waiting for his reply, she dashed off down the passageway. Drainage holes lined the ceiling here, lighting her way, but they also let the guards see her easily. And the passage did not split in many directions, so she had no chance to lose them in a maze.

Still, Loren had grown up running, and the guards wore heavy armor. Soon she had gained enough of a lead that she thought she might risk climbing out, and tried it at the next hole that looked low enough. This time she judged the height correctly, and her fingers clutched easily at the stone. She hauled up and slid out, emerging into the bright daylight. Below her she heard the furious shouts of her pursuers. Even as she watched, a mail-gloved hand seized the drainage hole's edge.

She fled blindly down the street as the guard emerged behind her, giving chase with a shout. Soon, Loren heard more voices join him. As she rounded the next corner, she looked about desperately to determine her whereabouts. They were in the wealthier district for certain, but beyond that she did not know.

More heavy boots tramped the street behind her. Trying to get her bearings slowed her down. She needed time to form a plan but would not get it so long as they followed.

Two constables froze and stared at Loren in shock as she rounded another corner. She darted down an alley away from them. But the guardsmen behind her did not lose the trail.

The roofs, she thought. *I need the roofs.*

Finally she saw one, its edge hanging low with two crates against the wall beneath it. She vaulted up the crates and seized the shingles, pulling herself up. Finding her feet again, she ran along the slope to the next roof, leaping the gap to reach it.

In the open air, she felt her head clear. Not far off, she spotted the familiar sight of the constables' jail towering over the other buildings. That, at least, told Loren where she was. And just like that, a plan appeared. It was mad, but madness must serve when reason cannot. She found a path that cut left and led her towards the jail.

On the streets below, Loren saw Damaris' men running parallel to her course. They dogged her steps, running below her like hounds trying to bring an eagle to bay. But they could not catch her, and by a stroke of luck she led them to an alley with no outlet. The men halted with furious shouts and turned to trace back their steps. Soon their voices faded behind her.

The jail grew ever closer. Soon she was only a few streets away. But Loren did not have Gem's knowledge of the city, and suddenly she came to a roof that led nowhere. No other building stood near enough to reach by leap or miracle, and going back would only send her to Damaris' men.

She was two stories up. Edging to the roof, Loren looked down to see a merchant's sign hanging from the building's front, suspended by a strong beam. It reached two paces into the street, and was fixed to the building halfway to the ground.

Loren steeled her nerves, took a deep breath, and dropped off the roof's edge.

She aimed for the beam, and her aim held true. But she hit it too fast. The wood slammed into her chest like a mule's kick, and her breath left her in a *whoosh.* She tried to grip the wood, but flew too hard and fell the rest of the way to the street. Her right ankle twisted hard as she fell, ripping a scream from her throat. A pang of agony struck her shoulder where Auntie had cut her.

She had landed in a busy thoroughfare of a street, and many stared at her in shock. Thankfully she saw no constables. Loren fought to her feet, wincing as she tried to put weight on her ankle. It would not bear her for long. But the jail stood close, only a couple of buildings away.

Hobbling like a lame old man, Loren limped for the gap between two buildings. On the other side lay the street before the jail. She was almost there. She would make it. She hobbled faster and faster, until she whimpered with each step.

Behind her she heard a cry of alarm. Someone had alerted the constables—or Damaris' men. The sound of boots filled her ears again.

Loren reached the street. Almost she fell as she came out into the open again, but somehow she stayed upright. There stood the jail's front door, with two constables standing guard with halberds before it.

And finally the stars and sky smiled upon her, for she recognized in one of them the squat and bulky frame of Corin.

Both men stared at her in shock, but Corin's face looked a perfect picture of incredulity. They stood rooted as Loren stumped towards them and finally let her ankle give way. She collapsed to the ground in the very doorway of the jail, and as she rolled to her side she saw half a dozen of Damaris' men behind her.

Loren ignored them, looking up into Corin's worried eyes. "Justice," she wheezed. "I throw myself upon the mercy of the King's justice."

THIRTY-SIX

CORIN STOOPED TO SEIZE LOREN'S ARM, PULLING her to her feet. Loren winced as her weight came down upon her ankle.

"Give us that girl, constable," growled one of Damaris' guards. Loren recognized him as the one who had failed to break down the door in the sewers.

"Are you mad?" growled Corin, glaring at the man. "I am a constable of the king of Selvan. I obey his laws and those of the High King—not you."

"She is nothing to you," said the guard.

"Nothing?" said Corin. "I have chased this girl for leagues, through forests and across rivers, over mountains and under the moon. She has escaped me once. I am glad to have her in my grasp at last, where she may be put to the question."

Even knowing it for an act, Loren's stomach clenched. *Be calm,* she reminded herself. *He cannot reveal himself.*

The guard put a hand to his sword hilt. The others with him did the same. Corin and the other constable lifted their halberds from the ground. Loren felt the air grow thick with tension.

"I warn you one last time," said the guard. "If you do not give her over to us, my lady will ensure you regret it."

"Threats?" barked Corin. "Threats against the law? What is your name, fool? And best that you give me the name of your lady as well, though I can well guess it. Mayhap the both of you could profit from time in a cell."

He slammed the butt of his halberd twice against the door behind him. It swung open, and three more constables emerged, each of them armed with a sword and broad shield.

The guards hesitated. Slowly, they removed their hands from their weapons. The leader said, "If you think my lady will enter your jail over this, you vastly underestimate her." But some of the fight had gone from his voice.

"Begone," said Corin. "Justice will be served. Stay any longer, and you will dine from its bitter dish."

The guard did not answer, but turned and walked away, taking his companions with him.

"What was that all about?" asked one of the other constables.

"Nothing," said Corin gruffly. "Only a few fools with heads too big for their helmets. Take my watch, brother. I will escort this one to her cell myself."

Corin handed over his halberd, and one of the newcomers took his place beside the door. Another swung the door wide, and Corin escorted Loren within.

The jail's front room seemed oppressively squat and small. A small fireplace sat in the corner, but no flames burned there. Against the far wall was a desk, and behind it sat a fat man with a bushy beard. Red leather armor barely contained his ample frame. A large book with many pages rested before him, along with a quill and inkpot.

"Who is this, then?" asked the clerk.

"Loren is her name, of the family Nelda," said Corin. "The one that Bern named."

Bushy white eyebrows shot for the ceiling. "Indeed? He will be well pleased to see her, I wager. I will check her for weapons."

"I have it," snapped Corin. He ran his hands down Loren's sides. She felt his hand pass over the dagger, but he made no mention of it. Her two bags of coin he left also. But he reached into her boot and withdrew her hunting knife, tossing it to the clerk.

"That is all," said Corin.

"Very well," said the clerk, and he bent to write in his book.

Corin took her to the stairs. Once they had climbed the first flight, he paused on the steps, loosened his grip, and pulled Loren closer.

"I am sorry about your knife, but it would have looked suspicious otherwise," he said in an urgent whisper. "Why have you returned?"

"A matter of desperation, I fear. I was pursued, as you saw." Loren winced as her ankle nearly buckled beneath her. "Be gentle, if you please."

Corin frowned. "I fear you may have guessed poorly at the situation. I cannot sneak you out, not now at any rate. Too many have heard your description from Bern, and not twice can I pull the farce of being overcome. I must place you in a cell."

"I understand. I will think of something." She hoped that would prove true.

"We have no empty cells, I fear," Corin went on. "We took many boys this morning, young urchins all. Bern led many men on a raid—to find you, actually. Do you know aught of that?"

Loren felt panic grip her. "You must not put me with them," she hissed. "They will kill me on sight. Their mistress, Auntie, is mad with hate for me."

Corin drew back to look at her. "Stars and sky, girl. What is it about you that draws such trouble?"

"A special talent, I am sure. One I must learn to break, before it breaks me."

"Indeed. I will empty one cell into the others. They will not be comfortable, but they will not have much choice."

"Thank you, Constable Corin. I am in your debt once again."

"We are both in the debt of greater masters, and you know it," said Corin cryptically. Loren flushed. She wondered what would happen if the constable discovered she did not work for the masters he thought.

Corin led her to the second floor. The stairs ended upon a landing with a door and a single guard.

The guard nodded and opened the door without a word. Beyond, Loren saw a long aisle with iron cells lining either side. A foul smell wafted from the place, the stench of human refuse. Loren felt ill.

"Come," said Corin. "This one needs her own cage. A valuable catch, and not one we will risk with any other prisoner."

The guard nodded and followed them in, where the stink grew ten time worse. A long way down the aisle turned left, leading to still more cages.

In every cell sat children—swarms of them. Many were Auntie's fighters, but many more were her wide-eyed pickpockets. These sat silent in huddled groups in the cells' centers, eyes wide and frightened as they watched her pass. Loren's heart nearly broke. These wretched creatures looked lost without their mother, mad though she might be. Now they suffered in darkness and silence, surrounded by nothing but the smell of their own waste.

"What will happen to them?"

"They will be out by the morrow," said Corin gruffly. "Not that you need worry about them, wretch."

Loren wanted to kick herself. *I must not reveal the game,* she thought. *Corin is my only friend here. I cannot lose him.*

They came to a cell with six of the urchins. The guard who accompanied them pulled a great ring of keys from his belt, picked one, and opened the door. Like a flight of birds, the children scuttled against the back wall. But the constable proved surprisingly gentle, ushering them out the door one at a time and to other cells while Corin stood guard to keep the rest from escaping.

When the cell was empty, Corin pushed her inside and slammed the door shut. He dismissed the other guard with a nod of thanks, and the man retreated down the aisle. Corin leaned in towards the door one last time.

"Is there anything I can do?" he whispered. "Any message I may deliver to your masters—or to any other man?"

Loren thought quickly. Other than Corin, she had only one friend within the city. "Do you know a man named Jordel?"

Corin's eyes widened. "Of course. I might have known. What do you wish me to tell him?"

What is that supposed to mean? Loren ignored it, for now. "He stays in the Wyrmwing. Tell him what has happened."

"What should he do?"

"He will know." Loren said it partly because she thought it was true—if anyone would know what to do, Jordel might—but partly because she herself had no idea.

Corin gave a curt nod and went, leaving Loren alone under the stares of Auntie's fighters in the other cells. None took their eyes off her. Even when she determined to ignore them, Loren could feel the weight of their gaze upon her back.

To distract herself, she inspected her cell. In one corner lay a pallet of straw. Loren moved it away from the iron bars beside it, fearful of one of the boys in the next cell reaching in and strangling her as she slept.

A chamber pot sat in the corner, and from what Loren could smell, it had not been emptied in a while. The room's only other feature was a window barred by iron and set high in the wooden wall. Not too high for Loren, though—she could reach the bars easily by stretching upon her toes. But the bars proved well mounted and did not give when she tugged. She could see nothing but blue sky through them.

She needed an idea, but she was fresh out of them. Throwing herself upon Corin's mercy might yet prove to be a terrible mistake.

The weight of the morning's battle and the sewers with Auntie descended upon her all at once, and Loren felt bone-weary. She sat on the straw pallet—but she did not wish to lie down. Loren did not wish to sleep if she could help it.

Everything fell to uncomfortable silence. A breeze blew in through the window above, a small stream of air somewhat fresher than the latrine stink of the jail. It was a small thing, but it helped. Despite herself, Loren dozed, leaning back against the wall. She only snapped awake at the sound of the jail's door slamming shut.

Corin. Or, hoping against hope, Jordel. It seemed too soon, but then she did not know how late the hour had grown. She stood and peeked out the window, but the sky looked as blue as before.

Loren went to her cell door. But her heart sank when she saw those coming down the aisle, and she wanted to crawl into a hole where no one would ever find her.

Corin came, yes. But beside him walked Damaris, her fine green dress sweeping along the floorboards, two armed and armored guards at her back.

Loren retreated from the door, returning to sit against the wall and wrapping her arms around her knees. She tried not to look up as Damaris stopped before her.

"Greetings, Loren of the family Nelda."

Loren said nothing.

"There," said Corin. "You have seen that she is here, as I said. Now you may go. By rights, none but constables are allowed to enter here."

"And yet you have already read the mayor's letter, constable. I am a friend to the crown, and I am to be given every possible courtesy. Did those instructions read unclear to you? I certainly understood them."

Corin only glowered.

"I wish to speak to her alone," said Damaris.

"I will not open the door," said Corin. "She's meant for the King's justice. Not even your pretty letter can stop that."

"That will not be necessary," said Damaris. "Only leave me alone with her. Words will pass easily enough through the bars."

"I will not. Besides, you will not be alone. Look around you." He waved at the multitude of prisoners.

Damaris snapped him a sharp glance and might have said more, but the conversation halted at the sound of the heavy wooden door crashing open again. The heavy stomp of boots came fast and angry towards them. Loren glanced up, but could not see their source for a moment. When she finally did, she wished she had not; Bern came to the cell door, standing beside Corin and Damaris, a vein in his forehead pulsing with fury.

"Caught at last, little jay," he said. "And not too soon. I thought we had lost you, but then dung always finds its way to the chamber pot."

"Ah, another admirer," said Damaris lightly.

"And what are you doing here?" snarled Bern, ignoring Damaris and rounding on Corin. "I left no question downstairs. You are not to stand watch over this one."

Corin drew up to his full height, though that still left him nearly three hands shy of Bern's impressive stature. "I, too, pursued her across Selvan. I will not be denied my justice any more than you will yours."

"Aye, pursued her, and then let her go once we had her. Well, not again. Return to your post, constable."

"You do not outrank me," said Corin staunchly.

"Not yet."

"Gentlemen, mayhap these measurements could be taken elsewhere?" said Damaris. "As I have already told you, I must needs speak with the prisoner alone."

Corin turned his glare on her. "And I have told you, no one is to be left alone with the prisoner, mayor's letter or no."

But Bern's face grew sharp, his eyes suddenly squint and glinting. It frightened Loren in a way that even Auntie's chilling laughter had not. He peered into Loren's cell and licked his lips.

"You do not speak for the jail's master at arms, Constable Corin. If he has commanded that lady Damaris' wishes be carried out, then carry them out we shall."

Corin stared at him in disbelief. "You would allow this one to have her way? After the north gate?"

Bern's lip curled. "I would do my duty. Can you say the same? Obey the authority that binds you to your post."

Corin's face grew red. Almost Loren feared he would strike Bern; she knew he would be lost if he did. But Corin turned and stalked off down the aisle. Bern stayed only long enough to give Damaris a mocking half-bow. "Enjoy, my lady." Then he, too, walked away.

The heavy wooden door slammed shut behind him, leaving only Damaris and her guard. Loren, meanwhile, refused to look up, studying her knees with exacting interest.

"Stars and sky," said Damaris. "So many interruptions. Now, Loren. There are many words to be had."

"There is nothing I wish to say."

"Nothing you wish, I do not doubt. But you will tell me where Annis is, and will not enjoy the consequences if you refuse."

Loren shrugged. "The truth, then?"

"Of course."

At last Loren raised her eyes to Damaris'. "I do not know. She ran from me when the constables took me the first time, and I have not seen her since."

Damaris stood silent for a moment. Loren could not read her eyes. Then the merchant sighed and shook her head.

"A brave attempt. You are gifted in the art of deceit, and if I did not know better I would take your words for truth. But the weremage gave lie to your words. She saw the two of you together in the sewers not two days ago."

"She is lying," Loren insisted. "I have searched for Annis since we separated."

"She did not lie," said Damaris. "Would you like to know how I can be so sure?"

Loren did not, and remained silent. She did not think she would like the answer.

Damaris reached into her cloak and withdrew a rope. No, not a rope, Loren saw. For as she pulled it from the pocket, the thing moved. Shiny cream scales shone in the daylight pouring through the window. The end twitched as it hung from Damaris' fingers. The top had a brown hood drawn around it, tied tight with leather.

Loren's heart stopped. "What is that?"

"This is a viper," said Damaris, "of a particularly unique breed and temperament. It is not . . . a kind-hearted beast. Its teeth seek flesh most eagerly. But what makes it particularly useful is its venom. Aside from being most fatal—which it is—in the painful moments before death, the victim's mind grows most pliable. It is quite a useful creature for extracting the truth."

Loren pushed herself harder against the wall, trying to sink into the wood. "Do not do this, Damaris."

"I do not wish to," said Damaris, and Loren heard genuine regret in her voice. "I do respect you, cherish you, even. You will never know how high you stand in my estimation, Loren of the family Nelda. But blood comes before all else, as the saying goes."

With a quick swipe, Damaris removed the leather hood to reveal a pointed head, spiked ridges running along both sides. The serpent hissed, but Damaris held it behind the neck so that it could not move. With a flick of her wrist, the merchant flung it between the iron bars to land upon the floor of Loren's cell.

THIRTY-SEVEN

LOREN CRIED OUT AND LEAPT TO HER FEET. THE snake's head snapped to the movement. It reared up, two handbreadths of its length rising from the floor, and swayed back and forth as it studied her.

"Stop, Damaris!" cried Loren. "I will tell you everything."

"Do so then," said Damaris. "And quickly. The serpent, I fear, is impatient."

The snake edged closer. A thin, milky film of skin passed across its eyes, and then retreated.

"Annis hides in the pauper's district," said Loren, the words rushing forth. "She poses as a beggar, wrapped in lepers' rags. She waits for me to find her so that we might escape the city."

"While you searched for your dagger, I suppose?" Damaris' mouth twisted in amusement. "A risky endeavor. One might say foolish."

"She said the same." Loren shoved her boots against the wooden wall and edged towards the cell's corner. It only bought her half a pace, and the snake edged closer at her motion. "And I see now I should have listened. But it is the truth, I swear it!"

"That is where we saw her," said Damaris. "But the paupers' district is large. You must be more specific, girl. Accuracy in all things."

Loren thought quickly. She must give them something, anything to earn more time. "There is a tavern! *The Princess Pig.* She waits in the alleys around it."

"How long will she wait?" said Damaris.

"As long as she must. She said she would remain until I returned."

Damaris turned to the guard beside her. "Very well. We must go there at once and find her, before she thinks to vanish again. My daughter is wise, and will know the foolishness of waiting for too long." With a whirl of her skirts, she turned to go.

"Wait!" cried Loren. "The snake!"

Damaris turned back, eyes frigid above a smirk. "Ah yes. My pet. But I have many to replace it, and will account it no great loss. And besides, my doomed dear, how did you think I would even recall it? Can *you* speak with a serpent's tongue?"

She stalked to the doorway and left, her guard close on her heels.

Loren screamed for help. None came, and the sound only made the snake rear up again, flicking its tongue out at her. In the cells to either side, Auntie's children studied Loren with terrified eyes, all of them edging as far away from her cell as they could.

Loren remembered her dagger, and in a flash the blade leapt into her hand. She brandished the weapon at the snake, now scarcely more than a pace away. She might as well have thrust it into the face of a river for all the notice she earned.

She could try to stab it, but if she missed it would strike her for certain. There was nothing to stand on except the chamber pot, and the rim was still within reach of the viper's fangs. If only she had a table, that would be something.

Her eyes found the bars of her window high on the wall. Reaching them would mean passing closer to the snake, but her options seemed limited.

Ever so slowly, she edged along the wall. The snake turned its head to follow, but it did not advance. Its tongue licked out, smelling the air, and its spiny ridges shifted.

Loren took another step. And another. Only two paces more now.

She sensed the snake's motion before it struck, and leapt high. Its teeth missed her by a hair's breadth, and she jumped into the air to seize the bars of the window. Quickly she scrambled up, pulling herself to curl in a ball against the wood. In a moment she hung a pace and a half from the ground, her boots planted against the wood while she held the rest of her body still higher.

The snake coiled beneath her. Its head rose into the air, mouth open, a thin hiss issuing from its throat. It stretched and snapped, but came short each time. Loren's arms burned with the effort of holding herself up, her body so tense she could feel her legs beginning to cramp. But at least she was safe. No power on earth would bring her down from the window, not even her exhaustion. The guards must come eventually, if for no other reason than to give the prisoners food and water. She would hang from the window as long as she must.

The snake coiled on the ground again, milky film blinking across its eyes. Loren watched it, wondering if she might drop her dagger point-first upon its head.

Then, in the next cell, a child's foot shifted across the floorboards.

The serpent's head snapped to the right.

"No!" cried Loren. "Here! Up here!"

The snake ignored her. Slowly it uncoiled, its head sliding across the wood towards the bars at the side of her cage, the rest of its body slithering after. The children cowered in fear, and with every movement of their feet upon the floor the viper seemed to move faster.

"Stop!" said Loren. "Stop moving! It can feel you!"

The children did not take their eyes from the snake, nor did they stop pushing themselves back, trying without hope to slip back through the bars and into the next cell. The snake was only a pace away.

Loren swallowed hard, and then dropped from the window, drawing her dagger as she thudded to the floor. The serpent stopped, head snapping back towards her. With a cry, Loren leapt at it, swiping madly in a wide arc with her dagger. Its head darted back, the blade missing by fingers. Fangs closed on the empty space where Loren's hand had been. She fell back a step, and the serpent snapped again. She swung the dagger madly back and forth, too afraid to get within striking distance but desperate to kill the thing.

One more step she took, and the viper paused. It settled back down, only the end of its neck still suspended in the air. Then its head pivoted again to the children in the next cell. Silent and swift as wind whispering through tree branches, it spun and darted for the bars.

Loren cried out and leapt. Her dagger plunged into its body, impaling it to the wooden floor. The viper writhed in agony, but in its flailing the head whipped around and the mouth shot open. Fangs sank into the flesh between Loren's thumb and forefinger, and she felt a burning as venom seeped into her blood.

She screamed, withdrew the dagger, and stabbed again. The blade pierced the serpent's head. Its tail spasmed, milky film blinked across the eyes a final time, and then it fell still.

THIRTY-EIGHT

THE BURNING IN LOREN'S HAND SPREAD SLOWLY—more slowly than she feared, and yet far more quickly than she wished. She screamed for the guards again, but no help came. With the serpent dead, the children sat silent and still, staring at her.

Surrounded again, and yet alone as ever, thought Loren.

She got to her feet and felt herself sway upon them. The poison. It had to be working upon her already. She silently thanked the stars that Damaris had left—were the merchant still here, Loren would no doubt tell her where Annis and Xain waited beyond the walls of the city.

Not that it mattered now, not to Loren at any rate. Here in this cell she would die, victim of a serpent's bite. Mayhap a fitting end for a great thief who built her home in the shadows. But she was not a great thief, not yet. Nightblade would be nothing but a dream in her mind, extinguished along with her life.

The idea held no justice. But then, none of this did, nor had Loren's life ever done so. Justice would not have given her to hateful parents in a tiny village, nor would it have seen her beaten almost every day of her life. Justice would not have offered her an escape from that life only to hound her with constables, ruthless merchants, and a mad weremage, all hungry for her blood. Justice, Loren saw now, did not come of its own accord. It found the weak only when the strong deigned to allow it.

Her thoughts grew hazy. She went to the bars of her cell and shook them. They did not budge in their iron fittings, and the burning in her blood grew worse.

She retreated to the corner of her cell and sank onto her pallet, eyes fixed upon the cream-colored serpent that lay dead on the floor, her blood still staining its fangs.

Shadow surrounded her in the crook between wall and floor, and Loren thought of Mennet in the burning house. He had knelt and prayed to the shadows, and they had come for him. They had wrapped him up, taking him for their own.

Mayhap they would do the same for Loren now. She rose to her knees, placing her forehead to the floor and splaying her hands out before her. The floor stank, but she ignored it.

Shadows that wreathe the world in darkness, thought Loren. *I beseech you, hear my plea. Save your daughter. Rescue me from prison and poison. Save me that I might serve you all the rest of my days.*

Nothing happened. Loren repeated the prayer, and then again. But the burning climbed to her elbow, and the words came more and more difficult to her mind. And all the while, dust motes danced in the beams of sun through the window.

"Shadows that wreathe the world in darkness. I beseech you, hear my . . . hear me and save me, your daughter . . ."

Loren stopped, realizing she had said the words out loud. All throughout the jail, the children stared at her. Even the older boys fixed her with looks of incredulity.

Save your daughter, thought Loren. *Save me, Father. No, Father never saved me. He only hurt me. Why would I want his help?*

I do not want his help. I ask only the shadows for succor.

She seemed to be talking to herself, and it occurred to Loren that she might be going mad. Had Mennet ever gone mad? She did not recall that story. Only that he prayed to the shadows.

And. And, and, and. And what?

She knew another tale. No, she knew a thousand tales of Mennet, every word about the thief that Bracken had ever divulged after her relentless hounding. But she always wanted more.

Why was she thinking of Bracken's stories? Ah, for Mennet. Mennet had many tales, and Loren knew them all. But why did she think they mattered? The shadow story did not matter. She had prayed. The shadows had ignored her. Why would she keep thinking of them?

No. Not the shadow story. Another. One she told Annis by firelight, in the darkness upon the road.

She straightened from the floor and looked again at the bars of her window.

Slowly she pushed herself to her feet, reaching up to clutch the bars. She shook them, but they did not move.

Loren looked down at her tunic. Idly, her mind wandering, her fingers found and played with its fabric. So rough. So coarse. She had not taken it off in days, not since she left the Birchwood. It stank.

She shook her head and forced her thoughts to clarity. The fabric was rough, too lightly woven. It would not do. She pulled at the cloak that still hung around her shoulders—Damaris' gift. Thick, like velvet, and strong. It hardly stretched as she pulled at it.

It would serve, or she hoped it would.

Loren removed the cloak. Almost she reached up and tied it around the bars, but then she stopped.

Not cloth alone. There had been another part to the story, the part she had withheld from Annis. Mennet had asked the Wizard King for water, and had used it to wet the cloth. That had lent the fabric strength, letting it conquer iron.

Loren looked towards the front of the jail, to the thick wooden door that led out. The guards had ignored her cries before—she would not get water from them. The chamber pot held only a thick sludge that made her retch. She backed away quickly, hand over her mouth. Her heel struck the head of the dead snake, and its body twitched.

She dropped the cloak on the floor against the wall, and then undid the drawstring of her pants and squatted. At first she feared she would not have enough, but finally her urine soaked the fabric in a thick stream. All around her, she saw that the children had some level of decency—their eyes had left her as she did her business.

Loren stood and retied her pants, nearly vomiting as she rolled the cloak into a short rope. But soon it was done, and she stretched up. Without too much trouble, she tied the cloak around the middle of the window's center bars. She pulled the knot, but not too tight. She would need some slack for what came next.

Her boots had wooden soles. Loren removed one. The sole she stuck through the cloth, and then gave it a half twist. The cloth wrapped tight around the boot, crushing the leather against it. She turned again. The cloth tightened further, and she saw—she *felt* it stretch.

Do not break, she prayed. *Please, do not break.*

Again and again she turned. With every movement, her head spun harder. She could not keep her feet, and soon was hanging from the wooden sole, letting it support some of her weight. But she did not stop turning.

She heard the cranky, groaning noise of iron bending.

Loren looked up to see the cloth had done its job. The bars bent in towards each other. To their left now showed a small gap, one she might slip through.

She withdrew her boot, slipping it back onto her bare foot before painstakingly untying the cloak. For a moment she had thought that she might leave it, but she could not bring herself to do so. It was too fine a gift, even now, stretched and reeking of piss.

She glanced over her shoulder one final time and found nearly every eye in the jail upon her. Silent they watched, the children and the boy fighters, and among the older children she saw no more hatred; instead they showed only awe.

"No cell may hold Nightblade," she said. Her voice came weak and cracked.

Loren leapt and grabbed the iron bars, hauling herself up. Her head was a tight fit, but it slipped through, and as her hair blew in open air she knew she would be free. One arm came through at a time, and then she hung suspended against the outside of the building.

Below lay the alley behind the jail. No constables patrolled the cobblestones below. She was only three paces up—an easy drop—so she hung as low as she could and let go. The cobblestones came hard and fast, and Loren tumbled prone upon them. The street felt deliciously cool against her face, and she let herself enjoy it for a moment. Almost she felt herself drifting off, until she remembered where she was. Then she leapt to her feet—head spinning mightily from the effort—and fled down the alley, into the darkness and the shadow that had turned a blind eye to her prayers.

THIRTY-NINE

LOREN STUMBLED FROM CORNER TO CORNER, ALLEY to alley, hiding from every flash of red leather armor. She missed one constable and walked right by him, but he did not seem to recognize her, and only recoiled from the smell of her cloak.

She could think only of Jordel. If any man in Cabrus could save her now, it had to be him. So she directed her feet to where she thought the Wyrmwing Inn might be, hoping the snake's poison had not dimmed her sense of direction.

All her arm burned now, and the sensation creeped into her chest. Worse, it moved faster now that she walked the streets. She knew something of poison, and knew that it crept through the body with blood. Now that she moved, her blood would move more quickly—and so would the poison.

It seemed a week before she spotted the Wyrmwing over buildings far away. Her steps quickened, and almost she burst into the street to rush headlong for the inn. Loren had to force herself to remain cautious, keeping an eye for constables.

At long, long last, she reached the square before the inn. Looking around, she could see neither the King's law nor any sign of men in bright mail. She took a moment to compose herself, stretching to her full height and steadying her steps. Then, as she had the day before—had it really been so recently?—she strode straight to the front doors. As before the guards started to see her. This time, though, she paused about three paces away, far enough that they would not smell her reek.

"I am here to see Jordel. I assume he has told you of my coming?"

What? she thought. She had meant to ask for Damaris, who the guards had already seen her converse with. Where had these words come from?

With a shudder she remembered Damaris' words. The venom had softened her mind, compelling her towards the truth when she would rather lie. She must not let that happen again. Without a tongue for deception, she stood no chance.

The guards exchanged a look. "No, my lady, but I will deliver your summons to his room—though I do not know if he is within."

"That will not be necessary," said Loren, forcing her mouth to produce the words. "He will not want to be disturbed." With that she set forth, brushing past the guards and into the common room. That would give them her smell, but she hoped it would be too late. And indeed, they did not follow her as she passed into the room and strode for the bar, behind which a serving maid stared at her incredulously.

Maintaining her composure took too much effort, and Loren slumped to the side as she eased between tables. Her hands came down hard on the back of a chair, her wrist cracking against the wood and making her wince. She clutched it with her other hand, thoughts swimming.

The burning.

The burning.

It had spread to her gut now, on some roundabout route to her heart that Loren did not understand.

"Are you all right, miss?" asked the barmaid. Loren feared she might call for the guards.

"Fine. Only a bit too much wine, that is all."

The maid relaxed. Drunkenness, it seemed was a familiar sight here, and one she could deal with easily. "And so early in the day. Fancy a bit more? We have a lovely brandywine I am partial to."

"No." Loren gripped the back of the chair. "I am here to see . . ."

Her mind swam. Why had she come here? She could not for the life of her remember.

The burning.

The burning.

Loren turned away from the maid and stumbled towards the back of the inn. Damaris. She had last come here with Damaris. She remembered the way. The steps were in the back.

"Are you all right, miss?" the maid called out, her words fired at Loren's retreating back. "Need help to your room?"

Loren waved her off.

The stairs seemed an insurmountable obstacle, a mountain stretching for the heavens. She climbed them anyway. Every step came like dragging an anvil up a tree's branches. The well-carved bannister, which she had found so smooth before, felt like a cat's tongue under her hand.

She reached the second floor.

Then, an eternity later, the third.

Finally she came upon the fourth landing, where she recognized the hallway leading to Damaris' room.

Where was Damaris? Guards stood at the end of the hallway, staring. Loren realized she must look a sight. She put a hand against her cheek before pulling it away to see. Her fingers were a ghostly white, like when they had found young Alden's body in the river in the Birchwood. The Birchwood, her home. This was not the Birchwood. What was this place?

Loren fought for clarity, and it came crashing upon her. The Wyrmwing. She stood before Damaris' room, with two guards looking nervous as their hands edged towards their weapons. But they had not attacked or taken her. That meant they did not know she had betrayed Damaris, which told her that no messenger had come here today, not since the dawn's attack on Auntie's hideout.

That clarity stood out as a rock in Loren's mind, and she clutched it like a drowning sailor. She stood a bit straighter and turned her voice harsh.

"Why are you still here? Did the messenger not come to retrieve you?"

The guards looked at Loren like a ghost. "What messenger?" mumbled one of them.

Loren gave an exasperated sigh. "There was a fight. Your captain was grievously wounded, and your lady's daughter stolen from the city. Even now she lies beyond the walls of Cabrus, and Damaris musters all her men to go and search. You should be among them."

The guards traded an uneasy look. "No one told us of this."

"I am telling you now. In the paupers' district there lies a tavern. *The Princess Pig.* You will find your lady there, but I do not suggest you tarry."

Again they looked at each other. "Who will stand our posts? If our lady finds her room unguarded . . ."

"If her daughter remains unfound, and Damaris takes it into her head that two more men in the party might have swayed matters, your punishment for leaving this place will seem paltry. If it will make you feel better, lock the door after I have retrieved what she sent me for."

"And what is that?" said one of the guards. Loren did not like how his eyes grew narrow and mean.

"That is the lady's business, and not yours. Let me pass, and then we may all three be on our way."

Loren drew herself up to her full height, but it left her woozy. Her mind began to drift again, and she knew she could not maintain this for long. Wisdom would dictate that she turn and flee, and let the guards stay for all she cared. But with clarity had come an idea, a sudden and certain knowledge. Just as Loren could not have left Cabrus without her dagger, she could not leave the Wyrmwing without taking care of one last piece of business within Damaris' room.

But her words had no effect on the guards. If anything, they grew more resolute as they stood their ground.

"If that were the case, Damaris would have sent another guard to tell us, or the captain," said the one with the mean eyes. "Not you."

Loren growled. "I have told you, Gregor is wounded. The trap fell on him as he tried to open the door."

The guards blinked. "What trap?"

Loren shook her head. Everything grew fuzzy.

"Nothing. I am injured, and the day grows ever longer. Stand aside and allow me within, and be quick about it, before you suffer Damaris' wrath. She will be most displeased with me. With you, I mean."

Now the both of them looked at her like a madwoman, and they drew closer together in front of the door.

She had no time for this. She must play one last gamble, and if it failed she would turn and flee as she knew she should. She found the last bit of focus within her and turned it to words. "Listen, you witless cretins. Do you know what this is?"

With a flourish she reached into her cloak and drew the dagger. The meaner guard placed a hand on his sword hilt and half-drew it, but the other's eyes widened when he saw the blade's designs. His gloved hand restrained his companion's fingers on the sword.

Loren focused on him. "Yes. You know it, if your dimwitted friend does not. Tell him what it means."

"Nicas, stay your hand," said the guard.

"Why? For some shiny knife?"

"It is not only that. Her words carry power."

Nicas drew back, pressing himself against the door. "A wizard?"

The other shook his head. "No. You must trust me. If this girl says that the lady has called upon us, we may believe her."

Loren let a small smile play across her lips. "One of you, at least, has some wisdom. Thank you for your support, and for knowing how displeased my . . . *masters* . . . would be by any delay. What is your name?"

The man shuddered as she said the word *masters*, and when Loren finished speaking he bowed so low that Loren thought his forehead might slap the floor. "Solon, if it please my lady."

"It gives me neither pleasure nor displeasure. But I will remember it. Be off with you, then. Already Damaris will be impatient with your delay."

Nicas still looked uncertain, as well he might, but he let Solon lead him away. Loren watched them go until they vanished around the first bend in the stairs. Then she looked down at her dagger, studying the lines etched across its shining steel.

One day it would be a problem. Today it proved an answer.

What was I doing?

The burning in her stomach intensified, climbing its way towards her heart. She could feel it in her chest now, singeing her insides with every breath.

She looked around at the hallway for a long moment before she focused again on Damaris' door. Of course. She had come to the Wyrmwing to find Damaris.

Or had she? It seemed she had come for another purpose, one she could no longer recall.

No matter.

She pushed the door open, taken aback again at the room's size. Her eyes roved across it. Empty. Where was Damaris? Had not Loren come to find her?

Her gaze fell upon the chest sitting near the bedroom door, and she remembered her purpose.

She picked up an iron fork that lay on a nearby table, and by sticking it in the doorjamb she bent off all but one of the tines. The final tine she twisted before approaching the chest.

It took her a long while to fiddle with the lock—much longer than it should have. Her head swam. The sunlight pouring through the window began to hurt behind her eyes, so she closed them. By feeling alone, she probed for the tumblers, tripping them one at a time.

The lock opened with a solid *thunk.* Loren seized the lid and lifted.

A mountain of brown cloth bundles met her eyes.

Damaris' secret cargo. The black crystals she hid from all eyes but those she trusted most. Stolen away outside the gates of Cabrus, and brought here to wait until she made ready to move them again.

Loren scooped them all out and scattered them across the room. She flung them into the walls and slid them along the floor. Black crystals spilled everywhere, some cracking open against the stone tile. Where they broke, they turned into a fine dust.

She threw a few into the hallway outside for good measure, ensuring they spread across the whole floor. Some even tumbled down the staircase at the far end. Finally, Loren went to the wide balcony and threw three bundles into the street. She heard a cry of alarm as one of them nearly struck a passerby, and then silence.

One bundle remained. Loren tucked it between her belt and her pants, and then she slipped out the door. She made sure to swing it shut behind her—it would not do to be a rude guest, after all.

The stairs echoed with hollow thuds under her boots, and many crystals crunched to dust beneath them. Her business was done. She must leave quickly and . . . and what? Where would she go now? Where could she go? The poison spread deeper with every passing moment. She passed the third floor and reached the second.

"Loren?"

The voice sounded a dozen leagues away. It sounded as though the speaker whispered in her ear. It was gone in a moment, and it echoed in her head for eternity. Her eyes roved, her head swinging around like a drunk.

A man stood four steps below, looking up in astonishment. Loren had to stare at him a while before she remembered his face.

"Jordel," she said in a soft whisper. "I forgot that I came here for you."

Jordel's lips split in a soft smile. "It is as I have told you, often and again. We are bound by more than common purpose."

Loren's head scrunched tight. "Oh, still your tongue, you great buffoon."

Then she collapsed down the stairs.

Jordel caught her after only two bounces, scooping her into his strong arms. Loren cradled against him like a child. She tried to wrap her arms around his neck, but they would not move. His nose wrinkled at the smell of her cloak, but he made no mention of it.

"Loren, what has happened?" said Jordel, and for the first time his voice did not sound soothing.

"A snake bite," said Loren. Had she spoken? She could not be sure. That voice sounded too small, too tiny. "It has spread to my heart. Deadly, Damaris told me."

"I must get you to the apothecary."

Jordel took the stairs two at a time and ran through the common room, ignoring the barmaid who asked if he wanted anything to drink.

Outside the Wyrmwing, a cluster of people had gathered. All of them studied the black crystals scattered across the ground, and many threw doubtful glances at the inn. Jordel ignored them, pressing through the crowd into open air.

"Forgive me," he said, and before Loren could ask him what for he pulled her hood down over her face. The urine had grown pungent, and Loren thought that she ought to drink more water.

"Did you have aught to do with the magestones?" he whispered.

"What? Oh, the crystals. They are not mine."

Jordel shook his head. "Never you mind. I should not have asked you to speak. Remain silent and still until we reach the apothecary."

"I will pay him myself. I have many coins. *Many* coins. I am a thief. I stole them."

Darkness descended, and Loren knew nothing more.

FORTY

BLINDING LIGHT PIERCED LOREN'S EYES, AND SHE rolled away from it with a groan. Her head, her body, every part of her hurt. Only stillness kept the pain from lancing back through her, so still she remained.

"You are awake."

Loren recognized the voice a moment before Gem rolled her on her back and cool water splashed against her lips. It spread across her face, and she pushed him away with a cough.

"Well, open your mouth then," grumbled Gem. Loren obeyed, and he poured enough water into her throat to choke her.

"Leave *off,* Gem!" cried Loren. Pushing him away hurt, but it seemed better than drowning.

Gem sniffed as he backed away. "I should fetch the apothecary in any case. A moment."

He vanished through the door.

Loren groaned again and slumped back onto the straw pallet. A short while passed before she could keep her eyes open long enough to study the room.

The blinding light that had woken her proved to be only the dim glow of a torch set in the wall. Its fire licked and danced against a ceiling of red stone. That probably meant she was underground, in a cellar or basement. And indeed, she could see many barrels stacked in the dark corners of the room, no doubt filled with the noxious chemicals apothecaries always kept on hand. Above the barrels hung many racks of herbs bound with string. Their odor filled the air, burning Loren's nose.

Gem returned with the apothecary, a surprisingly young man in the white robes of his trade. He came to her, shaved pate glinting in the torchlight, and without a word seized her face, pulling her eyelids wide open.

"Get off!" cried Loren. But she proved too weak to push him away, and the apothecary went on undeterred. She suffered his ministrations in a sullen silence. After her eyes he held open her mouth, looking over her teeth and gums with a concerned expression. Then he took her hands and inspected, of all things, her fingernails. Finally he sat back with a clucking of his tongue.

"None the worse for wear," he said easily.

"My head disagrees."

"As one should expect when tangling with clouded vipers," said the apothecary. "Or such is what I gathered from your tale of the snake's looks, though you half raved at the time. Jordel told me how you came to your disagreement with one, and if words may come freely, it is an unbelievable tale. As a consequence, I do not believe it. But it is none of my business, of course."

Loren eyed the man beneath hooded lids, wondering if Jordel had told the truth or some fiction—and which would be harder to believe.

"Where is he, anyway? Jordel, I mean."

"Upstairs, finishing breakfast. He will be down presently. I am Alin, by the by. I am just as honored to meet you as you seem to be to meet me."

Breakfast. Loren panicked, looking at Gem. "What day is it?"

"The day after your mad scheme," said Gem, glaring at her. "Which, I will say again, was a fool's notion, as is only further proven by each new bit of your foolery."

The day after. That meant tonight, Xain and Annis would ride on. Without her or Gem.

"We must go," said Loren, struggling up.

The apothecary pushed her down. "That is as may be, but take it slow. At least until you have spoken to Jordel and given your body some time to realize it has woken."

Loren settled back. She could wait a short while, she supposed. "Thank you, then. I imagine I owe you my life."

"Who, me?" Alin snorted. "Hardly. I only kept you comfortable and helped you wake a bit earlier, and with a little less pain. You would have slept for a week without me, but not forever."

Loren stared at him without understanding. "But . . . the snake bite."

"A clouded viper? They are as fatal as a garden snake. Do muddle the mind a bit, though. Powerful hard to tell a lie when their venom is in your blood. What I do not understand is how one found its way into Cabrus."

It would seem Jordel had not told the truth, then, or at least not all of it. Then again, he did not even know all the truth of her tale. Loren only half-remembered it herself.

With that thought, a bit more came back to her. The black crystals—magestones, she supposed. And the dagger. Her hand flew to her belt.

It was missing.

Eyes wide with panic, she looked to Gem.

The boy stood forth, sniffing importantly. "Good sir apothecary, might I have a word alone with my compatriot? Certain matters of great import must be discussed."

Alin glanced over his shoulder. "Oh aye, the children have many important matters, I am sure." He rose to his feet and made for the door. "Very well then, only I will say that Jordel will be down in a moment or two. Then, as I have told him often, I would be quit of you sooner than later, if given my way."

As soon as the door closed behind the apothecary, Gem knelt beside Loren, lowered his voice to a whisper, and said, "I have it." He reached under his shirt and withdrew the dagger, safe in its leather sheath. "I nicked it once their backs were turned, after I found Jordel walking with you through the streets and joined him."

She sighed with relief. "Why would you take it?" she grumbled. "Give it here."

Gem put it in her hands. She stuffed it beneath herself on the straw pallet.

"When you got here, you raved like a mad girl. You curled yourself around it and would not open your cloak, raving that Auntie would take it away again. So once they stepped out of the room to fetch you water and blankets, I whispered that I would hold it. That was the only way you would calm enough for them to help you."

"I thank you, then. Especially since you returned it in the end."

"Of course." Gem's face lit with a small, proud smile. "You are my new mistress, now. One never steals from one's mistress."

Loren scowled, but she reached out and tousled his hair. "I am no one's mistress. I work alone, with neither partner nor lackey."

"Oh, of course. And I will work alone with you."

She grinned. Then the door opened, and Gem backed away as Jordel swept into the room.

One look at his face told Loren something was wrong. Jordel's light blue eyes were clouded over with concern, and mayhap even anger. He looked at Loren as though he had never seen her before, and his whole body fairly shook.

"What?" said Loren. "What is wrong?"

Jordel glanced at Gem. "Leave us."

His voice radiated command, but even so, Gem drew up and placed his hands on his hips.

"I am no lackey of yours." He thrust a finger at Loren. "I am a lackey of hers."

"Gem, go." Loren did not know what troubled Jordel, but she yearned to find out.

The boy looked at her a brief moment, scowling, but he left. Jordel closed the door behind him, and then went to sit at Loren's side, legs crossed over one another and hands upon his knees.

"Loren of the family Nelda," he said, and it sounded like an intonation. "I must ask you something of the utmost importance—and it is of the same importance that you answer me true."

Loren shrank back a bit, looking at him in confusion. "Jordel, I ask again—what is wrong?"

"Where did you get your dagger?"

Loren balked, taken unawares. "Why?"

"Do not hedge with me. Give me your answer."

His hands balled into tight fists. For a moment, Loren feared him, seeing again her father before he struck. At that thought, resolve fled her.

"I stole it," she said. "When I left home. My parents held it close by for many years. I saw it once as a small child, and when I determined to run away from home I decided to take it with me."

Jordel's hands relaxed. "You swear this is the truth? You did not take it from any other? From a traveler upon the road, or from a corpse?"

"No!" cried Loren, aghast. "I am no grave robber!"

Jordel's head bowed. "That is good. That is most excellent, for both of us. And at last, at long last, I truly understand what has brought you and I together so often in so short a span of time."

"What? What is this thing? Some few seem to recognize it, and always they fear it, and fear me as well. Why, Jordel?"

His eyes flashed. "Well they might. But the story is far too long to tell now. We shall discuss it upon the road."

"The road?" said Loren. The conversation jumped and took so many turns that she knew not where to go next. "What road?"

"You aim to leave the city, do you not? I will come with you. It is now more urgent than ever that I find Xain and keep the two of you together—and safe."

"Safe? Safe from what?"

He leaned in close and answered with yet another question. "Loren, you asked once why constables would bow to me in the street. And when first we met, you did not remark upon my cloak except with a passing glance. Tell me: does this mean aught to you?"

He reached for the clasp that held his cloak around his throat. Loren stared again at the strange symbol: three rods of silver wrapped by a band, and mounted on silver wings that stretched wide.

"It has no meaning to me."

"It is the symbol of the Mystics, who count me among their number. Now, do you understand any better?"

Loren blinked and shook her head. "No. Why should I?"

Jordel stared at her, incredulous. "Stars and sky, from what rocky hole have you climbed, girl?" He shook his head and made to rise. "Never mind. It will have to be another tale for the road. One upon which I fear we will wander for a long time together, Loren of the family Nelda."

"Hold, please." Loren grabbed his wrist and kept him seated. His brows drew together. "Some questions may wait for the road, but some may not.

Alin told me the snake bite would not have killed me."

"No," said Jordel, and his voice grew soothing again. "In your raving you told him the shape of the snake. A clouded viper, I believe he called it. Alin said its poison disorients greatly, but does not kill."

"Damaris told me I would die."

"She lied," said Jordel with a shrug.

"But why?"

"I do not know."

Loren stared, but nothing else came. "That is all? You do not know?"

"What do you wish me to say, Loren? It seems Damaris did not wish to kill you, or mayhap she meant to do so later. She will have to wait awhile."

Loren blinked. "Why do you say that?"

Jordel cocked his head with a small smile. "Damaris has been run from town with the King's law hard at her heels. It seems that even her powerful friends could not protect her from the constables once they found a great mess of magestones scattered throughout her room."

Loren sank back with a sigh of relief. "That is one problem removed, then. And what of Auntie?"

Jordel shook his head. "I know not of whom you speak. But Loren, no matter what you wish to know, it must wait. We must be upon the road, and not yesterday. I must prepare the carriage."

He rose and left at last, and Gem returned with a bowl of broth. Loren did not recognize the taste, but only knew that it seemed the best she had ever eaten. Her stomach growled and gurgled, but it took every drop and begged for more.

"You get your wish," she said, when she had finished the bowl. "We are leaving the city with Jordel."

"His badge will get us through the gate, at least," said Gem. "Although you could probably flash your cloak at the guards and they would let you through. That is over here, by the way."

He went to the end of her pallet, where her travel sack waited atop the folded-up cloak. Loren waved it off.

"I have no need of it now. And I doubt it would scare the guards any more than would your rag of a shirt."

"Oh, but you are infamous now," said Gem, sitting beside her again. "There are whispers in every tavern in the city about you. Of course, they do not know it is you, but I do. They say you knelt in your cell and prayed to the shadows, and they filled your cloak. Then you wrapped it around the jail door, and it burst open at your touch. They say when you strode out, all the guards cowered in fear at the sight of you."

Loren's eyes bugged wide. "What? Who says this?"

"Everyone," said Gem. "Everyone who has a tongue to wag."

Loren cocked an eyebrow.

"Well, I have only heard one person tell the story, but that is no matter," said Gem, waving a hand airily. "It is all the same."

"The tale could not lie farther from the truth," said Loren. "I only—"

She paused, reluctant to discuss the finer details of her escape. It did not make for a glamorous tale.

But Gem took her hesitation for something else and tapped the side of his nose. "Of course. I understand. Any great thief must have her secrets. Only I wish I had known you were so mighty. Where was your magic when we fought Auntie?"

"It was not magic," said Loren sullenly, taking another sip of her soup. "Just never you mind."

Jordel returned before long to tell them the carriage was ready. Loren tried to find her feet, but she kept slipping back to the pallet and blankets. Gem helped her up, and Jordel fastened her cloak around her shoulders.

He pointed at the dagger on her hip. "Ensure you keep that hidden. Under no circumstances must you let anyone see it."

Loren nodded, mute and suddenly fearful of the weapon at her waist. Her hand closed around its sheath.

She could scarcely walk, so Jordel scooped her into his arms and took her to the carriage that waited behind the apothecary. They rode quickly through the streets, the driver pushing the horses to a trot whenever he could. Before long they reached the south gate, where guards stood forth with pikes to block the way. But Jordel emerged and showed them the symbol on his cloak, and the pikes parted.

Loren knew she should stay hidden, but she could not resist peeking through a raised corner of the curtain as they passed through the city gate. She poked her nose out the open window and took a long breath.

Free, clean air. She had not realized how deeply she missed it, but it smelled like life after the clustered mess of the city.

"Upon the road once more," she said. "I had forgotten how life felt when not surrounded by enemies in every corner."

"A relief to be sure," said Jordel. "Now, where did you arrange to meet the wizard?"

"Xain said he would ride south until sundown. There he would wait by the road for our arrival. If they saw no sign by the third day, they would move on."

"They?"

"He travels with our companion. A . . . a girl." Loren did not think Jordel would enjoy knowing Annis was Damaris' daughter any more than Xain had.

Jordel leaned out the window and urged the driver on. The man put whip to hide, and soon they clipped along at a rapid pace. The carriage bounced and jostled constantly, and Loren winced with every sudden movement.

Jordel looked at her with concern. "I could have him slow."

"Do not," she said through gritted teeth. "We must make haste. The day wears on."

To distract herself, she had the carriage stop once they were out of sight of the city, and took a seat beside the driver upon his bench. Looking at the open sky and the wide grasslands let Loren's mind wander from the aches in her body, and it would let Xain and Annis see them coming besides. But the bench had no cushions, and soon her rear grew sore from the jostling.

They did not stop for lunch, instead eating as they rolled on. The sun continued its long march across the sky, and soon went to greet the western horizon.

Loren kept a careful eye on the sparse woodlands that sprang up on either side. If she were Xain, she would have pulled off into hiding beside the road, waiting for Loren to appear. They would see her clearly atop the carriage so long as they kept watch, and Loren knew Xain would do so. If he did not, Annis would insist upon it, and probably scream at the wizard until he relented.

The sun grew ever closer to the horizon. Loren's search became frenetic. No one revealed themselves. She saw no other carriages.

The sun dropped below the horizon. The driver pulled off the road.

"Wait!" said Loren, as he climbed down from his seat. "We must ride on. They may still be ahead."

Jordel emerged from the carriage. "We cannot push on past nightfall. The road is not safe, and the horses will have trouble finding their way besides. Xain is gone, Loren."

His words hit her like a punch to the gut. She scrambled from the driver's seat, her head swimming as she reached the ground. Almost she fell, but she righted herself at the last moment.

"They would not have gone. Xain would not . . ."

She could not finish the thought. For of course, Xain *would* have left. He *had* left her, once.

"Annis," she said, grasping now. "Annis would not have let him."

"Xain is a man grown, and a wizard besides," said Jordel. "If he determined to leave, your friend Annis could not have stopped him. At most she would have found herself abandoned, and we have not seen her, either."

"They could be just over the next hillock! We cannot stop now!" Loren hated the desperation that crept into her voice, but she could not help it.

Gem emerged from the carriage and looked at her sadly. "They did not press their horses hard when they left, Loren. Like as not, we already passed the place where they would have stopped. Xain did not wait until the third day. If he waited at all."

Loren stood rooted, unable to move, unable to think. She could not fathom it. After all she had done to find him, the wizard had left her again. But Annis. The thought of Annis riding on without them struck her to the marrow.

She sagged to her knees, sitting cross-legged upon the ground. Mute, she could only watch as the driver hobbled the horses and built them a fire. Once it burned brightly, Jordel came to her.

"Come, Loren," he said softly, his voice soothing as always. "Sit and eat. We must ride hard tomorrow if we hope to catch them."

Loren blinked up at him. "Catch them?"

He gave a small smile. "Of course. You do not think I would give up so easily, do you? I have sought Xain from the High King's Seat to Cabrus. I will not give up the search now. Tomorrow we press on, and we will find them. You do not know why they left. Mayhap they were discovered, or hard pressed once they left the city. We will find them. Come."

Still numb, Loren let him lead her to the fire. Its warmth bathed her face, and she felt herself grow fuzzy again. It burned like the snake's poison, but gentler. Pleasant. She drew her arms around her knees and wrapped her cloak about her, reveling in the feeling while Gem, Jordel, and the driver made a meal of bread and salted meat.

"I trust Annis," said Gem, out of nowhere. He glanced at Loren as she looked at him in surprise. "If they left, they had good reason. I trust her. She would not have let them go otherwise."

"Mayhap you are right," said Loren. "Mayhap."

"I know I am," said Gem, sniffing and sticking his nose in the air. "After all, I could have been a scholar."

"So I have heard."

A restlessness seized her, and she reached to her belt to draw forth the dagger. As she pulled it from the cloak, it glinted sharp in the moonslight, shocking her. The glimmer died away, and she noticed a speck of dirt upon the edge. She wiped at it with her cloak. Looking up, she saw Jordel eyeing her from across the campfire.

She would expect a story from the Mystic, something to explain the blade and the hidden power it seemed to contain. But not tonight. Tonight she found herself content to sit quiet under the stars in the warmth of a fire. Tonight they had lost their friends, and tomorrow they would find them again.

Loren wondered how long the chase would run, and what would happen at its end. Again she found herself cast out upon the world with no plan or purpose beyond the one that had driven her from the Birchwood. A shadow in the night, a ghostly whisper passing between the gates of a city. Guards staring at each other, stricken by a nameless fear. Justice for the weak and terror to those who wielded their power ruthlessly. The purpose seemed no nearer now than it ever had, and yet it burned within her just as bright.

Gem sniffed again, took a final bite of meat, and unfurled a blanket upon the ground. He rolled away from her, drawing the cloth over his head.

"Until the morrow, then. Good night, Loren."

"Yes, a good night," said Loren, murmuring as if to herself. "And Loren I am. For now."

The dagger whispered back into its sheath, like the parting murmur of an old and trusted friend.

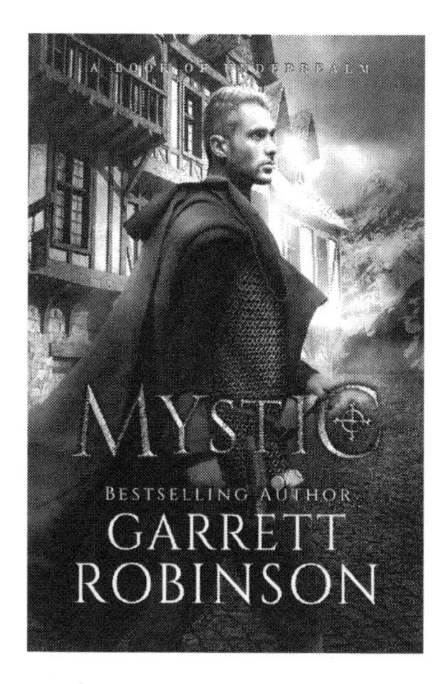

GET THE NEXT BOOK

You've finished *Nightblade*, the first book in the Nightblade Epic.

You can get an ebook copy of *Mystic*, the next book in the series, absolutely free. Just sign up for email updates from Legacy Books. You'll also get exclusive deals and sales on our titles.

Want to keep reading? Visit the link below now:

Underrealm.net/free-mystic

CONNECT ONLINE

FACEBOOK

Want to hang out with other fans of the Underrealm books? There's a Facebook group where you can do just that. Join the Nine Lands group on Facebook and share your favorite moments and fan theories from the books. I also post regular behind-the-scenes content, including information about the world you can't find anywhere else. Visit the link to be taken to the Facebook group:

Underrealm.net/nine-lands

YOUTUBE

Catch up with me daily (when I'm not directing a film or having a baby). You can watch my daily YouTube channel where I talk about art, science, life, my books, and the world.

But not cats.

Never cats.

GarrettBRobinson.com/yt

THE BOOKS OF UNDERREALM

Underrealm.net/Books

THE NIGHTBLADE EPIC

NIGHTBLADE

MYSTIC

DARKFIRE

SHADEBORN

WEREMAGE

YERRIN

THE ACADEMY JOURNALS

THE ALCHEMIST'S TOUCH

THE MINDMAGE'S WRATH

THE FIREMAGE'S VENGEANCE

CHRONOLOGICAL ORDER

NIGHTBLADE

MYSTIC

DARKFIRE

SHADEBORN

THE ALCHEMIST'S TOUCH

THE MINDMAGE'S WRATH

WEREMAGE

THE FIREMAGE'S VENGEANCE

YERRIN

ABOUT THE AUTHOR

Garrett Robinson was born and raised in Los Angeles. The son of an author/painter father and a violinist/singer mother, no one was surprised when he grew up to be an artist.

After blooding himself in the independent film industry, he self-published his first book in 2012 and swiftly followed it with a stream of others, publishing more than two million words by 2014. Within months he topped numerous Amazon bestseller lists. Now he spends his time writing books and directing films.

A passionate fantasy author, his most popular series is the Nightblade Epic. However, he has delved into many other genres. Some works are for adult audiences only, such as *Non Zombie* and *Hit Girls*, but he has also published popular books for younger readers, including the Realm Keepers series and *The Ninjabread Man*, co-authored with Z.C. Bolger.

Garrett lives in Los Angeles with his wife Meghan, his children Dawn, Luke, and Desmond, and his dog Chewbacca.

Garrett can be found on:

BLOG: garrettbrobinson.com
EMAIL: garrettbrobinson.com/be-a-rebel
TWITTER: twitter.com/garrettrauthor
FACEBOOK: facebook.com/garrettbrobinson